The

1 pretty

1 picturesque inn overlooking Hemlock Gorge

2 talented sisters even better at solving crimes
than they are at their day jobs

1 (or more) murders . . .

A WINNING RECIPE FOR MYSTERY LOVERS!

Don't miss these Hemlock Falls Mysteries . . .

A Taste for Murder
One of the year's biggest events, the History Days
festival, takes a deadly turn when a reenactment
of seventeenth-century witch trials leads to
twentieth-century murder. Since the victim is
one of their guests, the least Sarah and Meg Quilliam can do is investigate . . .

A Dash of Death
The Quilliam sisters are at it again, this time
trailing the murderer of two Hemlock Falls
women who won a design contest. Helena
Houndswood, the celebrated expert on stylish living, was furious when the small-town women
won. But mad enough to murder?

MORE MYSTERIES FROM THE
BERKLEY PUBLISHING GROUP...

DOG LOVERS' MYSTERIES STARRING HOLLY WINTER: With her Alaskan malamute Rowdy, Holly dogs the trails of dangerous criminals. "A gifted and original writer." —Carolyn G. Hart

by Susan Conant

A NEW LEASH ON DEATH   A BITE OF DEATH
DEAD AND DOGGONE   PAWS BEFORE DYING

DOG LOVERS' MYSTERIES STARRING JACKIE WALSH: She's starting a new life with her son and an ex–police dog named Jake... teaching film classes and solving crimes!

by Melissa Cleary

A TAIL OF TWO MURDERS   FIRST PEDIGREE MURDER   THE MALTESE PUPPY
DOG COLLAR CRIME   SKULL AND DOG BONES   MURDER MOST BEASTLY
HOUNDED TO DEATH   DEAD AND BURIED   OLD DOGS

SAMANTHA HOLT MYSTERIES: Dogs, cats, and crooks are all part of a day's work for this veterinary technician... "Delightful!" –Melissa Cleary

by Karen Ann Wilson

EIGHT DOG FLYING   COPY CAT CRIMES
BEWARE SLEEPING DOGS   CIRCLE OF WOLVES

CHARLOTTE GRAHAM MYSTERIES: She's an actress with a flair for dramatics—and an eye for detection. "You'll get hooked on Charlotte Graham!"
—*Rave Reviews*

by Stefanie Matteson

MURDER AT THE SPA   MURDER AT THE FALLS
MURDER AT TEATIME   MURDER ON HIGH
MURDER ON THE CLIFF   MURDER AMONG THE ANGELS
MURDER ON THE SILK ROAD   MURDER UNDER THE PALMS

PEACHES DANN MYSTERIES: Peaches has never had a very good memory. But she's learned to cope with it over the years... Fortunately, though, when it comes to murder, this absentminded amateur sleuth doesn't forgive and forget!

by Elizabeth Daniels Squire

WHO KILLED WHAT'S-HER-NAME?   REMEMBER THE ALIBI
MEMORY CAN BE MURDER   WHOSE DEATH IS IT, ANYWAY?

HEMLOCK FALLS MYSTERIES: The Quilliam sisters combine their culinary and business skills to run an inn in upstate New York. But when it comes to murder, their talent for detection takes over...

by Claudia Bishop

A TASTE FOR MURDER   A DASH OF DEATH
A PINCH OF POISON   MURDER WELL-DONE

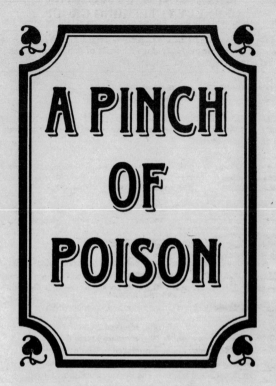

A PINCH OF POISON

Claudia Bishop

BERKLEY PRIME CRIME, NEW YORK

A PINCH OF POISON

A Berkley Prime Crime Book / published by arrangement with the author

PRINTING HISTORY
Berkley Prime Crime edition / December 1995

The Penguin Putnam Inc. World Wide Web site address is
http://www.penguinputnam.com

ISBN: 0-425-15104-2

Berkley Prime Crime Books are published
by The Berkley Publishing Group,
a member of Penguin Putnam Inc.,
200 Madison Avenue, New York, NY 10016.
The name BERKLEY PRIME CRIME and the BERKLEY PRIME CRIME
design are trademarks belonging to Berkley Publishing Corporation.

PRINTED IN THE UNITED STATES OF AMERICA

10 9 8 7 6 5 4

For Helen and Les,
with love

The Cast of Characters

The Inn at Hemlock Falls
Sarah Quilliam—owner-manager
Margaret Quilliam—her sister, gourmet chef
John Raintree—business manager
Doreen Muxworthy—head housekeeper
Dina Muir—receptionist
Kathleen Kiddermeister—waitress
Axminster Stoker—guest
Lyle Fairbanks—president, the Rudyard Kipling
    Condensation Society
Lila Fairbanks—his wife
Jerzey Paulovich—member, the Rudyard Kipling
    Condensation Society
Aurora Kent—member, the Rudyard Kipling Con-
    densation Society
Georgia Hardwicke—member, the Rudyard Kip-
    ling Condensation Society
Toshiro Sakura—former director, Sakura Indus-
    tries
Motoyama—his chauffeur
Kenji Sakura—his son, professor of art appreci-
    ation at Cornell University
Marco DeMarco—owner, DeMarco Construction
Eugene—engineer, DeMarco Construction

Members of the Chamber of Commerce
Elmer Henry—mayor
Harvey Bozzel—president, Bozzel Advertising
Howie Murchison—town attorney and justice of
    the peace
Freddie Bellini—director, Bellini's Funeral Home

Miriam Doncaster—public librarian

Marge Schmidt—owner, the Hemlock Hometown Diner

Betty Hall—her partner

Esther West—owner, West's Best dress shop

Dookie Shuttleworth—minister, the Hemlock Falls Church of the Word of God

Pete Rosen—publisher/editor, the *Hemlock Falls Gazette*

Mark Anthony Jefferson—banker, the Hemlock Falls Savings and Loan

Harland Peterson—president, Agway Farmer's Co-op

Petey Peterson—his cousin, owner of Peterson's Septic and Floor Covering

Norm Pasquale—principal, Hemlock Falls High School

. . . among others

The Sheriff's Department
Myles McHale—sheriff of Tompkins County
Dave Kiddermeister—deputy

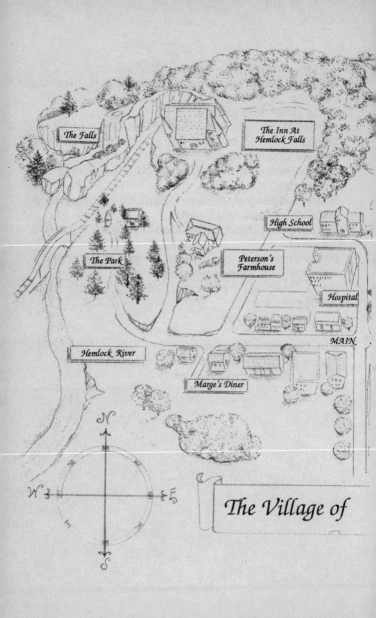

The Village of

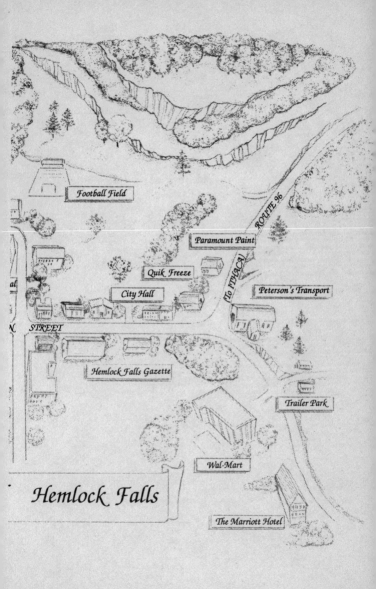

Football Field

ROUTE 96

Paramount Paint

to ITHACA

Quik Freeze

City Hall

Peterson's Transport

STREET

Hemlock Falls Gazette

Trailer Park

Wal-Mart

Hemlock Falls

The Marriott Hotel

CHAPTER 1

Margaret Quilliam flipped another page in the tabloid-sized newspaper, bolted upright, and shrieked, "My *god!*" She shook her head. "This is outrageous. Like discovering Martha Stewart's had a sex change operation, or that Julia Child binged on Twinkies. I can't believe I didn't take a look at this when it was published a week ago."

"We've been busy," said Quill shortly. "The new restaurant's taking up more time than I thought it would."

"Yeah, but, Quill. There's no excuse. With Doreen so annoyed with you—"

"Doreen is *not* annoyed with me."

"She's annoyed at both of us," said Meg comfortably. "Which is why she didn't let us know about this outrageous newspaper, I expect. I wish I'd gotten down to the diner for the gossip this week. It must be fierce. And, by god, it says the next issue's due out today. I'll bet everyone's all of a doodah. Well, you needed a murder to solve. Sure as heck somebody in town will knock this bozo off. Detecting will be good for you. It'll pull you right out of this depression you're in."

Sarah Quilliam ignored her sister, concentrating instead on the Arriving Guests list. She penciled "Query: Sashimi?" next to the names Sakura Kenji and Sakura Toshiro, then wondered where they'd find fresh fish. Ken Sakura taught art commentary at Cornell. Toshiro must be his father. She didn't really paint anymore, and it was too

1

much to expect that someone like Ken Sakura had heard of her, but still. Sushi would be nice. A gesture.

She dropped the list onto the wrought-iron tabletop and sighed. Meg's comment about depression was an exaggeration, like her reaction to the newspaper. If she, Quill, was a little down, it was because it was Friday and the Inn would be full by tomorrow. On the other hand, since a capacity crowd was unusual for the summer, it was probably the heat that was making her feel cross-wise.

It was hot even for August. When the kitchen thermometer in the Inn the sisters owned together hit eighty-eight (with a rise of ten degrees forecast for the afternoon), they'd headed outside to the gazebo by the waterfall to finish their weekly meeting over menus and the guest list. Quill scanned the items on her written agenda: review food to be served at their new boutique restaurant; assess inventory process improvements; verify menus and activities list for the upcoming week; discuss special menu requests from the customer survey results. Meg wasn't going to like that last one. Quill sat back and sighed. Even her elbows were sticky from the muggy weather.

The temperature had brought most of the Inn's guests out onto the lawn. Temporarily abandoning special menu requests, which was Meg's job, anyway, she wondered for the fourth or fifth time if they should air-condition the building. The Inn was situated high over Hemlock Gorge, and a breeze from the falls and the river usually cooled the Inn from the ground floor to the eaves. The heat was intolerable only two weeks out of the summer.

Maybe it wasn't as hot as it felt. Quill was wearing a light cotton skirt, sandals, and a flowered gauze blouse with full sleeves. Most of the guests had on less than that. Meg was in shorts, and she'd knotted her T-shirt above her waistband, but sweat trickled down her temples and her face was flushed. Quill lifted her own mass of hair to let the breeze from the Gorge cool her neck. It didn't work. It was as hot as it felt. She thought about the things she should be doing instead of sitting in the gazebo. She should grab the newspaper away from Meg and force her to plan her own bloody menus. And she should either talk to Mike the groundskeeper about dead-heading the roses or do it herself. The heat had forced an early petal drop, and things were looking shaggy. What she really wanted to do was go swimming in the clear water of the gorge and let the gardens, the Inn, the menus, and the guest list take care of themselves. She looked at the building, the grounds, and the garden filled with people whose relationship to her was defined by the limits on their credit cards. She sighed. Meg was right. She was depressed. Which was undoubtedly making her feel the heat even more.

Quill tried to convince herself that the Adirondack chairs placed at strategic intervals throughout the gardens were filled with guests drawn irresistibly outside by the sound of the falls and the scent of the roses, and not the muggy temperatures. A large elderly lady next to a four-foot-high bush of Apricot Nectar fanned herself with a copy of *Vogue*; her sigh of annoyance drifted accusingly across the lawn. Quill looked again at the estimate for air-conditioning, then grabbed an ice cube from her iced tea and ran it around the back of her neck. Now she was both hot and wet. She pulled a curl from behind her ear and looked at it. "Should I go blond?"

Meg glanced up, scratched her bare leg with one hand, and waved Quill's question away with the other. "It's been red since you were born. It's still red. Leave it alone."

"I'm going gray and I'm not even within spitting distance of thirty-four."

"That's not gray, that's Gruyère from the quiche at lunch. You're gorgeous, okay? Now, I wouldn't say you looked happy, or even pleasant, not for the past couple of weeks, at least. But gorgeous? Absolutely."

"Be quiet," said Quill crossly. "Put that thing down. I want to get to work."

"In a minute. You've got to see this after I'm through. Hedrick Conway never claimed he was going to publish a good newspaper. But this is ridiculous. It's not a newspaper, it's a joke."

"It looks like a newspaper to me. And I don't care what it is, anyway. How do you feel about sushi?"

"Sushi?"

"We have the Sakuras coming in. Do you know who they are? The father just retired as managing director of Sakura Industries, which is this huge multinational company."

"What's the former managing director of a billion-dollar business doing in Central New York? Need I ask. My cooking, naturally."

"His son teaches art appreciation at Cornell. He's Ken Sakura, the critic."

"Oh." Meg affected an air of unconcern. "We could unpack some of your paintings, maybe? He might want to take a look."

"I've quit."

"Quill . . ."

"My point was that it might be nice to offer a special Japanese menu."

"I don't know a thing about Japanese cooking except that you have to be licensed to serve fugu."

"Fugu?"

"It's a fish. The liver's poisonous. Kills you in something like two seconds." Meg mimed swallowing, clutched her throat, rolled her eyes, and made a sound like a garbage disposal with a fork in it. "You have to pass a test in cutting the liver away from the fish part." She looked thoughtful. "I wonder how they can tell when you've flunked? Now, there's a worthy subject for one of the nutty statistical studies you've been messing with recently. The morbidity rate in fugu inspectors on the island of Honshu."

"I would really appreciate it," said Quill stiffly, "if you'd cut the crap and give me a hand here."

Meg raised her eyebrows, said nothing for a moment, then saluted. "Yes, ma'am."

Quill flushed. She was willing to admit to a slight—very slight—depression over her breakup with Myles McHale, but it was not making her—what had been John Raintree's adjective? *Touchy.* Or was it *bitchy*? Maybe it had been a little bitchy to tell John to stick to minding the general ledger. Now, telling him he was not the Inn's resident shrink and to butt out of her private life would qualify as bitchy, since John was a friend of long standing as well as being their business manager. She didn't think she'd gone as far as that. At least not in so many words. Anyway, business was business, and the sooner everybody at the Inn figured that out, the better off they'd be. "Which," she said aloud—and to Meg's slight confusion—"we came out here to do, anyway, so we should get back to it."

"If you're talking about next week's menus, let me finish this newspaper first, and then I'll be your willing slave. How much do you suppose Hedrick Conway and his family invested in it anyway? He's going to lose his shirt."

Quill, perversely, found herself in sudden sympathy with the Conways, whom she had never met. She dampened her fingers and scrubbed at the gray strand in her hair. "You remember what everyone said about us when we opened up six years ago." Having determined that the gray was in fact Gruyère, she interrupted herself, considered a haircut, and bunched her hair together at her chin line. "You think I should go short?"

"No," Meg said without looking up. "It's nice the way it is. And yes, I remember what people said when we moved here and opened the Inn. Nothing. Nobody talked to us for a year."

"Well, when we *did* start making a few friends, they wanted to know why we were wasting our time and money on this junk heap and were we made of money or what?"

"What's that got to do with anything?"

"Nothing would ever get accomplished if people didn't take risks. Make sacrifices. Make tough personal decisions. Like my deciding to quit painting for the time being. And . . . other things. I'm getting the same kind of negative reaction to my efforts to improve the way things are done around here that the Conways are getting to their newspaper. 'You stick to what you do best. What do you want to mess around with stuff for when the Inn practically runs itself?' Runs itself, hah! I'd like to see some people run this Inn and find out how easy it is.''

"So Doreen *did* talk to you this morning! She told me she'd had it up to here.'' Doreen, their head housekeeper, was a fiftyish widow whose three husbands had not, as occasional opinion would have it, died from being nagged to death. "She's got a right to be mad at you. I'm a little annoyed with you myself over this sudden immersion into all this quality improvement stuff.'' Meg tapped the agenda in a way loaded with significance. "Doreen's got her own case of . . . what's your euphemism for your lousy mood? 'Slight irritability,' that's it. Anyhow, ever since that miserable Axminster Stoker took up residence in the Shaker suite and the two of you started harassing her about how he can help her be more efficient, she's been more than slightly irritable, she's been pissed.''

"It wasn't just the process improvement stuff,'' Quill said in gloomy agreement, "it's the boutique restaurant. Despite the fact that we've been planning it for months and included the staff every step of the way, Doreen hates the idea. She was complaining about the restaurant again this morning.''

"Did you tell her she could put her Amway catalogs near the cash register? As soon as you do that, she'll come around to our way of thinking. You haven't changed your mind about the boutique, have you?''

"No.''

"Good. I think it's terrific. And the mall design is neat. The town needs the tax revenues. I'll be able to try some snazzy little dessert thingies that aren't right for the main dining room. I need the creative space that a little restaurant like that can give you. I can improvise. I can—''

"If you need creative space,'' Quill interrupted, "why don't you start with some Japanese food? The feedback from this new customer survey Mr. Stoker suggested says that people like to eat the things they're familiar with. And the Japanese are familiar with sushi.''

"If people want familiar, they can stay home.'' Meg's

face flushed with more than the heat, well past the ninety-degree mark now. "This sort of thing is exactly what Doreen was complaining about. You're brooding over Myles and making the rest of us jump through hoops. Process improvement for Doreen. Menu changes for me. Investment projects for John. No painting for you. I was sympathetic for a while, but you were the one who decided not to marry him."

"I am not brooding over Myles," Quill said carefully.

Meg opened her mouth, caught her sister's eye, and closed it. "I'm sorry. I didn't mean to . . . never mind. Why don't I get us some more iced tea? Stop thinking about the Inn. Forget Myles. Take three deep breaths."

Quill sat very still.

"Are you breathing?"

"Yeah."

"Really, truly just sitting there and forgiving me for being a tactless jerk?"

"Yes." Quill cleared her throat and wiped carefully under each eye with the back of her hand. There'd been a family saying for years when they were little, and she used it now. "It's just so hot my eyeballs are sweating."

Meg laughed a little, squeezed her hand hard, and released it. "One of the many advantages of having an older sister is they never completely let you forget your childhood. Here. Read this. I'll be back in a minute and we can talk about your next project. It'll be a real community service. Trust me."

Determined to be diverted, Quill took the paper.

The village of Hemlock Falls (population three thousand four hundred and fifty-six) had two newspapers for the first time in its three-hundred-year history. The venerable and conservative *Hemlock Falls Gazette* had carried hog and cattle prices and covered birthdays, weddings, graduations, and funerals to the exclusion of news stories for over seventy years. If anything so cataclysmic occurred that even Dookie Shuttleworth (the amiable but absentminded minister of the Hemlock Falls Church of the Word of God) was aware of it, the *Gazette* would refer to it in terms so elliptical that no one could possibly take offense. Natural disasters such as the Blizzard of '88 were usually apologized for: QUITE A BIT OF SNOW IN TOWN had been the headline reporting forty-eight inches. Man-made disasters, such as the murder investigations into which Quill and Meg had been involuntarily drawn several years before, were alluded to indirectly, if at all: UNFORTUNATE INCIDENT INTERRUPTS HEMLOCK HISTORY DAYS and PAINT FACTORY PRODUCTION SLOWS were the *Gazette*'s response to a total of five corpses. Town opinion had it that the *Gazette* was more properly a medium for amiable social exchange than an organ designed for the balanced analysis of events.

The town had been in shock when Pete Rosen had put the *Gazette* up for sale. When Hedrick Conway, his mother, Louisa, and his sister, Carlyle, purchased the vacant Nickerson Hardware building (the hardware business had fallen victim to the new Wal-Mart on Route 15) and announced the successful purchase of the *Gazette*, Hemlockians had been dubious. The old newspaper had an editor-publisher related to half the folks in town. A man, moreover, who knew that real news was published at Marge Schmidt's diner over Sunday breakfast. Best thing that could happen was the flat-land foreigners get their clock cleaned and return to wherever they had come from, flat broke.

Meg had rolled the paper into a cylinder with the address sticker uppermost. Quill read: Mrs. Sarah Quillam, Manageress, Hemlock Falls Inn, One Hemlock Road, Hemlock Falls, New York 14562. At least the ZIP code was right. Quill and Meg had both retained their maiden names after Quill's divorce and the demise of Meg's husband; they both preferred to use *Ms.* although *Miss* would do in a pinch; they spelled their name with two '*i*'s; the Inn was named the Inn at Hemlock Falls; and the term *manageress* had gone out with World War II, if not Warren G. Harding.

Even Dr. Watson could deduce quite a bit from something as simple as an address label. She frowned thoughtfully at it. The Conways were probably sweet, certainly elderly, obviously retired. Hedrick was probably fulfilling a lifelong dream of running a hometown paper in the Eden-like setting of Hemlock Falls. Hedrick's mother undoubtedly had pure white hair and a bravely wielded cane.

Quill decided to take out a subscription, maybe even an ad. People (like, for instance, Myles McHale), were unreceptive to those who tried to change the course of their daily lives. Especially if that person was a thirty-three year old artist turned Inn manager who preferred to remain single. Who wasn't sure she was tough enough to have a husband whose job took him into dangerous, life-threatening situations at all hours of the day and night. Especially a husband who wanted children. Not, Quill thought, the paper crumpled in her lap, her eyes on the water cascading over the rocks to the Hemlock River below, that babies weren't a pretty good idea in the abstract. She just wasn't sure about the particular.

A red-tailed hawk swept the narrow ledge of the gorge and shrieked, hunting to feed its ravenous young.

She shook herself, smoothed the tabloid over her knees, and read:

THE TRUMPET!

Premier Issue no. 1 vol. one
FREE COPY ONE TIME ONLY!!!

Underneath the banner was the headline:

DOG'S RUN WILD IN THE STREETS!!!

"Holy cow," said Quill.

Meg, back from her trip to the kitchen, set a fresh pitcher of iced tea on the table and settled into her seat. "Told you."

"Dog's run wild in streets?" said Quill. "In Hemlock Falls? A dog's what, anyway? Good God, listen to this! 'It was a dark and stormy night when this reporter took to the streets and alleys of our fair village. . . . ' "

"Tuesday, I should think," said Meg with a judicious air. "That's when it rained last, three nights ago."

" 'A dark shape followed this reporter as this reporter patrolled the muddy alley. A ferocious growl made menacing noises.' A ferocious growl?" Quill peered around the paper's edge. "Behold my wild surmise."

"I think he must have been behind Esther's shop. That's the first place in the village to get muddy when it rains."

"Got it. And the ferocious growl?"

"Buddy, Esther's poodle. She lets him out at seven-thirty for what she discreetly refers to as his constitutional. Doesn't fool a soul. Turn the page."

Quill turned the page. A photograph of "this reporter" filled the upper right quadrant. A banana-nosed man in his early thirties held the bottom of his loafer toward the camera with an expression of extreme distaste.

Quill shrieked.

"He stepped in it." Meg's grin was reluctant. "The editorial's about leash laws. He wants the town council to enforce leash laws—"

"No!"

"As you see. But that's not the worst part."

"Does it get worse?" asked Quill, fascinated. She skimmed the rest of the story. "Of course it gets worse. He wants the sheriff's office to issue citations for canine 'infractions.' "

"Now that's a good thing," said Meg. "It might make more dog owners aware of heartworm. August is a terrible time for heartworm. But that's still not the worst part."

"How do you know that about heartworm?"

"Andy told me."

"Andy's a people doctor, not a vet."

Meg shrugged, the slight blush with which she was liable to greet mention of the Falls' best-looking (and only) internist. "He's a dog-loving people doctor. Read on. See page four?"

Quill was cheered at the prospect, however remote, of six-foot-four Myles McHale chasing Esther West's yappy poodle to give it a ticket; Buddy was a notorious ankle-biter. She turned to page four. Her amusement faded. ''Oh, no! He's printed the police blotter!''

''Cute, huh?''

''It's awful! As if there weren't enough gossip in a town this size. 'A juvenile, aged ten, of 256 Maple Drive, was arrested on a charge of petit mal larceny at the Wal-Mart store on Route Fifteen.'' Quill threw the paper on the table. ''Honestly. Everyone knows it's just Benny Pasquale swiping gum. He's done it since he was eight years old. His parents make him give it back and work it off at the store. I think he just likes to stack cartons. And petit mal larceny? What the heck is that?''

Meg shrugged. ''Not quite as funny as the 'infarction-infraction' mistake. Half the town is going to think Bennie's an epileptic and the other that he's kiting bad checks or stealing cars.''

''This is too bad. His poor parents. That poor kid.''

''There's more. Look at the bottom of the page. Pete Rosen would *croak* to see what's happened to the good old *Gazette*. I wonder if anyone's sent him a copy in Florida.''

Quill picked the paper up and peered at the boxed item under the police blotter. '' 'Next week. Mini-Mall or Mighty Mess? Is the Entire Chamber of Commerce on the Take?! The *Trumpet!* has uncovered the true facts behind the construction—or should this reporter say *destruction*—of Hemlock Falls' most expensive venture in town history. Mayor denies cover-up!' '' Quill dropped the paper on the table, and stared at her sister, astonished. She fished the lemon slice out of her tea and bit into it. The sour taste helped pull her scattered thoughts together. ''This is just cheap gossip! Have you met these people? These Conways? Hedrick and Louisa and what's-her-name? Carlyle, his sister?''

''Nope.''

Quill spit a lemon seed into her hand. She felt like throwing something. Not a large something. Just a gesture of disapprobation. Mike the groundskeeper had edged the gazebo with Old Spice sweet peas. It'd been a hot, wet summer, and the plants grew lushly cream, pink, scarlet, rose, and lavender around the latticework. She tossed the seed into the heavy foliage and pitched the rind in after it. "This is ridiculous. When I think of all the work that's gone into that stupid mini-mall—and the hours of time I've spent at chamber meetings taking endless notes." She stopped. "There can't be anything in this. Can there?"

Meg shrugged. "Who's to say? On the face of it—or maybe I should say the sole of it, given that stupid picture—he's more likely a Geraldo Rivera wannabe. I'll tell you who would know if there's anything criminal going on at the mall."

Quill, who knew quite well whose name was about to surface, since he was the only real law in town, tore the paper into three long strips and said firmly, "Dookie Shuttleworth is head of the Mall Committee, as you very well know. And he couldn't be involved in anything crooked to save his soul. He's a minister, for Pete's sake."

"What about Harvey Bozzel?" asked Meg.

Quill pulled her lip. Harvey was Hemlock Falls' premier (and only) advertising executive. While Harvey's basic honesty was undeniable, his cupidity was problematic. With the best will in the world, Harvey had an eye for the main chance. "Nah. Marge Schmidt's on the committee. I could see Harvey getting involved with something crooked out of sheer dumbness, but Marge would put her size nines flat on his sweaty little neck. She's shrewder than the entire bunco squad at the FBI."

"Oh, sure," said Meg. "There's a superior comparison. If you're talking about the guys who didn't know their chief liked to wear a dress and bet mob money on the horses. What about the fact that nobody, but nobody in town is actually working at the site? The carpenters and electricians are all from out of town."

"Bull. We checked out DeMarco Construction thoroughly. At least, the committee did."

"And who was on that committee? Harvey Bozzel. And the Mayor. Neither of whom are up for Nobel prizes in investigation."

"So was Howie Murchison. And he's no fool. The best thing to do with this rag is ignore it. It's obvious, isn't it? Conway's a yellow journalist. He's trouble."

"Right here in River City," Meg chanted. "With a capital *T* and that rhymes with *P* and that stands for—"

"Poo!" they shouted together. Quill smiled and shook her head. "This is low-grade, bottom-of-the-barrel schtick humor, Meg."

Meg smiled back. "Whatever it takes. That's the first time I've actually heard you *laugh* since you packed up your paintings and decided to give Myles the boot."

Quill balled the paper up and stuck it under the chair. "Let's forget about it. We need to get through this agenda. Then I want to go swimming. It's been a tough week."

"No-no-no-no-no! Look. We got most of the full-time employees involved in this new restaurant of ours, right? One of your ideas about how much more appreciated they'd feel if they were truly a part of the business."

"You thought it was a good idea!"

"I still do. But what if there *is* something behind this mini-mall exposé? We have a clear responsibility to ourselves and our staff to find out the truth. My goodness, Quill, all our savings are in this project."

"Good God. You don't think there's something funny going on, do you?"

Meg shrugged. "Wouldn't hurt to find out. And who better than you to do a little discreet investigation?" She waved her arms dramatically. "Who was it that captured the Paramount Paint murderer? Confronted the History Day's killer? You're secretary of the Chamber of Commerce. Everyone in town likes you. It's perfect. So you'll do it? Maybe start with a quiet little interrogation of the Horrible Hedrick?"

"Well. You may be right."

"So you'll do it?"

"It's probably worth a look."

"And you'll start right now?" Meg's glance at the To Do list, which was uppermost on the stack of files on the gazebo table, was artfully innocent. "No time like the present. Can't hurt to start right now. Think of how cheerful you are when you're detecting. And how few lists you make."

"We'd have utter chaos without the To Do list. And

there is absolutely nothing wrong with my moods.''

''Well, let's talk about that. Before we get to the list.''

Quill frowned, her hilarious mood evaporating as quickly as it'd come. ''Okay, okay, maybe I've been a little—dour—lately.''

''Dour! Try surly, cranky, tetchy.''

''Not that bad,'' said Quill, startled.

''Let's stick with grouchy. We can all live with that. It's the hyperactivity that's tough. You throw yourself into all this useless work. I mean, look at this stuff.'' Meg pulled a file from the stack they'd brought from the kitchen and opened it with a dramatic flourish. 'Order Entry Process for Inventory.' What the heck is that? All these stupid little boxes showing Doreen how to do a job she's done perfectly well for the last five years.''

''Axminster Stoker's been helping me. He was a process manager for a Fortune 500 company before he took early retirement.''

''And you wonder why Doreen's been telling you to mind your own business? With you and this boob Stoker zooming all over the Inn with your slide rules and these dopey charts? Come on, Quill. It's impossible to have a decent conversation when you're depress—sorry, grouchy and defensive at the same time.''

''I am *not* defensive!'' Quill shouted. Then subsiding to a less bellicose tone, ''Keep your voice down. Mr. Stoker's sitting right over there. It's not a dopey chart, it's a process chart. It's supposed to make us more efficient. Reduce costs. Improve profitability.''

''My sister the Wizard of Wall Street. What about this other stuff?'' Meg tossed the Order Entry Process for Inventory to the gazebo floor and fished another file from the stack. ''Customer surveys. 'Rate your satisfaction with the quality of dinners during your stay at the Inn. a. Very Unsatisfactory. b. Unsatisfactory. c. Satisfactory. d. Very Satisfactory.' ''

''We received an eighty-six percent 'Very Satisfactory' rating from that survey. Axminster says that's extraordinary for a business that's just getting into Total Quality. You should be proud. I've told you that, already.''

"Fine. Swell. Good. Pretty nice," said Meg in an apparent—and in Quill's opinion—lame attempt at Total Quality humor. "So what did you do about the fourteen percent who thought my food was awful?" Her expression, innocently inquiring, didn't fool Quill at all. She was conscious of trepidation. Her sister's temper, serene only when she was cooking well, was volcanic when aroused.

"They didn't think your food was awful. They had suggestions for improving the menu, that's all. Some very, very small suggestions."

"So you asked the fourteen percent what I could do to improve," said Meg with a dangerous calm. "And why they hated my cooking. All you had to do, Quill, was ask me why they hated my cooking. You want to know why? I'll tell you why. . . . " Meg, her face pink, began to tug at her short, dark hair with both hands—a bad sign.

"They didn't hate your cooking. They loved your cooking. A basic quality principle, according to Mr. Stoker, is that everything can be improved. They loved your cooking so much, they had ideas for it to get even better. It's not a criticism, Meg. It's feedback. It shows the customers are involved."

"Oh. I see. Of course." She picked up a survey response at random and read: " 'Herring no good.' Silly, silly me, to have no-good herring. Dammit! I don't serve herring at all!"

"You have to know how to interpret these things," said Quill wisely. "That may sound like our herring was no good, but what it means is that it wasn't good that we didn't have herring. I'm pretty sure that this was from the reunion meeting of the Finns Who Found God. They eat a lot of herring, Finns do, and which was just the point I was making about our Japanese guests. People like it when you serve food familiar to them."

"Oh? What about this one?" Meg's nostrils flared. She read: " 'We want tits!' "

"Well, that one . . . you remember?"

"The Society of Swamp Reclamation Engineers—the ones who wanted to know how come there were no topless joints in Tompkins County? How could I forget?" Meg's face got pinker. Her eyes narrowed. Her voice rose. "I am *not*, I repeat *not* going to change a. my cooking, or b. my menus, or c. remove my T-shirt to suit *anybody!* And that includes the President of the United States himself! Do you hear this? If the President himself showed up and asked for herring I would refuse! This quality stuff sucks!"

"Will you hush, Meg? Mr. Stoker—"

"Who cares!?"

"Okay," said Quill cautiously. Then, "I'm sorry. You have a point about the T-shirt."

"You bet I do."

"But not about the herring."

"Jeez!" Meg said. Her hair began to resemble bed-springs.

"Just think about adding a few specials to the menu to make the guests feel more at home. Not every day. Not all the time. Just once in a while. Like maybe sushi. It'll give you creative scope. I admit, I can see your point about the feedback—"

"Stuff the feedback. It's not the feedback. It's the fact that you think these people have the right to change the way I cook that's driving me bananas. All these dopey statistics tell you is that the Swamp Reclamation Engineers should have gone to Atlantic City and the Finns to Nantucket. You want feedback? I'll give you feedback. You and Mr. Stoker can take these statistics and—"

"Will you keep your voice down, please? The poor man can hear you. The entire town can hear you. I'm changing my mind about spending money on air-conditioning. At least we can argue in the kitchen, where nobody can hear us."

"Pooh! I'm not saying a single thing to you that I wouldn't say to that fussy little process gearhead myself."

"Airing these differences can be a good thing," said a dry voice in Quill's ear, "but only when the parties involved share a common vision for excellence." The clipped precise speech was an aural representation of a lawn mowed within an inch of its life.

Quill closed her eyes, turned in her seat, and opened them to see Axminster Stoker standing at the entrance to the gazebo. "Hi, Mr. Stoker."

Mr. Stoker was small and sinewy with a buzz cut and a stiff blond-gray mustache. He looked as though he wore khakis even when he didn't. His eyes were the color of little blue marbles. "Margaret? I can tell you what you are feeling now. You're feeling threatened. This is a normal response to those unacquainted with Total Quality principles. I am, however, always glad to have the opportunity to enlighten the uninformed."

"It's enlightening enough to know somebody who's been named after a carpet," said Meg tartly. "We have an Axminster in the conference room. Were you born on one?"

"My family," said Mr. Stoker, with the air of someone who has had to explain this before and is rather pleased to do so, "came from the village in England. I sense that you are feeling offended as well as threatened. This, too, is a common reaction to my ideas for process improvement. Made worse, I might add, when inadequately explained." The birdy-blue eye fixed itself on Quill in impersonal accusation. "I do apologize for the intrusion, but I couldn't help but overhear the lamentable interpretation of Total Quality principles. May I sit down?" He stepped into the gazebo, settled onto the bench facing Meg and Quill, and drew a deep breath. "To begin with, there is no human activity that cannot be flowcharted."

"Terlits," said Doreen Muxworthy.

Quill jumped. Their head housekeeper, skinny and tough as a piece of barbed wire, placed both freckled hands on the gazebo railing and glared at Axminster Stoker. Quill wondered why voices carried in the humid air and footsteps didn't. She decided, crossly, that Doreen had crept up on them on purpose. "What is it, Doreen? I didn't hear you come up."

"D'ja hear me now?"

"Of course I hear you now. Anybody within a mile could hear you now. What about the toilets?"

"The maintenance of toilets," said Axminster Stoker, "lends itself in particular to a process flowchart. All it takes is an initial commitment to doing things right the first time.''

Doreen's eyes narrowed, but she said nothing. Quill cleared her throat and said brightly, "What about the toilets?"

"Backed up." Although her mouth moved, Doreen's regard of Axminster Stoker's face was otherwise totally motionless, reminding Quill of a National Geographic Special she'd seen on lionesses stalking in the Kalahari. "Ground floor. Second and third floor like to go as soon as this lot sitting out here goes back to their rooms. Which'll be pretty soon. They been drinking iced tea like it's going out of style."

"Oh, dear." Quill got to her feet with a guilty sense of relief. She fully appreciated Axminster Stoker's advice, but it was advice that benefited from coffee with a high caffeine content and cooler temperatures. Otherwise it made her sleepy. "I suppose I'd better go. Doreen, did you call Petey what's-his-name?"

"Peterson," said Doreen. "From Peterson's Septic and Floor Covering. I already done that. So you can stay right here."

Her steady gaze was beginning to discomfit Quill, who couldn't imagine why it wasn't unnerving the apparently nerveless Mr. Stoker. "And leave you to deal with this on your own? I'd be a pretty poor manager if I did that." Familiar with the opinion Doreen seemed about to express, she hurried on, "Is Petey coming soon? It's Friday, you know, and I'm pretty sure I mentioned that we've got twelve people checking in this afternoon. Those Japanese guests, and the members of the . . . the . . .'' She scrambled hastily through the file on guest preferences. "Rudyard Kipling Condensation Society. Now, that might interest you, Mr. Stoker. Do you like Kipling? You look as if . . . I mean with your family background and all."

" 'Though I've belted you and flayed you, by the living God that made you, you're a better man than I am, Gunga Din,' '' said Axminster unexpectedly. "Yes. I like Kipling."

"Dina Muir, our receptionist, should be able to tell you

all you need to know about them. The Society sent ahead
some literature. They give recitations on request, I guess,
wherever they go.'' Drawing on six years' experience of
managing guests prone to an astonishing variety of behav-
iors, she guided Axminster out of the gazebo and onto the
lawn. Doreen swiveled her head to follow them, rather like
the gun turret on a tank.

''I'm quite interested in Kipling,'' said Axminster, ''but
wouldn't you say that I was needed here? Prioritization
is a key quality concept. Toilets are too critical to be left
to chaos—''

Behind her, Doreen made a sound Quill hadn't heard
before and was pretty sure she didn't want to hear again.
''I wouldn't dream of asking you to use up your precious
vacation time on plumbing problems. You've already been
far, far more helpful than necessary. We are all in your
debt. Will you be eating here tonight? If you decide not to,
there are a number of places I can recommend. Or what
about taking the wine tour? The van leaves this evening at
six-thirty from the foyer.''

''I have already signed up for the wine tour,'' said Axminster, a little pathetically. ''It will be my fourth such
foray. You feel it would be worthwhile to go again?''

''You learn something new every time,'' said Quill
firmly, ''especially on the all-day tour. You can catch that
one tomorrow.''

''I sense that you may be backing off from your leadership commitment, Sarah. I am disappointed. Ladies? Good
day to you.''

Quill watched him march off with dismay. ''I think I
hurt his feelings.''

''I think you saved his life,'' said Meg, her eye on Doreen.

Quill turned to Doreen, ''No,'' she said.

Doreen's eyes widened in cagey innocence, which gave
her the look of a startled rooster. ''No terlits?''

''You know what I mean. No mops left jammed under
Mr. Stoker's door in the morning. No slippery puddles of
soapy water on the bathroom floor. No foreign substances
in his food. And don't you dare call any religious organi-

zations to convert him. Understood? Now. What about the plumbing?''

Doreen blinked. ''Petey says we gotta pump the septic.''

''How long will it take? When will he get here? The Kipling people are due to check in at four o'clock. And most of them are booked into the first-floor rooms.'' She thought a moment. ''Maybe we can move the Kipling people to the third floor.''

Doreen brightened. ''We could throw out this Stoker. He's in the Shaker suite. Put a couple of the Kiplings in there.''

''Mr. Stoker booked the Shaker suite for three months. And paid in advance. We can't afford to offend a guest like *that* Doreen.''

''Up the proletariat,'' muttered Doreen. Quill groaned. Marx, after Amway, would be too much. ''Doreen!''

''If they're into Kipling, they at least have pretensions to the literary,'' Meg intervened. She waved the tattered *Trumpet!* ''We can search the trashcans all over town and get them copies of this rag. They'll be laughing so hard they won't think twice about toilets. Come to think of it, it'd be a good investment for you, Doreen. Benny Pasquale's dad has probably thrown most of them into the incinerator by now. They'll be collector's copies by next week and worth a bunch. I can't believe the guy will have the nerve to publish another issue.''

''Oncet a week,'' said Doreen.

''Petey's going to have to come once a week?'' said Quill, once again preoccupied with plumbing. ''How much is this going to cost us? I'm seriously thinking of getting the air-conditioning people in this afternoon. And they want half of the payment for the installation up front.''

''That thing.'' Doreen pointed a callused thumb in the direction of the *Trumpet!* ''Comes out oncet a week. Mr. Conway told me that himself.''

Meg raised her eyebrows. ''Hedrick Conway? The publisher of this piece of junk? I didn't know you knew him. Have you met him before?''

''You ain't?''

''Nobody's met him, far as I know.'' Quill thought a

moment. "Howie Murchison must have. He handled the real estate closing for the Nickerson building."

Doreen shrugged. "He come out here to look for you a while ago."

"Hedrick Conway did? Then where is he?" Quill scanned the Adirondack chairs. She was familiar with all the guests and they all belonged there. Hot, but registered.

"Right here, Mrs. Quilliam." A very tall, banana-nosed man unfolded from behind the mass of sweet peas like a stork coming up for air. A lemon seed stuck to his forehead like an afterthought. "Ladies? Can I quote you on why you refuse to serve the President?"

CHAPTER 2

Meg gripped the sides of her wicker chair, threw her head back, and screamed. Judging from the cheerful look on her face, it was a satisfying scream. "And," said Meg, "you can quote me on that." She stood up, brushed off her shorts, and retied her T-shirt, exposing another few inches of flat stomach. Hedrick's pale blue eyes bulged. "Quill? I'll take this stuff back to the kitchen. Doreen and I will take care of the menu planning. I'll turn the guest list over to Dina. That leaves you"—Meg gave her a look loaded with significance—"to handle things here." She nodded briskly to Hedrick Conway, swept the files off the table, and marched out of the gazebo, trampling the tattered remnants of the *Trumpet!* underfoot.

Quill, trying to recall just when she'd pitched the lemon seed over the side of the gazebo, had come to the reluctant conclusion that Hedrick had heard all; it had occurred far too early in their derisive discussion about the *Trumpet!* to make social niceties credible. With a baleful eye, she watched her sister cross the lawn: the same conclusion had obviously occurred immediately to Meg. At least, her own decision to discover what lay behind Hedrick Conway's promised mini mall exposé had been thoughtful, determined, and unvoiced. Just like Lew Archer, the least verbal of all the great detectives.

"Quite a place you got here." Conway shifted from one very large foot to the other, crushing a particularly vivid spray of crimson sweet peas. The heat had plastered his coarse blond hair to his forehead. He was thin, except for a round ball of stomach. A white cotton shirt laundered far past its useful life fitted badly over his sloping shoulders. Baggy pale brown chinos and soft white suede shoes made him look like a marshmallow handled by too many Boy Scouts.

"Yeah," said Quill laconically, in true Archer style. "I'm Sarah Quilliam. That's Quilliam with two *i*'s. What's up?" This, Quill realized even as she said it, was rude even for Lew Archer. And, to paraphrase what one vice presidential candidate had once said to another, she was no Robert Mitchum, she was the manager of a public hostelry, and constrained to be hospitable. "It's very nice to meet you. Can I offer you something cool to drink?"

"Wouldn't mind a glass of iced tea." Ignoring the graveled path that ran parallel to the sweet peas, he trampled through the plants to the gazebo entrance, thudded into the shelter itself, and sat in the chair Meg had so sensibly vacated minutes before. "The glasses are dirty," he pointed out.

"Well," said Quill inadequately. "This is . . . is there . . . I mean, did . . . Let me get you a fresh glass." She turned and looked for Kathleen, who was nowhere in sight. "The waitress will be out in a bit."

A brief silence reigned. Quill, momentarily discomposed, and in search of a conversational gambit, remembered that Hedrick wasn't solely responsible for the *Trumpet!* "Are your mother and sister with you today?"

"Nope, nope. They went to Syracuse. Shopping. You know gals. I was just roaming the streets of the village, looking for news. Carry this with me, at all times." He rummaged in the pocket of his chinos and withdrew a thick red spiral notebook. "It's all in here. The goods book. Not the Good Book, y'see, but the goods book. Get it?"

Quill got it. She eyed the book with a high degree of interest. "You keep your story ideas in there?"

"It's my bible." He descended to the practical with an abrupt change of manner. "Also, I stopped by to see if you got your free complimentary issue. Thought I'd better introduce myself, seeing as how people probably would like to know the person that runs something like the *Trumpet!*"

"Um," said Quill. Under her feet the *Trumpet!*'s second page fluttered in the breeze from the Falls, the picture of Hedrick's disgraced loafer flapping back and forth like a small flag. Hedrick *tsk'd* in distress and picked it up.

"This didn't happen in delivery?"

"The wind," Quill improvised, "blew it under the chair."

"You probably didn't read the old *Gazette* until now." He smoothed the paper with a loving hand. "I told Ma, we're going to make some changes. Time this town had a real paper, tackling real issues. Take this f'instance." He began to read aloud. " 'It was dark and stormy when this reporter—' "

"Yes," said Quill. "The leash law issue." She smiled in what she hoped was a winning way, and perjured herself without a qualm, something Archie Goodwin did frequently in the pursuit of justice. "I was just fascinated by the paper. This whole approach is such a departure from the way Paul Rosen used to run the *Gazette*. Especially the story you're going to write about the mini-mall."

Hedrick smiled complacently. "Made you sit up and take notice, huh? That's the mark of a good story. I suppose they know who I am in this town, all right. You see the police blotter?"

"You're going to make that a usual practice, are you?"

"It's Hemlock Falls first. That sheriff, what's his name?"

"Myles McHale."

"Yeah. Gave me a little lip about printing it. But I know my rights." He shook his head and laughed genially. "These small-town police. You gotta know how to handle 'em."

"I don't know that I'd call Sheriff McHale small town, precisely. Did you get the small-town impression because of his reaction to the story you're going to write about the mini-mall?"

Hedrick ignored this gambit. "Well. You been around a bit, like I have, you'd know what I mean." He narrowed his eyes at the sprawling building. "How big is this place, anyway?"

"This place? You mean the Inn? Twenty-seven rooms."

"Occupancy rate?"

"I'd have to ask John Raintree about that," said Quill, a little stiffly, "our business manager."

"Reason I asked is, with twenty-seven rooms, you'd probably want a good slug of papers every week. What can I put you down for, say, forty copies a week?"

"Forty?" Quill decided it wasn't the heat, but Hedrick's goatlike leaping from crag to conversational crag that was making her dizzy.

"Good business like this—if it is a good business, and you're not just blowing smoke like a lot of small-timers do—you'd want a copy for each room plus lobby copies, plus one for you and a couple of the staff."

"Well," said Quill cleverly, "we might think about a subscription—maybe even two—if we had an idea about upcoming features. For example, this story about the mini—"

"Quill? Meg sent out some refreshments." Kathleen Kiddermeister stepped into the gazebo, tray in hand. "And she said to tell you she'll think about the sushi, but she's got another way to impress this art critic guy."

Quill, normally glad to see Kathleen, was frustrated at this interruption of her subtle interrogation. She jumped to her feet and grabbed at the tray. "Thanks, Kath. You didn't need to do this. I'll take care of it."

Kathleen held on to the tray and dropped one eyelid in a surreptitious wink. Clearly, Hedrick Conway and his lunatic journalism had been a topic of discussion in the kitchen. "You just sit down, Quill, and let me clear this for you." With the deft efficiency that made her one of the Inn's best waitresses, she put the pitcher and the used glasses on the tray, folded the remains of the *Trumpet!* into her apron pocket, and set down a bowl of strawberries, plates, and a fresh pitcher of tea.

"So," said Quill. "Thanks."

Kathleen, curiosity all over her freckled face, said, "About the plumbing?"

"Mr. Peterson's here. He's taking care of it. So. Thanks."

"You know the toilets in 101 and 102 are like totally backed up."

"Plumbing problem?" said Hedrick alertly. "Toilets, huh?" He began scribbling and muttered, "Inn at Hemlock Fall Evacuated." He repeated this with a pleased air, then regarded the waterfall. "Any chance the sewage'll flood the Gorge? Sure there is. 'Will Environmental Disaster Close Inn?' "

"Jeez," said Kathleen.

Quill raised her eyebrows at Kathleen and sent her a fierce mental message—an activity recently promoted by the Reverend Dookie Shuttleworth, who was currently experimenting with extrasensory-perception sermons—to beat feet. She braced her feet against the footer at the base of the gazebo with an assumption of careless ease. "Thanks for bringing the tea and fruit out, Kathleen. I'll be in after Mr. Conway is finished here."

"Nothing else I can do for you here?"

"Not a thing."

"Wait a minute, there, girlie." Hedrick took in Kathleen's soft peach uniform, her starched apron, and the loaded tray. "You a waitress?"

Kathleen, bridling over the "girlie," said rather tartly that, no, she was a shortstop for the New York Jets.

"Before you were a waitress?"

Quill stated the obvious. "The Jets don't take women players, Mr. Conway. Kathleen's been a waitress for six years, ever since we opened the Inn."

"Thought so. Hang on a bit, Mrs. Quillam. I got something to ask this little lady." Hedrick reopened the red notebook with a flourish. The pages were much-thumbed and filled with small, surprisingly neat writing. "Got a report I'm following up on here, ma'am, about policies regarding the serving of guests. You ever been instructed not to serve some people? You know, like some political figures?"

Kathleen blinked at Hedrick. "Refuse to serve some people?"

"F'instance, did Mrs. Quillam here ever tell you to kick some folks out? Not to serve them?" Kathleen's bemusement seemed to register on him and he added in an explanatory way, "Say, f'instance, the President comes to Hemlock Falls. Not that he has or anything. But say that he does. Mrs. Quillam here let you serve him?"

Quill intervened, "Mr. Conway, you've misinterpreted something you overheard a few minutes ago from my sister. Meg frequently overstates—"

Hedrick held up a fleshy palm. "No fair coaching. So, Katherine, say you got the President wanting to eat in your dining room."

"The President's coming to dinner?" said Kathleen. "Our President? You're kidding! Does Davy know?"

"Davy?" asked Hedrick with a clever air.

"My brother. If it's true, he'll need to know right away."

"Your brother, huh?" Hedrick licked the end of his pencil. "Local political activist? What's his name and address?"

"The Inn's full," said Kathleen with dismay. "Where are we going to put the President?"

"So you'd let your brother know, first thing," said Hedrick. "He's what they call a subversive, your brother?"

"*Stop!*" shouted Quill. Behind her the low murmur of the guests in the Adirondack chairs came to a sudden halt. Quill controlled her voice. "Mr. Conway, Kathleen's brother, David Kiddermeister, is Myles McHale's chief deputy. He'd be busy with security matters if the President visited, which, Kathleen, he *isn't* scheduled to do. Go back to the kitchen." Kathleen began to straighten the dishes on the table. Quill ignored her. "Mr. Conway, would you like some strawberries?"

"Strawberries?" He peered suspiciously at the bowl of fruit. "They're not canned, are they? I never eat canned food."

"We've made our reputation on the quality of our food," she said with determined cheerfulness. "Now. You were just about to tell me all about the mini-mall story. I read all about it in this week's *Trumpet!* and I can't wait to hear more."

"Well, now." Hedrick frowned. "My information's confidential of course, but . . . Quillam, Quillam," muttered Hedrick, paging through his notebook. "Sure. Here we go. Mini-mall. Chamber of Commerce. Payoffs to Mayor." He looked up at Quill alertly. "You're the alleged secretary of the Chamber of Commerce? Would you care to comment on the stories circulating in town about fraudulent activity in the mini-mall project?"

"Alleged? Alleged? I *am* . . . Mr. Conway, there is *nothing* fraudulent about the mini-mall project. What are your sources of information?"

"Quillam . . . denies . . . involvement . . ." muttered Hedrick, scribbling.

"Involvement in what! Are you referring to something specific?"

"I'm referring to the truth, ma'am. That's all I'm after. You involved in this mini-mall investment all by yourself?"

"We all are," Kathleen interrupted nervously. "Quill and John Raintree gave all us employees the chance to invest in the new boutique restaurant. Is there something wrong? Did somebody steal our money? You know what? I'll see if I can find John. He knows all about our new restaurant there. That sound like a good idea?"

"No," said Quill. "Kathleen, please—"

"Raintree, Raintree, Raintree . . . now where did I hear that name? Aha!" Hedrick held up a minatory hand, read to himself, lips moving, then looked at them with an expression Quill found incredibly sly. "He have something to do with this deal?"

"John Raintree is our business manager. And yes, we made the decision together to invest in the mini-mall project."

"Raintree? That a white name?"

"I beg your pardon?"

Kathleen coughed nervously. "Quill. John's going over the supplier bills in the office. I'll be back with him in two seconds." She hurried across the grass, the glasses on the tray jingling.

"Raintree. Doesn't sound like a white name." He raised

his eyebrows expectantly. "It's important for a newspaper-man to be accurate. First thing they teach you."

"John's a member of the Onondaga tribe. He has an MBA from Cornell and he's been with us four years. He handles our accounting and all the finances."

"So you don't have a hand on the checkbook. That's very interesting." Hedrick made a small finicky note in his book. "Can't say as I blame ol' John. Don't like to let either one of my ladies out of hand myself."

Quill stared at him, open-mouthed.

"Hello? Hello?" Hedrick rapped on the table. "Are we communicating here?"

"We're certainly exchanging words, Mr. Conway. But I have to say, I don't in the least understand what you're doing. Now, if you could just explain a bit more about this mini-mall story."

Hedrick leaned forward. His breath was unpleasant. "I've got the most important job there is. To publish the best paper I can. I'm a newshound, first and foremost. Like Eddie Murrow and Ernie Pyle, which is why I have to be on the alert for news all the time. Walking the streets of this town day and night, finding the news." He sat back, with that wild veer into the pragmatic Quill noticed before. "And I'm a publisher, which is why I have to find out about subscriptions, at least until I can find a circulation manager. You wouldn't know anyone who'd be interested in the job, Mrs. Quillam?"

"It's spelled Q-U-I-L-L-I-A-M," said Quill tartly. "And I am not married. I'm sure you'll agree that the first obligation of a good reporter is to get the facts straight." She fanned herself and took a deep breath. The first rule of innkeeping, she and Meg had agreed long ago, was not to belt guests in the mouth, even under the severest provocation. A change of subject was in order, if she wasn't going to violate rule one. "I'd be fascinated to know where you got your ideas about how to run a newspaper. I know Syracuse has a fine program. The S.I. Newhouse graduate program?"

"You mean did I go to journalism school? Nah. I guess I could teach so-called professors a thing or two about what sells papers. Nope, this issue of the *Trumpet!* is my first.''

''You're not an experienced newspaperman, then?''

Hedrick lowered his notepad and gave her a look compounded equally of incredulity and hurt. ''I guess maybe you didn't mean that the way it sounded.''

Quill apologized, then hoping further digression would result in a more sensible conversation, said pleasantly, ''Is there a reason why you chose Hemlock Falls for your first venture?''

''That him coming? The Indian?'' Hedrick interrupted. ''Got that brown skin and black hair. Must be.''

Quill twisted around in her seat. ''Yes, that's John.'' She waved. John smiled, his long legs covering the distance between the Inn and the gazebo with easy athleticism. He nodded to Hedrick as Quill made the introductions.

Hedrick, brow furrowed, mouth lightly agape, burrowed in his book like a mole after a grub. ''Heard about you.'' He flipped the pages. ''Here it is. Thought so. Got a record, right? Arrested on suspicion of murder a couple years ago. Served time for murder before that.'' He tucked the notebook into his shirt pocket with a nod of satisfaction. ''Thing is, I was thinking maybe of doing a series of stories with a punch. Y'know, human interest. 'Will I Kill Again?' That kind of thing. Grabs the reader.''

Quill's breath went short. She felt as though she were encased in glass, as if there were a transparent, sound-proofed barrier between Hedrick, herself, and the rest of her world. The skin on her scalp contracted and her fingers curled into fists. ''Out.'' Her voice just above a whisper, she got to her feet. ''Get out.''

''Quill.'' John's voice was quiet, removed from her by that glass wall of rage.

''You heard me,'' said Quill to Hedrick Conway. She picked up the iced tea pitcher and pulled her arm back. She thought of Darryl Strawberry.

Hedrick smirked and waved the red-covered book as he left the gazebo and shambled across the lawn to the Inn's parking lot.

''Quill.''

The world righted itself. She smoothed her hair. Her

hands were shaking, and she sat down hard, bumping her head on the latticed wall of the gazebo.

"Hey." John squatted next to her chair. His coppery skin was redder than usual, but his expression was calm. "It's true."

"It's not true. Not the way he said it. It made you sound . . . guilty."

"I was guilty."

"Of manslaughter, John. No one in their right mind could blame you for what you did. That little muckraking *toad*! Has the *nerve*! I could just kill him!"

"No offense, Quill. But I can take care of him myself. And if I don't want to rearrange his nose down to his socks, why should you?"

"You don't?"

"Well . . ." The skin around John's eyes wrinkled in amusement. "Maybe a little. But what can he do to me now? Everyone in town knows what happened. If he reprints the story, so what? It's a nine-day wonder, and then it's over. You know Hemlock Falls."

"I guess I do. And you're right. But—! What a little twerp!"

"I'll buy that. Come on." His hand was warm in her own. He pulled her to her feet, "You'll be glad to know that Petey Peterson's pumping the septic tank and the toilets will be functioning again. That sounds like a tongue-twister, doesn't it? And the Kipling Society's due momentarily. We'll go back to the kitchen and see if we can talk Meg out of some of the *sorbet* she's made for tonight while we're waiting for them to check in."

"There's something wrong with this picture," Quill complained as she followed him across the lawn.

"Wow!" John cocked his head to one side, a funny note in his voice.

"I should be comforting you, and as usual, John, you end up comforting me. Wow, what?" She squinted. "My goodness. Does that look like an advance party of the Kipling Condensation Society to you?"

"If it is, I'm joining."

Two women emerged from French doors that led from

the Tavern Bar to the flagstone patio. The younger wore a pink halter top that just barely contained a generous pair of breasts. They looked exactly like a pair of giant rolls in a wicker breadbasket. Even at this distance, Quill could tell she was chewing gum. Her sister was older, slimmer, and better-dressed. Even at this distance, the two women's sexuality was as blanketing as the August heat. Quill poked John in the side, hard. "Stop that."

"Stop what?"

"Drooling over that pair of sisters. They're poking holes in the lawn with their stiletto heels. You know how Mike hates that."

"I never drool. Except when it's deserved. It's deserved." John chuckled. "And they aren't sisters."

The women walked toward them like peacocks picking their way through a barnyard.

"Mother and daughter?" said Quill dubiously. "You're right, that's a heck of a face-lift on the mother. I wonder who they are?" The younger blonde was carrying a large paper shopping bag that read: SAKS FIFTH AVENUE AT THE SYRACUSE MALL! "Oh, nuts. More Conways."

"There's more?"

"Sure. You remember what Marge told us last Sunday. Louisa's the mother, the daughter's . . ." Quill frowned. "I keep thinking Thomas, but that's not right."

"Carlyle."

"That's it." A wave of heavy perfume hit Quill before the women came within hearing distance. "Giorgio. Phew! At one o'clock in the afternoon?"

John slipped her a sideways grin. "Snob."

They stood and watched the Conways wind their way through the rosebushes. Mrs. Conway wore a white linen suit—probably Armani, Quill thought—possibly Ungaro. Her daughter's halter, short skirt and gold-trimmed handbag were definitely Escada. Mrs. Conway's shoes would have paid Doreen's salary for a week. Although neither of the women looked directly at John, Quill knew in her bones that the animated conversation between them was for his benefit. They subsided into self-conscious silence as they neared the gazebo, then the elder extended her hand. "Ms.

Quilliam? I'm Louisa Conway. My daughter Carlyle. We have to apologize for the gum; she's trying to quit smoking." Louisa Conway's hand was cool and firm, the nails buffed, not polished, the skin well-cared for. "Carlyle, this is Sarah Quilliam—you're familiar with her work? She's the artist?"

"The flower studies?" Carlyle shifted the gum from one cheek to the other, and said rapidly, "You did that terrific series of roses a while back. I saw the show in New York. They called you the heir to O'Keeffe, didn't they?"

"Just O'Keeffe's flower work, Cay. Ms. Quilliam's work is nothing like the desert studies." Mrs. Conway, with the air of a script prompter in a bad play, gave her a nod.

"Thank goodness for that, I say. O'Keeffe terrifies me. Do you hang any work here at the Inn?"

Quill blinked, opened her mouth, and said, "Not really."

Up close, the Conway women resembled nothing so much as heavy cream. Neither had a beautiful face; Quill could see the resemblance to Hedrick in both of them, especially around the mouth and eyes. But they had something: both had thick translucent skin, heavy-lidded eyes, full mouths, and hair the color of bronze, thinly beaten. Like plush cats with glossy fur, Quill thought. Except that she liked cats, and she didn't like these women at all.

"And you," said Louisa, "must be the famous Mr. Raintree." She widened her eyes and wriggled her shoulders. John's answering grin irritated Quill profoundly. "We've heard about you from some friends of ours who stayed here last year. The Ferragamos? No relation to the luggage people, but just as nice as can be. Theobold said you truly know your wines. When Cay and I eat here, you'll have to give us your personal attention."

John said, "I'll be happy to show you around the Inn, if you've got a little time. Excuse me, Quill. I'd like to show Carlyle and Louisa the koi pond."

I'll just bet you would, Quill thought, resisting the impulse to kick him. "We've got a fairly large party checking in in about twenty minutes, Mrs. Conway, but I could take you on a quick tour of the first floor." She patted the curl behind one ear, hoping she'd scrubbed off all the Gruyère, vowing she would not, under any circumstances, fluff her hair or check her lipstick.

"We've come at a bad time," said Louisa, raising and lowering her long lashes at John.

"You must be terribly busy, John," said Carlyle.

"I'll be happy to give you all the time you need. You go on ahead to the kitchen, Quill." In his haste to brush by her, John stepped on her foot.

"Thank you so much!" Quill's sarcasm might have been bird droppings, for all the notice John took.

Louisa's large blue eyes looked directly into John's. She smiled slowly, and—as Quill told Meg later, if she hadn't actually seen it with her own eyes she never would have believed it—ran her tongue around her lower lip. "We'd love to take the time, wouldn't we, Cay? Although, actually, we stopped by to find my son. Has he been here?"

"Yes," said Quill.

"He's so proud of that darn newspaper. Cay and I fully support it, of course, but it's definitely Hedrick's baby."

"You aren't going to be involved in it, then?"

"Oh, goodness, no. Cay and I travel quite a bit, and we've just established a home base in Hemlock Falls. We won't be here much at all."

"And Mr. Conway, your husband, I mean? Is he going to be joining you?"

"Aren't you sweet," said Louisa. "Mr. Conway died six years ago, unfortunately. Leaving me to bring the children up by myself."

"Mother," said Carlyle, "as though you didn't have a raft of nannies and servants to do it for you."

They laughed, like slow-breaking china: Hah-hah-hah.

"He was a dear, dear man, my Connie." Louisa's tone was absentminded in the extreme, as though she had trouble recalling his name. Quill would have bet a quarter's income that she knew his estate to the nickel. "HC Pharmaceuticals, you know. *Big* money, I'm afraid. Cay and Heddie loved him as though he'd been their real father, and he loved them. It was truly a love story, Ms. Quilliam. All four of us, together. It was so sad when he died."

Quill, who couldn't think of any tactful way to inquire who'd fathered the horrible Hedrick, asked if they intended to make their permanent home in Hemlock Falls.

"God, no!" shrieked Carlyle.

"Not that we don't love it here," said Louisa. "But Cay and I are used to a little more activity at night than we've found here so far."

"I wouldn't mind a little nighttime activity with that sheriff," said Carlyle with a full-lipped smile at John. "My brother's asked us to make some calls around town, just while he's starting into the business, you know, and we stopped by the courthouse yesterday, and ran into him. Myles McHale. Mummy, didn't he remind you of that gorgeous banker we met in Saint T.?"

"Jean-Paul? Cay, you're right. He did!"

They both gave a little shriek.

"Saint T.?" asked Quill, who found she had to make an effort to unclench her teeth.

"Saint Tropez," Carlyle tossed over her shoulder. "Mom, this heat! Could you take us out of the sun, Mr. Raintree?"

Louisa leaned toward John, placed her lips near his ear, and said ruefully, "Daughters!"

"Just trying to save you money, Mummy. We could buy this place with what I spend on the dermatologist. I'd far rather spend the money at something more fun than repairing sun damage."

"Anything for you, precious. Although I claim seniority, and the right to this darling hunk of maleness." Louisa slipped one hand through John's elbow, the other through Carlyle's. The three of them ambled back to the Inn. Quill, trailing like a neglected puppy, was so astounded at the sudden transformation of her business manager that she tripped on the flagstone patio. At the French doors leading to the Tavern Bar, John stepped aside to let the women precede him. "God, your painting's gorgeous!" said Carlyle as they stepped into the warm shade. "Look at the lily, Mother."

"Actually, that's a print of O'Keeffe's," said Quill. "One of her most famous. When your average, everyday art lover thinks of O'Keeffe, that's what they think of. The lily.''

"Quill's work is in storage," said John. "Although we're set up to display them anytime she cares to bring them out. We painted the north wall deep teal to set them off.''

"This floor's terrific," said Carlyle. "It's so shiny!" Her thin heels clicked on the wood. She stepped daintily, like a chicken looking for worms.

"So shiny!" Quill mouthed behind her.

"Mahogany," said John, "like the wainscoting and the bar itself. All of this dates from the mid-nineteenth century, when the Inn was owned by General C. C. Hemlock.''

"I'll just buzz on into the kitchen," said Quill loudly. "If you'll excuse me." She waited a moment. John gave her an absentminded nod. Louisa ignored her altogether. Quill walked through the Bar to the foyer, from there to the dining room, and into the kitchen, planting her sandals with loud, definite slaps. Meg was bent over the butcher block counter, peeling grapefruit. She looked up as Quill came in. "There you are. Good grief! What's the matter?!''

"Not the least little thing. No, ma'am.''

Meg looked dubious. "If you say so. I can't find Dina, by the way, so I sent Doreen to look for her. The Kiplings are due to check in at any minute. It's not like her to take off in the middle of a shift.''

"Maybe some muscle-bound cretin in a sleeveless T-shirt came slouching through the front door with a cigarette hanging from his lower lip and sweat rolling off his biceps and seduced her away.''

"What?''

"Nothing. It's hot. It's August. I feel . . . witchy.''

"So what's new? Did the Horrible Hedrick Reveal All?''

Quill decided she was too mad to answer the question. She settled onto a stool opposite her sister and picked up a section of grapefruit.

"Do you want to answer my question?''

"No.''

"You want to sample the *sorbet*?''

"No.''

"Just no? Not 'Your *sorbet*, Meg? Your fabulous sherbet! I would kill to get a teeny bit'? I've got blueberry, strawberry, banana, and grapefruit. And I've been sweating in this kitchen for hours and hours making it, so you owe me.''

"It is hot in here," Quill conceded. "I'm going to call the air-conditioning people."

"Oh, it's all right. The breeze usually comes right through there." She nodded at the long row of windows lining the far wall of the kitchen. "I can take a little heat. And you know what they say, if you can't take the—"

"Stop. I'm in no mood."

"So was Hedrick as horrible as he looked?"

"Worse."

"As bad as his paper?"

"Worse than that." Quill swallowed the grapefruit.

"Worse than that," mused Meg. "Did you find out what's behind the mini-mall scandal?"

"No."

"Quill. This attack of taciturnity is *most* unlike you. What'd he do?"

Quill told her.

Meg frowned. "This little red book—"

"Great minds think alike. If we could get our hands on it, we could find out just what the heck he thinks he's doing."

"Yeah. With any luck, Quill, the poor schmuck'll go broke in three weeks and slink on back to Syracuse."

"I don't think so. He's not a poor schmuck, Meg, he's a rich schmuck, or at least his family is."

"Hedrick Conway's rich? What he'd do, win the lottery?"

"You could say that. If there's a sort of demonic lottery that randomly assigns gold-digging mothers and sisters to people like Hedrick, he's absolutely won that lottery."

"You met his mom and his sister?"

"I met them." Quill picked up another section of grapefruit.

Meg snatched it out of her hand with an exasperated 'tch!' "It takes me a long time to pith these properly, Quill.

Get an unpeeled one from the bowl. So, what are they like?
Are they something?''

''John thinks they're something. She—Carlyle—thinks
Myles is something.''

''Hmm.'' Meg peered at her. ''It's a free country.''

''That it is.''

''And Myles is a free man.''

''Yep.''

''And you've been worried that John hasn't had a date
for several months, so what's the big deal?''

Quill selected a grapefruit, began to peel it, then set it
down with a frown. ''It's what they know about us. When
I met Louisa and Carlyle, they had this little spiel all prepared about how I was this well-known artist and how the
flower studies resembled O'Keeffe—''

''You *are* a well-known artist,'' said Meg loyally.

''They claimed to have seen that show I had last year.
You know, the Hemlock Falls studies.''

''It wasn't so little.''

''Meg. Get real. It was at the rear end of Dan Feinman's
shop in SoHo, and barely anyone saw it. Nobody here even
knows I held it.''

''Myles went,'' said Meg. ''And so did Andy and I. And
it was written up in the *Times,* in the Art section. June
twenty-third. I remember.''

''That's not the point.''

''The point is . . . ?''

''The three of them know way too much about John,
about me, about God know's what.''

''And what are we supposed to do about it?''

''Kick 'em out,'' said a familiar foghorn voice.

Quill jumped. ''Doreen, don't do that!''

''Do what?'' The housekeeper stumped into the kitchen,
her lower lip at a belligerent angle.

''I swear you listen for exactly the right entrance line.''
Doreen exchanged a look with Meg.

''She's not grouchy, actually,'' said Meg. ''At least, she
is, but she has a reason, this time. Did you find Dina, Doreen?''

"Yep. This crisis you got—have to do with the plumbing?"

"No," said Quill.

"Then I ain't got time for it. Got a crisis of my own."

"What kind of crisis?" asked Quill.

Doreen folded her hands under her apron and regarded Quill with satisfaction. "You got to kick that Stoker out on his keister."

Meg chuckled, then took a large bag of ice from the Zero King and put it in the Cuisinart, a clear signal that she refused involvement. As it usually did, the Cuisinart noise drove Quill and Doreen into the dining room.

"I told you," said Doreen. "That Stoker's a menace."

"Look, Doreen. I know Mr. Stoker can be a little difficult, but I honestly think he can improve the way we do things around here."

Doreen came to a full stop, placed both hands on her hips, and glared. "He told Dina to do the registration different, right?"

"He didn't tell her any such thing. He sat down with her in a team meeting and brainstormed a solution to the problem of registering guests more efficiently." Quill cocked her head, distracted. "Did you hear anything unusual?"

Doreen ignored this last question, fierce in the pursuit of her point. "We ever overbook before?"

"Well, no. What *is* that bunch of thumps?"

"Bill got out that hadn't ought?"

"If you mean have we over-or underbilled in the past, no, not that I know of. Doreen, you didn't hang Mr. Stoker up by a rope or anything, did you? That sounds like kicking. Like somebody's kicking."

Doreen remained immovable. "And we've always collected from Visa and that, right?"

"Right. What *is* that noise?"

"So what I want to know is how come this Stoker was sticking his nose into somethin' that dint need to be fixed in the first place?"

"Everything that you do can be made better, Doreen. It's a basic principle of Quality Improvement. That kicking's coming from the lobby."

"You're durn tooting it's coming from the lobby."

Quill hurried, Doreen following like a grouchy sheepdog; she'd spent a lot of time selecting the Oriental rug that covered the oak flooring, the two huge urns that flanked the desk, and the creamy leather sofa that stood in front of the cobblestone fireplace. The lobby was an elegant introduction to the Inn. Holes in the wall wouldn't improve it.

A large Slavic-looking gentleman in an orange brocaded waistcoat, dark trousers, and Norfolk jacket was on his knees, rhythmically beating the wooden registration box against the floor. A middle-aged couple with a Victorian air stood by with mild looks of concern. The woman wore a filmy, calf-length dress with blue ribbons at the waist; her husband—or so Quill guessed, since they had that indefinable sameness that usually comes from a long marriage—held a parasol in one hand and a Gladstone bag in the other.

Two women sat on the couch, the first elderly and dressed with neat precision in a beige pleated skirt and light jacket. The other, perhaps in her late fifties, was hugely fat in a bright caftan; she responded to Quill's astonished survey of her lobby with a warm, attractive chuckle.

Axminster Stoker shifted from one foot to the other in the midst of this small invasion. "You *all*," he said with a querulous snap, "were supposed to have read the instructions all the way through."

CHAPTER 3

"Z'ere is it," said the orange waistcoat, with a final thud of the box against the floor. He set the box down and picked up a credit card.

"*The*re it is," corrected Mr. Stoker fussily. "And it wouldn't have been there in the first place if you'd read—"

"I've never heard of such a thing," interrupted the blue-ribboned woman with soft indignation. "This is supposed to be a four-star—"

"Three star, sweetheart, three star," said her parasol-carrying husband, in the thickest Texas drawl Quill had ever heard. "There are three degrees of bliss in the Gardens of Paradise, you know."

"Three star, of course, darling . . ."

"And whether this is Paradise remains to be seen," said the old lady tartly. "And the rating's for food, after all, not accommodations, or service. Although I must say the room rates would lead one to anticipate a more courteous welcome."

"Lot more than a shilling a day, hoy, Jerzey?" said the parasol husband to the orange waistcoat.

The large lady in the caftan chuckled again. Then all five of them shouted, " 'Shillin' a day, bloomin' good pay— Lucky to touch it, a shilling a day!' "

They applauded themselves.

Quill took advantage of momentary good humor. "You

must be the Kipling Society. How do you do. I'm—''

''Not Cecily Cardew!'' interrupted the husband, who was apparently inclined to be boisterous.

''And not Wilde,'' said the old lady, to Quill's momentary confusion. She adjusted the pearls at her neck and regarded Quill with kindness. ''You must think we're quite mad, my dear. But it's been a long ride in that miserable rented van, and we are fatigued. I take it you are Ms. Quilliam? I am Aurora Kent, spinster of this parish, as Mr. Kipling might say. May I introduce you to Mr. and Mrs. Lyle Fairbanks?''

Mrs. Fairbanks smoothed the ribbons at her waist with a slim white hand and nodded gracefully. Lyle Fairbanks bounced forward, took Quill's hand, and kissed the air above her wrist with a flourish.

''And the gentleman in the waistcoat (she pronounced it ''weskit'') is Mr. Jerzey Paulovich, of Poland.''

''And I am Georgia Hardwicke,'' said the large woman in the caftan. Quill decided she really liked her chuckle. ''I'm fairly new to the Society, and I'm not sure how the Poet would describe me. Widow of this weald, maybe. Let Ms. Quilliam's hand go, Lyle. Then maybe she can straighten this out.''

''I'm sure I can,'' said Quill. ''Has Dina gotten you all checked into your rooms?'' She looked at the reception desk. ''I see she's not here. I have to apologize. Something must have happened. We were expecting you, of course, and Dina's an excellent receptionist. . . . ''

''There's a receptionist?'' asked Mr. Kent.

Doreen gave a loud meaningful sniff. Mr. Stoker cleared his throat nervously once or twice.

''Of course. Dina Muir. She's a very good one. Except that she doesn't seem to be here.''

''Well,'' said Mrs. Fairbanks, drifting to the tapestry chair by the couch, ''I did wonder about the propriety of checking ourselves in.''

''Checking yourselves in?'' said Quill.

Doreen's freckled hand shot under her nose. It held a card printed in large red letters.

THE RECEPTION TEAM SAYS

DO IT YOURSELF!

(A Total Quality Project from
the Inn at Hemlock Falls)
(Please refer to instructions on lobby desk.)

"Do it yourself?" Quill took the card, studiously avoiding Doreen's gimlet eye.

"If you'd just *read* the instructions," said Axminster Stoker, "this would have gone smoothly—and efficiently. That's the Quality Way."

"What instructions?" Quill asked him. "Dina's supposed to check guests in. Guests aren't supposed to check themselves in. They don't know how."

"The instructions are right here." Lyle Fairbanks took a sheet of paper from the top of the reception desk. "Miss Kent, Mrs. Hardwicke, and I managed all right, but Jerzey's English, although gettin' better, isn't all that great. When he dropped his credit card in the box, he was followin' instruction number seven, as you can see. Then he realized that you don't accept the Discover card here, like it says in instruction number twelve, and he tried to get it back."

"It sucks," said Doreen loudly.

"It does not 'suck,' Mrs. Muxworthy," said Axminster Stoker. "The team did not anticipate non-English-speaking customers. That is all. Significant savings in labor can be demonstrated almost immediately if the receptionist position is eliminated from payroll."

"You fired Dina!" said Quill. "You fired our receptionist?"

"In the spirit of continuous improvement, staff cuts are inevitable," said Mr. Stoker.

"On'y thing that'd improve around here is you get your skinny butt back to Detroit, or wherever it is you come from," said Doreen loudly. "Swiping this poor soul's credit card . . ."

"I get it back," said Jerzey hastily. "No problem."

"And harassing these-here guests. What's next? They warsh their own towels? Make their own beds? Mop the kitchen floor?"

"There's a very good Marriott on Route fifteen," said Mrs. Fairbanks in an undertone to her husband.

"We passed a charming bed-and-breakfast on Route ninety-six," said Aurora Kent to Georgia Hardwicke. "Marvelous roses out front, too. What do you think, my dear? I can assure you that this is not at all what we're used to in our travels. Generally the places we've selected for our little conventions are very attentive. The service is usually quite Japanese."

"Japanese?" said Quill.

"Benchmark," said Axminster Stoker, as if this were supposed to make sense.

Georgia caught Quill's eye. She winked and turned her attention back to her colleagues. "I think we just hit a little hitch here. Why don't we stay one night at least? Give poor Miss Quilliam a chance to straighten things out."

"Please don't even think of leaving," said Quill hastily. "I'm sorry that you were greeted by this... this... confusion. If you can give me just a few moments, we'll get all this settled." She grabbed Mr. Stoker by the arm and hauled him into the dining room.

Doreen marched after them, "Told ya," she said in simple satisfaction when they were safely out of earshot. "You boob," she said to Mr. Stoker.

"Mrs. Mux—"

"Where's Dina?" Quill asked him.

"Pursuing her graduate studies, I should imagine," said Mr. Stoker. "I'm extremely sorry about—"

"Please find her," said Quill. "Explain that you acted totally without my authority. Ask her to come back and see me immediately."

"Very well," said Mr. Stoker. "I shall explain my error."

"And apologize, you," said Doreen.

"I most certainly will. If I had any idea—"

"John will have my head in a basket if we lose this

business," said Quill a little ruefully. "So you might apologize to him, too. And Mr. Stoker . . . I think we need a moratorium on this Quality Training."

"Durn right," said Doreen. "If that means what I think it means. We can shoot this bozo here, too, for all of me."

"Doreen, please go find John and ask him to come help me register the Kipling Society, if they're still in the lobby by the time I get back."

"We're all still here," said Georgia Hardwicke cheerfully.

Quill started.

"Sorry. Didn't mean to sneak up on you. Just wanted you to know that the promise of the perennial gardens have tempted Aurora to stay, and the king-size bed the Provençal suite featured in your brochures was what attracted Lyle and Lila Fairbanks, God bless 'em, and I wouldn't miss your sister's food for all the rice in Tokyo."

"And Mr. Paulovich?" asked Quill with hope.

"Well, he got his credit card back, so he's just as happy as a clam. I have to say, though, that he was muttering something about crime in America when the box wouldn't give it up."

"You," said Quill with relief, "are a peach."

"You looked a little harassed," said Georgia. "Glad to help."

"Doreen. Please find John—he's with Carlyle and Louisa Conway giving them a tour—and ask him to talk to Meg about a high tea for the Kiplings. On the house." She turned to Georgia. "Do you think that everyone would come into the dining room for a cream tea while we get the luggage situated?"

"I'll go ask." Georgia disappeared into the lobby in a swirl of green and gold, to reappear moments later with the remainder of the Kiplings in tow. Quill, having dispatched Mr. Stoker and sent Doreen to find John, greeted them with relief.

"We are delighted to take you up on your offer," said Miss Kent.

"Ze food is free?" asked Jerzey Paulovich.

"Lyle, darling . . . the view!" said Lila Fairbanks, drifting to the window overlooking the Falls.

Quill, pulling chairs away from the large table by the windows, indicated with a smile that they should sit.

"You know," said Lyle Fairbanks, settling into his chair with a benevolent air, "we-all'd be delighted to sing for our supper."

"Oh, yes?" asked Quill.

"The Indian cycle," said Miss Kent. "That always goes over well."

"Too long, too long," said Jerzey. "We condense it, yes? What do you think, Mz. Quilliam?"

"I'm afraid I don't . . . Just what *is* the Kipling Condensation Society?"

"It would not be too ambitious to claim that we are Kipling scholars," said Miss Kent. "Lyle and Lila in particular."

"Absolutely not, Aurora," said Lyle gallantly. "You are far more experienced than we are."

"Be that as it may"—Miss Kent acknowledged the tribute with a gracious nod—"at any rate, I cannot claim credit for the original idea. For that we must pay tribute to G and S."

"You mean Gilbert and Sullivan?" asked Quill.

"Yes!" shouted Jerzey. "Prezisely. We condense the poet's works into an hour performance."

"All of them?" asked Quill.

"We select." Jerzey threw back his head. "This I condense myself. 'Now in Injua's sunny clime, where I used to spend my time, if you can keep your head about you, you're a bloke. By the living God that made you, there's nothing else that will do, when a woman's just a woman, and a good cigar's a smoke.' "

"Needs a little work," said Lyle critically, "but you get the idea."

"Perhaps the beauty of the poems in full might be better," said Lila with an anxious eye in Quill's direction. "He wrote the most touching poem about dogs: 'Master, this is thy servant, he is rising eight weeks old. He is mainly Head and Tummy. His legs are uncontrolled.' " She broke off, tears in her eyes. "And of course, it ends with . . . you know . . . the doggie's . . ."

"Death," said Georgia, patting Lila's hand. "That one always gets to me, too. Doug and I had the most wonderful little cocker spaniel."

"At any rate," said Lyle, "we are always ready to perform, for those who'd appreciate it, of course."

Five pairs of eyes looked anxiously in Quill's direction.

"If it'd be any trouble . . ." said Lila.

"Well," said Quill, floundering.

"At one of our stops last year," said Miss Kent, with a crisp twinkle, "the inn owners staged a garden party . . ."

"Under an August moon," said Jerzey.

"And the other guests kept us there for hours. Simply hours." Lila sighed. "It was wonderful."

"And you in that gauzy dress," said her husband gallantly.

"I suppose," said Quill doubtfully, "we could—"

"Only if it's no trouble. . . . "

"We wouldn't want to impose. . . . "

"Zis America," said Jerzey, with an expansive gesture, "is *not* filled with crooks, I guess."

"I'd be delighted," said Quill, "to talk to my staff."

In the kitchen Meg was folding puréed grapefruit into the crushed ice, whistling softly to herself. The *sous* chefs worked quietly. Quill summarized, ending with a suggestion that the Kiplings entertain the other guests at the Inn the next evening at a small cocktail party. The Finn, who was new, dropped a copper kettle with a clang and a muttered "Phut!" at Meg's shriek, "Kipling!! How many poems in an hour?! Are you *crazy*!?"

"Shush!" Quill settled into the rocking chair by the fireplace with a sigh. "I think we can keep them to half an hour if it's handled tactfully. Handled tactfully means no shrieking. And maybe a lot of free food."

"For the whole Inn!" Meg added grenadine to the *sorbet* and scooped the mixture into a large glass bowl.

Quill propped her feet up on the hearth and closed her eyes. "They were threatening to check out!" She took a deep breath. "Just give me a second. I want to settle this stuff about Dina getting fired first, then we'll—"

"Dina? You fired the best receptionist we ever had! What the heck is going on here, Quill? Have you lost your mind!"

"Meg. It's been a bad day. There's only one way it could get worse. . . ."

The back door to the kitchen opened with a bang. "Quill? What in the name of God is this business about evacuating the Inn?"

"And that's it," said Quill, opening her eyes at the all-too-familiar baritone. "Hello, Myles."

CHAPTER 4

Myles was always tanned in the summer, which turned his gray eyes silver, and he never seemed to sweat. Quill pushed apologetically at the damp tendrils of her hair, suddenly conscious of her appearance all over again.

"Hey, Myles," said Meg. "Have some *sorbet*."

"I can't stay too long. Just following up a report that the building's unsafe."

Meg shrieked. "Hogwash!"

"Hedrick Conway. That idiot." Quill tugged at her blouse. It'd been weeks since their last, painful conversation. "The plumbing's backed up, that's all. We've already taken care of it. Conway was here when the problem came up and thought it would make a good headline. He called you?" She straightened in alarm. "Did he call the EPA?"

"He wanted to know if the Tompkins County Sheriff's Department had an evacuation procedure."

"Do we?" Quill asked.

"We do."

"Quill threw him out," said Meg with relish. "So it's pretty clear he's got an ax to grind with us. And you couldn't have possibly thought that we would jeopardize the guests, Myles. So how come? Ah. Never mind. Myles. Sit down. Stay a while. What do you know about this guy? Have you seen the *Trumpet!*?"

"Yes."

"It's a load of trash. How could you let him have the police blotter?"

"Didn't have much choice, I'm afraid."

"I'll bet Davy gave it to him," said Meg shrewdly. "You would have sent Conway packing."

"He threatened an injunction. The blotter's public information. The result would have been the same. The public has a right to that information."

"There's no problem, though, Myles. So thanks." Quill bit into her third piece of grapefruit.

"If there's no problem here, I'll be going. Good to see you both."

"No problem here?" shrieked Meg after a shrewd glance at her sister. "How can you say that? If you've seen that miserable rag of a newspaper, you know there's a big problem here. Are you just going to let this bozo run loose?"

"There's not a great deal Myles can do," Quill said. "Conway has First Amendment rights like everyone else. And as long as the stories aren't actionable . . ."

Meg, shaking her head in disgust, filled a small bowl with her grapefruit mixture and determinedly shoved Myles onto a stool. "Here. Quill was just going to make coffee." She raised her voice as Quill took a breath to say she had no intention of making coffee, "Sit down, Quill." She filled the kettle from the jug containing spring water and took the coffee beans from the freezer. "I'll make the coffee. Do you want caffè làtte or cappucino, Myles? Caffè làtte, I'll bet. Of course outright lies are actionable. What about this mini-mall exposé he's threatening? That's actionable. Unless there's something in it."

Quill sat at the counter and looked past Myles's left ear. "Do you have any idea what Conway's up to? You probably don't know this, but we've invested quite a bit in the mall project. If there's something funny going on, we should probably know about it."

"I don't think you should worry. Not yet. He showed up at the Courthouse to check the site proposal and the property deeds filed with the county clerk. He made a copy of the engineering drawings for the leach field and of the budget proposal. He also requested the incorporation documents for Hemlock Mall, Inc., which are kept at the county seat in Ithaca. I have no idea whether he picked those up or not.''

''So,'' said Meg. She pursed her lips. ''Very interesting. *Very* interesting. Wouldn't you say it's interesting, Quill?''

''What's interesting is that Conway and his family seem to know a lot more about Hemlock Falls than they should after being here less than a month. Myles, he threatened to write about John, dragging up all that old business again.''

''Did he?''

''Yes. And his mother and sister pretended to know something about ... um ... painting ...'' For a moment, she acknowledged, she'd really thought they might have heard of her, and she was a little miffed.

''Miffed? Why?''

Quill hadn't realized she'd spoken aloud. ''Just that ... Never mind. It'd be good to know where they're getting all this information. It's so specific—as if someone in town were feeding them gossip on a regular basis.''

''They could have picked up the talk about John, and you for that matter, at Marge's on Sunday.''

''Myles, John's history is old news. And no one gives a hoot about my career.'' There was an uncomfortable silence, which Quill broke rather hastily, ''Who talks to flatland foreigners anyway? You know how insular this town is. If we had a malicious busybody in Hemlock Falls, I could see it. But we seem to have been lucky that way. I can't think of a single person who likes to make trouble just for the heck of it.''

''We were at Marge's on Sunday,'' said Meg. ''We didn't see Hedrick there. We didn't see you there, either.''

''Carlyle and Louisa dropped in after you'd gone.''

So Myles had met the voluptuous Carlyle at the Courthouse and again at Marge's. Quill wondered if the meeting at the diner had been by arrangement. Except that Myles's Sunday morning activities weren't her business any longer.

''I'll tell you what we need,'' said Meg suddenly. ''We need that little red book.''

''What little red book?''

''He called it the 'goods' book.'' Quill pleated her cotton skirt between her fingers. ''He referred to it when he met

John for the first time. With," she added, looking squarely at him, "a certain amount of glee. Apparently he's spent the last week collecting all kinds of gossip and recording it in the thing."

"Distasteful," said Myles. "But not a felony. Or even a misdemeanor." A slight, very slight, warning note sounded in his voice. "Now, appropriating that book without Hedrick Conway's consent would be a misdemeanor."

"Maybe we could snatch it at the party tomorrow."

"About the party?" asked Meg.

"I could call and invite him. Tell him we wanted coverage in his awful rag. Of course they'd all probably show up. Yuck."

"How big a party?" Meg demanded. "And how much food did you promise?"

"It's a small party. I didn't promise a lot. Just some hors d'oeuvres, and perhaps a couple of cold soups."

"How *many* people, Quill?"

"Well. How would you feel about most of the guests? It's a little hard to leave people out. The Kiplings seem to need a large audience."

"The whole Inn? That's . . ." Meg counted rapidly to herself. "That's roughly fifty people! How much are we charging a head?"

"Um, I hadn't really—"

"We're not getting paid for this! I thought you and John said you would never, ever offer free food and drink without discussing it with me and with him. Fifty people for *free*!"

"It's to make up for a bad start to their visit, Meg."

"Oh, *God*! All right! I suppose I ought to count myself lucky I got twenty-four hours' notice." Meg flung open the door to their oversized refrigerator and stared into it, muttering.

Quill caught Myles's grin, and smiled back.

"So," he said, "about this party."

No, thought Quill, I won't. Besides, the only reason he wants to come is because Carlyle and her halter top might be there—and to keep me from committing a misdemeanor. Myles's gaze shifted to the floor. There was a slight stiffening in his shoulders. Nuts, thought Quill. I do miss him, dammit. "Let's say at seven. That okay with you, Meg?"

"What? The time or the fact that you should have asked Myles before he had to ask you? It depends," she said into the awkward silence, "what you want me to serve. Beluga's a snap. I just have to have a lot of ice. Of course, we'll be broke for the rest of the quarter, since it's on the house, but the preparation time is zero. Zip. Nada. If, on the other hand—"

"That Jap's here," said Doreen, opening the dining room door and sticking her head into the kitchen. "Unless you want him to beat feet like the others almost done, you better get him checked in. 'Course, I could call that-there Axminster."

"For God's sake, don't you ever use that word, Doreen! It's Sakura, Mr. Sakura. The Japanese list their last names first."

"He's a durn snooty little cuss," Doreen grumbled. "Snapped his fingers at me like I was somebody's pet."

"We've talked a lot about guest courtesy, Doreen." Doreen sniffed, unimpressed. "Well, the first Sakura's here, Meg. What about sushi?"

"I'll see what I can do. It depends on the supplier. Yellow-fin tuna shouldn't be too hard to get, but it's got to be fresh. And Quill? There's a little surprise in the lobby, or should be, if Mike's gotten to it."

"What kind of a surprise? Did you find Dina?"

"That Stoker did," grunted Doreen. "She's pret' mad, but she's coming back to work."

"So what other surprise waits for me in the lobby?"

"That picture you did of the two of us a few years back."

"Meg!"

"Hey. The son's an art critic. The father's richer than God. Why not?"

Quill slid off the stool. "I've got to go check in Mr. Sakura, Myles. See you tomorrow, I guess."

"Thanks for the invitation."

"Men," Doreen said with vague disapprobation as she followed Quill through the dining room.

"Who? The sheriff? Or Mr. Sakura?"

"Sher'f." Doreen stopped cold, folded her hands underneath her apron, and said, "That's a good man, there."

"And?" prompted Quill.

"And nothing. This modern way of gettin' together? It sucks."

"Doreen!"

"Thing is, you get the eye, you give it back, you try it out, you get married. That's the way I done it. And that's the way I'll keep on doin' it. Three times. You don't," Doreen added fiercely, "have to go through all this touchy-feely stuff."

"What touchy-feely stuff?"

"You know. I tell you something—guy's decent in the sack and brings home his pay, what more do you want?"

"This conversation is ridiculous."

"On'y if you expect men to be something they ain't."

"And what is it they 'ain't'?" asked Quill in a lofty tone.

"They ain't," said Doreen, resuming her march to the foyer, "wimmin. Mr. Sakra, this here's my boss, Ms. Quilliam. Aloha."

Sakura Toshiro, managing director of Sakura Industries, had booked a suite and a single for a week through a New York City travel agency that dealt chiefly with the wealthy and influential. The small elderly man with the belligerent lower lip standing in front of her didn't look like the head of a multinational, multibillion-dollar conglomerate, but then Marge "the Barge" Schmidt didn't look like the wealthiest person in Tompkins County, either, but she was. Quill, who had diligently reviewed a copy of *Japan: The American Businessperson's Guide to Political Correctness* the week before, folded her hands together and bowed. "*Ohio gozaimaisu, Sakura-san.* I am Sarah Quilliam."

Sakura Toshiro bowed back, a hint of arrogance in his back and neck. "This so-beautiful picture, Miss Qurriam"—he nodded at the painting hanging behind the reception desk—"yours?"

Quill rarely tried portraits; she was too young, she thought, and hadn't lived long enough to really paint what lay behind flesh and bone. But she had painted herself and

Meg seated on a red couch last year. Meg was looking off into the distance, a slight smile on her open face. Quill sat beside her, one arm protectively over the back of the couch, her head turned to look at Meg. She'd used a photograph for the charcoal sketch that began the painting, and her internal eye to finish it. She'd packed it away months ago.

"Yes?"

"You?" He made delicate brush strokes in the air.

"Yes," said Quill, and blushed. He sucked air through his teeth, which, Quill recalled, was a gesture of appreciation.

"My son, Sakura Kenji. Terrs me you are velly famous. Velly." He smiled with an appreciative twinkle. "My Engrish." He shrugged, shook his head in apparent regret. "Kenji-san, nei? He come. Velly good Engrish."

A little appalled to find herself speaking slowly and distinctly, as though to a backward child, Quill said, "The travel agency indicated that Sakura Kenji will check in the day after tomorrow. In the meantime, I'm sure we can manage. We have the room ready now for you and is it Mr. Motoyama?"

"Motoyama. *Hai.*" He bowed.

Quill returned the bow. "And is Mr. Motoyama here now, Sakura-san? May we take both of you to your rooms? The suite is ready."

"Motoyama. *Hai,*" said Mr. Sakura.

"If this Motoyamer's a little skinny Jap older than God, he's outside with the van they come in," said Doreen. "He's a servant, like."

Mr. Sakura's shrewd black eyes slid over Doreen with the slightest flicker of contempt. Quill's own understanding of French was far better than her ability to speak it, which was apparently true of Mr. Sakura's English. Her face warm, she bowed and said "Mrs. Muxworthy meant no disrespect, Sakura-san. Is Mr. Motoyama also ready to check in?"

"*Mo*toyama." Mr. Sakura gestured, driving with his hands.

"Your chauffeur," said Quill.

"*Hai,*" said Mr. Sakura. "Prease." He withdrew a sheaf

of papers from his immaculately tailored suit coat and presented them to Quill.

She glanced at it. "You've been communicating with the
mayor?" said Quill in surprise. "About the mini-mall?"

Mr. Sakura made driving motions.

"You'd like to see the site," Quill guessed. She handed
the letters, which hinted at investment, back to him. "Mike
will be happy to drive you both there. You don't need to
trouble your chauffeur. When would you like to go?"

"Velly soon."

"This afternoon?"

"Velly soon."

"Them Kiplings are takin' the van for a tour," said Doreen "You want I should tell Mike to take the Ja—I mean
these fellas, too?"

" 'Gentermen rankers out on a spree damned from here
to eternity,' " said Mr. Sakura. "Kipring. Velly good.
Hai." He nodded toward her painting again. "Velly beautiful. I may see more?"

"Sure," said Quill, dizzy. "Perhaps later?"

"After Motoyama dlive."

"Yes, but there's no need to have Mr. Motoyama—"

"*Mo*toyama," corrected Mr. Sakura, with a frown.

Quill, whose democratic principles frequently collided
with her commitment to courteous service, smiled, ducked
the issue of honorifics altogether, and once again offered
the services of Mike and the van. "It will be easier for you
to find the construction site. And the van is much more
comfortable than the rental car."

"A Toyota?"

"Oh, dear. No. I'm afraid it's a Chevy Lumina."

"*Hai.* Yes. Velly good, then."

"Ms. Muxworthy," Quill addressed Doreen, feeling an
obscure need to make her democratic principles clear,
"would you let Mike know? They can all go together."

"So, you want I should get these bags up to the room
first, or what?"

"I'll take the bags up."

"Hell, no. You go back to the kitchen. Tolt the sher'f

you'd be right back. I'll take care of Mr. Sakra, then I'll get a holt of Mike.''

Mr. Sakura watched this fine example of employer-employee relations with interest. ''Fine,'' said Quill, reminding herself good managers never minded a bit of affectionate bullying. In front of other people. Who understood more English than one could wish. She bowed to Mr. Sakura, who bowed politely back, and went to the kitchen to find that Myles had left and Meg was giving the last of the dinner instructions to the kitchen help. The *sous* chefs, she noticed crossly, never bullied Meg. Quill sat in the rocker by the cobblestone fireplace and brooded.

The *sous* chefs and dishwashers dispersed. Meg stowed her clipboard neatly in the shelves she used as a desk. ''So, you asked Myles to the party?''

Quill roused herself from a confused contemplation of Kipling, men, the proper way to address a chauffeur, and a strong desire to show some really marvelous work to Mr. Sakura and his billion-dollar corporation. ''Myles asked himself to the party. And, you recall, he asked himself to the party after I said I'd invite the Horrible Hedrick and his relatives, specifically the sister with the overlarge hooters.''

''This Carlyle must be a ripsnorter.'' She narrowed her eyes. ''But that sort of thing's never bothered you before. What's really wrong?''

''Mr. Sakura recognized my work.''

Meg gave her a self-satisfied grin.

Quill stretched restlessly in the chair. ''Of course, he seems to be fond of Rudyard Kipling, which says a lot about his politics, so make of that what you will.''

Meg rolled her eyes. ''Don't sulk, Quill. Here's what you do. Take some time off this afternoon.''

''Time off?''

''It's hot. Go swimming.''

''I can't. There's a Chamber meeting this afternoon.''

''Sure you can. It's not until four o'clock. It's two now. Nothing like exercise to get those endorphins up and circulating.''

''I'll go if you go.''

"As soon as I settle the menu for this party you've arranged. What do you think about tapanade?"

Glad to concentrate on something concrete and practical, like a menu, Quill said that she loved tapanade. "But we ought to have something a little more conservative to offer the Kiplings."

"Tapanade and Parmesan-artichoke cheese dip, then."

"Don't get sarcastic."

"You started it."

"Never mind." She pulled at her lip. "About the sushi, I've already made arrangements for the fish. And the usual cheeses and fruits. Okay. Did you decide to go swimming?"

"Yes."

"Good. I'll go with you. You can contemplate your future and get some exercise at the same time."

"How's about if I just swim?" Quill sighed. "Just once I'd like to do one thing at a time. Just once, I'd like to get up in the morning and have no schedule, no meetings, no feelings to soothe, no guests to coddle, no nothing. Just time. Lots of time, stretching ahead of me like a lovely trail with no beginning and no destination."

Meg shook her head. "That's not going to help. You'll just go frantic concentrating on all the meetings you're missing and all the soothing you're not doing. You remember what helped me for quite a while after Colin died."

"Work."

Meg nodded. "Work lets your subconscious take care of itself. That first year after he'd gone, I barely remember parts of it. But I do remember the cooking."

"But I don't have time to paint! That's the whole point!"

"No. Not that kind of work. Cooking isn't like painting. I can cook and have a life outside of cooking. The way you've been tackling painting, you can't. Painting consumes you. There's nothing left over for the outside. That's part of your struggle with Myles and kids, and for a long time, Quill, me. Because you took time out of painting for me, to help me. You wouldn't be here running the Inn if it weren't for the fact that I needed you that year. You'd be back in SoHo, getting paint in your hair.''

"You forget why I left and moved here. I had just as compelling reasons as you did. I didn't have anything more to say on canvas. Not then. But now. Now it's coming back. Slowly. And now I do have a decision to make.''

Meg's flush subsided. "The question's whether there's room for Myles and the art, then.''

"Myles and children and the art. Myles and the art, yes. He surrounds it, Meg, he doesn't share it, but he surrounds it with an odd kind of reassurance that I think I may be lost without. But babies? They take it out of you, all of it. Oh, my God. I don't know what to do. Children are as consuming as art. They take that part of you. I know it. I know it.''

She wept, standing in the middle of the kitchen.

Meg put the recipe cards back in the file and made coffee. She ground the beans, then filled the kettle with spring water and set it to heat, then pushed Quill into the rocking chair and stroked her hair, saying nothing, but humming a wordless little tune with the cadence of a lullaby. The water rattled, just on the boil, and she poured it carefully into the filter. She brought the cup to Quill, who sipped it, with the sense that she was recovering from the flu. "Here's what we do, chief. We go swimming. Forget about Myles and art and just let it work itself out in your subconscious. Listen, we'll plan to get back by three, so I can pull the rest of tomorrow's dinner together and you can set up for the Chamber meeting. And''—she smiled sunnily—"What you want is a rational, practical problem to solve, with no feelings swamping up your brain. While we're swimming, we figure out a way to separate the Horrible Hedrick from that bloody little goods book. Whatever we figure out will take enough time to divert you to let the old subconscious do its decision-making stuff. And besides, that damn book's important. We have to find out what's inside. We can't have the Bozo of the Year wrecking our new boutique restaurant, can we?''

Quill wiped each eye with the back of her hand, sniffed, and went to get her bathing suit.

• • •

"So seducing the little red book out of Hedrick is totally out of the question?" asked Meg, floating on her back and gently kicking her feet. The pond at the park had been filled with kids, and they'd swum over the submerged sluiceway gate leading to the river. Even the current was lazy in the heat, and they paddled with it like wood ducks bobbing on the surface of the clear green water. The granite cliffs rose on either side of them, hands cupping jade.

"I'm not offering up this fair white body," said Quill. Meg was right. Concentrating on this problem was better than Prozac. It was a neat little puzzle, free of emotion. "And Andy'd take violent exception to donating yours, even in the cause of justice."

"Undoubtedly," said Meg, with a hint of complacence. "The two of us have arrived at the state where exclusivity in dating is a priority. What about good old breaking and entering? They're all living in the apartment over the print shop, right? Piece of cake to sneak in and rifle the place."

Quill dived, considering this. She opened her eyes underwater. A brown trout gave her a startled glance out of one doll-black eye, and curved away like a question mark. She rose to the surface and exhaled. "When it's not on his person, I'll bet he sleeps with it under his pillow. We've got to figure out a way to get it out of the sports coat."

"Not bad. You stand next to him batting your eyes admiringly. I create a diversion. You slip your hand into that ratty sports coat and grab it."

Quill shook her head. "Too risky. And pickpocketing's a misdemeanor or something. We've got to get him to take the jacket off, and drape it over a chair or whatever and while I'm hanging it up, I slip my hand in the coat and get it. If Myles finds out, we can always say it fell out of his pocket and we're returning it to him."

"If we get him to strip, we're back to seduction again."

"Meg! What is this bee in your bonnet about seduction? No. We invite him to the party tomorrow night, and if it's as hot as this, of course he'll take his coat off—"

"What if it's in his pants pocket?"

"You haven't seen it. It's too big to fit into a back

pocket. He'd have to curl it up. And even if he does that, it'll be duck soup to get behind him and slip it out. You could create a diversion.''

Meg addressed the sunny sky overhead. ''The old diversion trick? What a new idea. There must be an echo in here.'' She contemplated the shoreline. ''What do you think's in the book, anyway?''

Quill attempted a shrug and took in a mouthful of water. ''Who knows? Myles said he'd asked for the names of the bidders on the mini-mall project. Maybe he's found out something about one of them.''

''You want to swim downstream and see how it's going?''

''We'd have to walk back over the rocks. And we wanted to be back by three.''

''Somebody will give us a lift.''

''In our suits?''

Meg rolled her eyes. ''Jeez. Come on. First one there has to spend twenty minutes listening to Axminster Stoker after dinner.''

Quill, disinclined to that much activity even in the river-coolness, breast-stroked pleasantly along, her mind empty of everything but the sensation of water and sky and sun. The gorge sloped abruptly to a riverbank a quarter mile ahead, an ideal place for a mini-mall with a view of the river. Ahead of her, Meg reached the small beach which fronted the mall property and treaded water, waiting for Quill to catch up.

''We can ride back with the Kiplings,'' said Meg. ''Didn't you say that they were touring the site with Mike and the van? Isn't that one of them now? That Georgia what's-her-name?''

Quill waved. Georgia waved back, her arms describing a wide semaphore.

''That's odd,'' said Quill.

''I agree. People dedicated to furthering the works of R. Kipling, the last of the male chauvinist Victorian male poets, are *very* odd.''

''No. The rescue truck's there. See the lights?''

''Rescuing the carpenters from another version of *Gunga*

Din, I'll bet. But we can go up and look." Meg turned herself around and began to float toward the beach head-first. She had a peculiar version of the backstroke, rather like an upside-down dog paddle that involved a minimum of breath. "Ooonnn the road to Mandalay," she sang tune-lessly, "where the flying fishes play, aaannnd the dawn comes up like thunder out of China across the bay ... tumpty um ... tee ... tumpty um ..."

"Elephants are piling teak in the sludgy squidgey creek," Quill joined in. "Where the silence ... oh, god!" She bolted upright, sank, and her foot struck the thing again.

Hair like seaweed, in the river.

CHAPTER 5

When Quill entered the kitchen the day after she'd discovered the body of Louisa Conway in the river, Meg was contemplating a pile of chicken liver, her slight figure cool in a thin T-shirt, cotton shorts, and a hideous pair of tennis shoes. Like the rest of the Inn, the kitchen hid technological efficiency beneath nineteenth-century charm. The cobblestone fireplace was fitted with the latest open-hearth grill, and birch wainscoting concealed the oversize Zero King refrigerator. A late-model Aga stove, flanked by hardwood and granite counters, dominated the large room. When the sisters had updated the three-century-old Inn, they'd decided the one concession to modern comfort they were unable to make was the flooring. The floor in the kitchen was the original brick, uncomfortable to stand on for long periods of time. Meg—who preferred to cook in ancient sportswear—solved the problem with battered pairs of Nikes designed for heavy-duty basketball players.

"Hey," said Meg, plunging her hand into the pink-brown pile as Quill stamped into the kitchen. She hefted the liver with an absent air. "Equal parts butter and minced liver, with a heavy dash of Cointreau and a bit of tarragon. What do you think?"

"Sounds like a heart attack waiting to happen."

"I'm sick of *cuisine minceur*. It's boring. I want scope." She swept both hands through the air, scattering bits of liver. "My experience tells me that the guests are sick of *cuisine minceur*. The world is turning its back on the rabbit-food menus of the eighties and forging toward cholesterol overdose. And high time, too. *Geeve me butter!*'' she roared, with a sudden veer to the Teutonic. "Geeve me *beef!*''

Quill glumly settled into the rocker by the fireplace and contemplated nothing in particular.

"So you found another body," said Doreen, stumping in the back door, the light of battle in her eye. "Maybe now you got this to think about, we can get rid of that-there Stoker."

"Mr. Stoker just needs a firm hand," said Quill. "And I already told Meg last night, I don't want to talk about the body. How are you this morning?"

"J'a know right away it was Louisa Conway drownded in the river? You din't step on her face did you?"

"Dor*een!*'' Meg complained. "It's bad enough to find a corpse in the river, without you acting like somebody out of Salem's Lot after the vampire shows up. Poor Quill." Meg patted her shoulder sympathetically, then settled comfortably at the counter with her liver pâté. "*Did* you feel her nose or anything? I mean, you knew it was a body right away, right?"

"I knew right away."

"How?"

"Never mind how." Quill flexed her sandaled foot and resisted the temptation to scrub at it again with a soaped sponge. It'd been the teeth, and the sensation was going to be with her a long time. She shuddered.

"Anyone get to that Mr. Conway to say they're sorry his mother fell in the river?" asked Doreen. "And what about the funeral? They gonna bury her here? We could take a ham, I guess. I could go over since he don't know too many people in town, yet."

"His mother knew one of them well enough," muttered Meg.

"What d'ya mean?" Doreen's face was alight with interest. Quill knew that look. It wasn't an avid or an unhealthy interest, since Doreen was far too nice a woman underneath the tough exterior to delight in a grisly death for the excitement. She'd seen The Look before, the time when Doreen converted (briefly) to Christian evangelism. And again when Doreen had signed up to sell life insurance, and yet a third time when the housekeeper began attending Amway sales-training classes. Quill hadn't been around for Doreen's flirtation with Nu-Skin and the Tupperware business, but there was no doubt of Doreen's entrepreneurial bent. "Doreen," said Quill, suddenly suspicious. "We got a copy of *Armchair Detective* in the mail this week. I didn't take out a subscription. Did you, Meg?"

"Huh-uh."

Doreen put her thumbs in her dress belt and hitched her shoulders forward.

"Bogart," said Meg accusingly. "Oh, nuts." The sisters exchanged a meaningful glance.

"Some of them guys," said Doreen, whose intuition was acute, "get twenny bucks an hour."

"You think Hedrick Conway's going to pay you twenty dollars an hour to investigate his mother's murder?" shrieked Meg. "Pooh!"

"So it *was* murder," said Doreen, thoughtfully rubbing her chin.

"No, Doreen," said Quill. "No and no and no. You are *not* going to go into business as Doreen Muxworthy, P.I."

Doreen pointed out that not only had Meg and Quill solved several murders, but they'd done it for free; she, Doreen, was merely turning an eye to the profit possibilities, which, if word-of-mouth were true about Hedrick and Carlyle's millions, would be considerable.

"And what if the kids did it?" Meg demanded. "Who'd pay you then?"

"Huh," Doreen said, considering.

"And let's not forget that we have a perfectly capable sheriff in town with an extensive background in investigations of this sort," Quill added. "I mean, he was Chief of Detectives in Manhattan before he left the N.Y.P.D., and a man like that—"

"My, my, my," murmured Meg. "The post-discovery interview with Myles must have been interesting. He was pretty brief with me. 'Did I see anything floating along the river?' 'Nope.' That was about it."

"Was it murder or wasn't it?" Doreen demanded.

"Was," said Quill briefly. "The classic blunt instrument. Louisa Conway was hit on the left temple with something like a hammer—"

"Something like, indeed," murmured Meg.

"—and fell or was thrown into the gorge, sometime between one-fifteen, when she was last seen at the mini-mall, and two-fifteen, when I step—that is, when we found her in the river."

"There's somethin' not right about that place," Doreen muttered. "Went out there myself to see how our investment's goin'. Them workers give me the creeps."

"Really?" Quill pulled at her lower lip. "I've never been all that comfortable there myself. Why, do you suppose?"

"Them guys don't talk much. Never see 'em in town. DeMarco brings 'em in on buses and takes 'em out again. There's allus at least two of 'em together. Thing folks in town is astin', was she interfered with?"

"You mean rape? I don't have the least idea." A troubled frown appeared between Meg's eyebrows. "That'd be a heck of a note. A rapist in Hemlock Falls."

"She didn't look interfered with," said Quill cautiously. "I mean, she was fully dressed and all her clothing seemed to be in place. There was just this gash on her head."

Meg shook her head and went, "Brruh! It's going to be a heck of a case to investigate. Quill and I counted; there must have been at least fifty people there. The construction crew, the electrical people, some of the Chamber members checking on the progress of the site, the entire membership of the Rudyard Kipling Condensation society, as well as Mr. Sakura and that weird little driver of his. For my money, Hedrick and his sister Carlyle *could* have done it. They all arrived together; Hedrick and Carlyle decided to leave a little after one-thirty and started to look for her."

"So how'd j'a know about the hammer?"

"Oliver Doyle, with the rescue service. You remember him, Meg. He was here with the volunteer ambulance crew that time you made Keith Baumer so—"

"Yes. Yes. Yes," said Meg testily, who clearly recalled some aspects of their first case years ago with little enthu-

siasm. "I remember Olly Doyle. He's a carpenter and vol-
unteers on the ambulance. I hardly think he's qualified in
forensics."

"If you hadn't been so busy being squeamish over the
corpse, you would have heard him, too. One of the Kiplings
found a hammer with blood on the claw at the lip of the
gorge where they think Louisa went over."

"Oh," said Meg.

"What was Louisa nosin' around the site for?" asked
Doreen.

"I don't know. She had a camera with her." Quill shuddered. "It was tied around her neck. Hedrick got everybody
at the site—the plumbers, the electricians, the carpenters,
and the sewage guy—to start looking for her, and called
the rescue truck. The Kiplings volunteered to search the
woods at the south end of the development, and that's
where they found the hammer."

"So what do you think, Doreen? You still want to take
on this case?" Meg asked. "I think you'd be a terrific addition to our detective team. You could go out, poke around
the site, figure out who saw Louisa last, and where the
hammer came from. Of course, that's on top of scheduling
the household staff and seeing that the rooms are clean."

"That-there business about the pay . . ."

"No pay. Strictly in the interest of good citizenship."

"Seems to me a good citizen would do something about
that-there Stoker."

"You are not to do a thing about poor Mr. Stoker." Quill
was firm.

"Then I guess I'll figger out somethin' else." Doreen
brightened. "Think those Kiplings might be inn-erested in
Tupperware? They do all this stuff in a group."

"No!" said Meg and Quill in unison.

"Then tell me what's on for today, and I'll get to it."

Quill breathed in relief and looked at her watch. "There's
an emergency Chamber meeting this morning, to replace the
one that was canceled yesterday. But the Kiplings' party has
been rescheduled for tomorrow, so we don't have to worry
about that. We don't have any checkouts today, so the staff
will have to work around the guests."

Doreen pursed her lips and stumped out the back door to get to work.

"That," said Quill, "was a close one."

"You mean you aren't fascinated by this opportunity to solve yet another crime?"

"I am not," said Quill firmly. "The opening ceremonies for the mini-mall are scheduled for Tuesday. This is Saturday. We'll be lucky to get through the next few days with our nerves intact, without adding amateur detective work to the list."

"You know who might be a good addition to the team?" asked Meg thoughtfully. "Georgia Hardwicke. I really like Georgia Hardwicke."

"There isn't going to be a team, Meg."

"Right," said Meg absently. "First thing is we can find out more about the scene of the crime. And then we need to find out if she died of the hammer blow or drowned. Maybe Georgia would be interested in a little legwork."

"Meg, we're going to leave this one to Myles. And why would Georgia want to be a detective anyway?"

"She was pretty efficient, yesterday. She was the one who organized the search for Louisa. And she was the one who prevented that engineer Eugene something from picking up the hammer and messing with the evidence. And Doreen told me that she's got a lot of detective stories in her room. Besides, I like her."

"Then maybe the two of you can solve this one. Count me out."

"Quill?" Dina Muir, the receptionist, poked her head through the kitchen door. "The Chamber's been trying to settle down to session for almost an hour. The mayor's looking for you."

"It's good to see you back. I think I told you how sorry I am about the mixup with Mr. Stoker yesterday."

"I told him he'd better check with you," said Dina indignantly. "I knew you wouldn't let him do it. But, I wanted to go shopping for a new dress for the opening ceremonies anyhow, so it worked out all right. Shall I tell the Mayor you're coming soon? He's in pretty much of a fidget."

"This murder's upset everyone. I don't blame him."

"Oh, it's not that. The new edition of the *Trumpet!* is supposed to come out today. They're all just wild about it."

"Oh, Lord. Tell them that I don't think even Hedrick would take the time to publish that rag the day after his mother's death. And let them know I'll be right there."

Dina gave her the high sign and withdrew.

"Good," said Meg. "Pick up as much gossip as you can."

"Gossip?" said Quill with raised eyebrows as she left. "At the Chamber? Gossip? Never in this life!"

" 'Bout time you got here," Elmer Henry groused to Quill. "Now maybe we can get somewhere. You ready to take the minutes?"

"We heard you found the body!" Miriam Doncaster said as Quill sat next to her in the conference room where the Chamber's weekly meetings were held.

"Stepped into it, like," said Marge Schmidt with a fat chuckle.

"Heard it was no accident," said Betty Hall, Marge's partner in the Hemlock Hometown Diner (Fine Food! And Fast!).

Miriam, who was town librarian, blinked her large blue eyes, "Not another murder!" she whispered to Quill. "Are you and Meg going to . . . I mean now that you and Myles . . . that is, if it's true about you and Myles. . . . "

Elmer *thwacked* the official gavel on the table and demanded the Chamber's attention. The twenty-four Chamber members settled like geese landing on a pond, their gabbles and squawks smoothed into an expectant quiet.

Quill reached for the meeting notebook and produced a pen. She'd vowed to straighten herself out after her renunciation of Hemlock Falls' sexiest (and only) sheriff, pay strict attention to taking complete, coherent, readable minutes, and not stray from the point of the meeting to make sketches of the members (she'd given up being an artist), or make grocery lists when she should be taking attendance. She hesitated. It probably wouldn't hurt to take note of any suspicious behavior—just in case Meg grilled her about possible Chamber suspects. Meg, when her interest was caught, had the tenacity of the better breeds of pit bulls. Quill flipped to a fresh page, and wrote: INVESTIGATIONS.

Elmer Henry, rotund and red faced, surveyed his troops with a slightly troubled air. "Revrund Shuttleworth? Would you lead us in an openin' prayer?"

The Reverend Mr. Dookie Shuttleworth, of the Hemlock Falls Church of God, unfolded his storklike length, and gazed benignly on his flock. "Let us pray," he said and compressed his lips. Dookie, although amiable in the extreme, and possessed of an unnerving goodness, tended to phrases without nouns or predicates, which severely impaired the quality of his penitents' progression toward enlightenment. He'd completed a three-month-long correspondence course in "Christian mentalism" some weeks before; C-Ment appeared to be based on a sort of religious ESP. C-Ment sermons, Dookie had explained to his bewildered but receptive parishioners, were delivered through mental messages, and not the traditional verbal peroration. He was touchingly pleased when church attendance jumped the Sundays following his announcement. Christian mentalism made post-sermon discussion at Marge's diner (a test rendered by the more severely religious Hemlockians as an edge against laxity) blissfully nonspecific.

The silence in the conference room stretched on. Quill thought about the hammer that had killed Louisa, and Hedrick's little red book. "Amen," Dookie said and sat down.

"*Thank* you, Revrund," said Elmer. "Our first order of new bidness—"

The room erupted into discussion in which Hedrick Conway's name, the manner of Louisa's demise, and the next issue of the *Trumpet!* (due momentarily, according to several indignant voices) figured prominently. Elmer pounded the gavel with increasing irritability. The furor rose, primarily, Quill suspected, so that people could hear themselves over the hammering.

Elmer, whose Southern roots were very much in evidence when under stress, threw the gavel on the carpeted floor and scowled down the length of the table. "I'm orderin' *silence!* We'll get to the Conways when we get to it, and not before. This here's a bidness meeting of bidnessmen and women and not a hog calling. First order of bidness, last week's minutes.''

"There ain't gonna *be* any 'bidness' in this town if that damn fool Conway runs lies in the paper about us!'' shouted Harland Peterson. "I heard he was up all night after his ma's unfortunate accident in the river, runnin' that damn printing press.'' Harland, the president of the local Agway Co-op, and cousin to Petey (Septic and Floor Covering), slammed a meaty fist onto his thigh. "I say the first order of business is to run that bum out of town.''

"I say the wrong Conway got bumped off,'' Marge Schmidt added in her assertive baritone. "That Louisa didn't have anything to do with the damn *Trumpet!* 'cept bankroll it. So a good question is, who'd want to kill her?'' Marge swiveled a small blue eye at Quill. "What went down at the site today anyway?''

Quill, a little alarmed at the overt hostility being exhibited at the table said, "Well, well, well,'' in a deprecating way, which Marge greeted with a snort of contempt. Quill cleared her throat. "I guess there was a bit of a problem.''

Marge rolled her eyes at the ceiling in mute appeal. "Somebody got a bit free with a hammer. That right?''

"Apparently,'' Quill said.

"Think maybe Hedrick done his ma in for the bucks?''

"That'd work out all right,'' said Harland. "Then we could run the murdering bastard out of town.''

Harvey Bozzel rose to his feet, trembling. "You're being a bit hasty here. And it just doesn't do to be hasty. I think we should sit down and discuss the whole problem calmly like the rational people we know ourselves to be.''

"Siddown,'' snarled Marge.

Harvey jutted his jaw and ran a hand just above his moussed blond hair. "The man's got an image problem. I grant you that. And Bozzel Advertising is well situated to deal with image problems, particularly in the publishing and media areas. Crisis management, it's called, and Boz—''

"Just shaddup, Harve,'' said Marge. "We all know you're angling for a piece of the creep's business!''

Howie Murchison, town attorney and justice of the peace, rapped his knuckles on the table in fair imitation of

a judge quieting a rowdy courtroom. "Shall we start by
defining the problem here?" he asked with a mild glance
over his half-glasses. "A discussion of whether or not
Louisa Conway was murdered, and by whom, isn't a suitable topic for our agenda."

"You wanna know the problem?" shrieked Betty Hall.
"You saw last week's newspaper! You saw what that lyin'
snake wrote: that he's got something on the mini-mall project. And today's the day the next paper's gonna come out,
and who the hell knows what-all lies he's gonna print! I
got all I saved invested in that mini-mall!"

"And since his ma gets knocked on the head and tossed into
the river," added Marge, "it's gonna piss him off something
fierce, is my guess." She ruminated a moment, her massive
jaw working slowly. "Less, like I said, he did it himself. Since
somebody knocked his ma on the head with a hammer, who
knows what he's gonna write about us next?"

Elmer said they'd know soon enough, as he'd asked Esther West to pick up a copy of the *Trumpet!* as it came off
the press at the Nickerson building.

Marge suggested the meeting adjourn to the Nickerson
building so they could stuff Hedrick into his press if the
Trumpet! offered calumnies of any description. Harland Peterson said it was too hot to walk downtown, even for that
scum, reminded Marge of the existence of his Norwegian
cousins who farmed west of the village, and were notable
for their ability to wield ax handles and had excellent night
vision. A surge of approbation met this suggestion for a
nighttime raid on the Nickerson building.

Quill, strongly in mind of a lynch mob, made an alarmed
face at Howie, who winked at her in a reassuring way before saying, "What precisely has Conway written that's
actionable or even alarming, so far? This"—he drew a
neatly folded section of the first *Trumpet!* from his sports
coat pocket—"merely indicates that revelations are to
come. He hasn't specified what those revelations are, and,
indeed, if the front-page story is any indication, that's all
the story's going to amount to."

"Dog shit," said Marge.

"A direct if inelegant description," said Howie. "Now,

as soon as Esther brings the latest copy of the *Trumpet!*, we can determine the most appropriate way to pro—''

"Coo-ee!" Esther West posed at the conference room door like Gertrude announcing Ophelia's demise in a particularly bad production of *Hamlet*. Like Gertrude, she took an unconscionable amount of time to get to the point. "I had to stop for gas, because I was almost out, and I couldn't find anybody but Gordy Michealson's boy Odie at the newspaper office, and he didn't want me to take a copy without Mr. Conway's approval. *Quelle dommage!* I said to him." (Esther had renamed her dress shop Ouest's Best, after signing up for conversational French at the local junior college.) "This paper is for the public, *n'est-ce pas?* That means 'is it not so,' Marge. Is it not so? I said to Odie."

"J'a bring the copies?" demanded Elmer.

"I guess it is so, I said to him. So here's your five bucks, I said."

"Five bucks!" Marge interrupted in dudgeon. "What the hell. Five bucks!"

"And Odie didn't know how to make change . . ."

"We ain't gonna pay no five bucks for that sleazeball paper!" roared Harland.

"I don't care what it cost!" said Elmer. "*Did you get it!*"

"I got ten copies," said Esther primly. "Fifty cents each. I'd appreciate quarters, please. I can't make change myself." She rummaged in her capacious shoulder bag, withdrew a sheaf of newspapers, and unfolded one: MALL MADNESS!! screamed the front-page banner.

The air stirred with the members' expelled breath.

"Forty-point headline," said Harvey helpfully.

"Lemme see that," demanded the mayor. Esther passed the pile to Howie who scanned it with the grave deliberation appropriate to his position as town attorney and justice of the peace. Norm Pasquale, principal of Hemlock Falls High School, grabbed the pile, took one, and passed the rest to Harland as though it were the pregnancy statistics for the cheerleading squad. Harland passed the rest to Miriam, who passed it on to Harvey, who turned it over to the mayor with a hope-filled smile.

The mayor read for a lengthy moment, his face crumpled like a frustrated baby's. "Gol-dang!" he said. "You hear this? 'Is the sewage system safe? Will toilets be backed up all over Hemlock Falls as a result of the hasty and cheap installation of the leach field at the Hemlock Falls Mini-Mall? Will the citizens of this fair village be soon awash in rivers of unspeakable filth? This reporter will have the answers to this and other tough questions in the next edition of the *Trumpet!* The mayor of this fair city, it seems, has a lot to answer for.' " Elmer's pudgy hands tightened on the newsprint. There was a ripping sound. "He can't do this, Howie. He can't say those things about me—I mean the Chamber—here. Hasty? We done it quick, is what we done, because we promised we'd be done in time for the holiday sales. And cheap? We went and did it cost-effective, which is why we got that DeMarco and that out-of-town work crew doin' it so cheap. There's nothing wrong with that leach field, let me tell you. Why, Harland's cousin has been putting in leach fields all over Tompkins County for twenty years or more, and if he don't know leach fields, I'd like you all to show me somebody who does know leach fields. He's been down there four, five times tryin' to talk to that DeMarco about lettin' him in on it, and he says it's bein' put in proper."

Was Louisa, Quill wrote in her minutes book, getting pictures of the septic system when she was killed?

Howie gazed at the mayor over his wire-rimmed spectacles with a benign and reassuring expression. "Hang on to your pulse rate, Elmer, and let me finish." Halfway down the page he sat up with an exclamation. "Payoffs!" he demanded incredulously. "My fee for handling the anchor store contracts was not only legitimate, it was twenty percent less than my normal billing rate! That big banana-nosed son of a bitch!"

Dookie cleared his throat in a mild though meaningful way. Howie subsided, cheeks reddened.

"Hold on to your own durn pulse rate," said Elmer with a regrettable degree of satisfaction. "See what I mean?"

Quill, with a vague intention of making everyone a little more comfortable, suggested lunch. Elmer rather sourly in-

timated that "lynch" was more to his liking. This was sec-
onded by more than one outraged Chamber member; Norm
Pasquale went so far as to suggest that Sheriff McHale arrest Hedrick.

"Guys," said Quill, who hadn't managed to get her
hands on a copy, "isn't there anything at all about his
mother's death?"

"This boy hasn't got a word about his mama?" Elmer
paged frantically back and forth through the paper. Quill
was surprised and a little disturbed at the intensity of his
search,

"Holy crow," said Miriam. "Here it is. It's outrageous!"

There was a rustle of papers. Quill grabbed Miriam's
copy and read:

OBITUARIES

Conway, Louisa, aged
54, suddenly at her home
in the summer resort of
Hemlock Falls. Survived
by a daughter, Carlyle,
and son, Hedrick. Dona-
tions to the Volunteer
Ambulance Fund.

And below that, a boxed item, reading:

DO YOU HAVE INFORMATION LEADING TO
THE ARREST OF "MINI-MALL" PERPETRA-
TORS? EARN A FREE!! YEAR SUBSCRIPTION TO
THE TRUMPET! CALL TRUMP-27 TOLL FREE!

"That's it?" demanded Elmer. "His ma bites the big
one and that's it?"

Marge tossed her copy contemptuously to the floor. "What a pile of crap. That boy's taste is all in his mouth."

Harland Peterson gnawed his lower lip. He picked up the paper, set it down, then shoved it to the center of the table. "So we wait for next week for more bullshit."

Howie folded his paper into neat quarters. "A bit of an incitement, that boxed item underneath the obituary," he observed.

"Incitement to what?" asked Quill.

Howie pursed his lips and said nothing.

"Mr. Mayor," said Miriam primly. "I take exception to the scatological turn of this meeting."

"You what?" Elmer wiped his forehead with a large handkerchief. "You going to air-condition in here, Quill?"

Quill, who had written, "Uh-oh. The mayor?" under the INVESTIGATIONS heading in her meeting's notebook, gazed thoughtfully at Miriam.

"Scatological," said Miriam. "All this reference to bodily functions. I'd appreciate a little more decorum. I mean, the opening ceremonies are in three days. . . . " Miriam's hands crumpled a tissue into a ball, smoothed it out, then crumpled, smoothed, crumpled, smoothed, crumpled, smoothed, until she caught Quill's startled eye. Tissue-crumpling was not at all like Miriam. Nor were her objections to Marge and Harland's pungency; she'd known both for years and was prone to an occasional "Oh, shit!" herself. Quill wrote "MD: NO!!??" and sketched a little alarmed face next to it. "Howie," she said suddenly. "Could you give us some possibilities?"

"Possibilities?"

"You know—best case, worse case." Quill looked up and down the table. "The thing is, I'm not sure just what's at risk here. What . . . um . . . crim—I mean, scandalous activity could he discover?"

"You mean what criminal activity is possible in a project like this? Jesus Christ, Quill, the possibilities are endless."

"They can't be," Quill urged. "I mean, Mr. Conway's mentioned payoff twice. Payoffs for what? This is a private investment and most of the town bought into it, and the records and transactions have been reviewed by every regulatory office in the entire state. What could be crooked or devious about that?"

Howie removed his glasses, polished them, then fitted them carefully over his nose and peered at her over the rims. "You don't understand how the state works. Or the county."

Lawyers, thought Quill, had a trick of putting you on the defensive even when all you'd asked was a simple little question.

"This is not a simple little question," said Howie. "Just offhand, although if the Chamber wants me, in my capacity as town attorney, to prepare a summary memorandum for them, I'd be happy to do so. So my present response is by no means complete. By no means."

Caveat Avocat, thought Quill, and was so pleased with this that she wrote it down in the meetings book and sketched a frowning Howie shaking a minatory finger. The figure looked so much like Richard Nixon that she erased it.

"Everyone's aware of the more obvious areas of defalcation, fraudulent behavior, and criminal activity. Bids can be rigged. It's a simple matter, for example, to sneak the lowest bidding figure to a favored contractor, and award the job to him. Or her. Simple, but illegal. It's possible to bribe inspectors, or to use cheaper-grade materials when more expensive items have been specified. The mini-mall is forty thousand square feet. Concrete is sixty dollars a yard. You pull a bag or two of cement from each yard of concrete, and the illegal profit can be considerable."

Quill scanned the assembly for telltale twitches, guilty flushes, or suspect indifference. She thought she was being unobtrusive until she met Marge's affronted glare.

"Our initial proposal for the mini-mall stipulated that no one individual could own a controlling interest. Opportunities for collusion here, of course, are rife. Rife," Howie repeated complacently. "I suspect, however, that Mr. Conway is after smaller fish. As a former state employee . . ."

"He was employed by the state?"

"The Department of Motor Vehicles," said Marge. "'Till Louisa up and married some rich old coot who died."

". . . he is undoubtedly aware of the many, many ways in which an individual—or even a corporation—can be in violation of a state code or a municipal regulation."

Quill, who spent a lot more time than she wanted to mediating disputes between Meg and the DOH, began to get an inkling. Take the intense opportunism of Hedrick's prose. Add the power of any media to form public opinion in a country where injustices were the price to pay for freedom of speech. Mix the sad truth that Meg refused to pull the Aga away from the wall to clean underneath more than once a year, with the fact that DOH regs required "frequent" cleanings, the degree of frequency to be determined by the local inspector. Meg hated inspector Arnie Cunningham with a passion equal to Jael's for Sisera. The passion was reciprocated. Result?

INN KITCHEN CLOSED FOR FILTH!!!!

Her mind's eye saw the headline all too clearly. She poked at her copy of the *Trumpet!* with dismay. "Wow," she said. "I begin to see what you mean. If the OSHA inspections for a mini-mall are anything like the DOH regs for our kitchen—"

"Oh, it's not just OSHA. It's the DEC. It's NIST. It's state regs, country regs, village regs, municipal regs." There was, Quill noted, a pleased satisfaction in Howie's voice. "It's thousands and thousands of pages of government manuals—some with conflicting requirements."

"J'a know that OSHA's self-funded?" asked Marge. "Fact. Those guys come out to inspect and don't find nothin', they get whacked when they get back to the office. They're supposed to bring in enough money in fines to cover their salaries and overhead."

"You don't know that they get 'whacked' when they get back to the office," said Howie sternly.

"May not know," said Betty, "but we can guess."

"Well, it's my opinion that that's what Conway's doing.

Guessing. But a guess is as good as a bull's-eye in a project like the mini-mall. Something's bound to be out of spec. It always is. Some contractor may have not placed a prepayment in a trust account; that's a lot of trouble for a small operator, and expensive to set up, although it's a strict requirement of New York State's. There are, in short, very fertile fields for Mr. Conway to plow.''

"Oh, my," said Quill. "Maybe we should just ignore the whole thing." This was met with varying degrees of scorn, which was, Quill admitted somewhat justified. The meeting wound down several hours later; the sole area of consensus: Hedrick Conway had to be stopped.

Nobody mentioned Louisa.

CHAPTER 6

"It's a shame, this Conway guy slipping a snake into your Eden." Georgia Hardwicke looked over the balcony to the herb gardens; beyond the purple lavender and scented geraniums, the Falls flowed white under a bright moon. She was wearing a purple caftan trimmed with gold threads. The gold glittered cheerfully in the darkness of late evening, a little, thought Quill, like Georgia herself. "This is just gorgeous, Quill." She'd responded to Meg's invitation to dinner in Quill's suite with alacrity, having been Kippled, she'd said, almost to screaming boredom; she'd love an opportunity to discuss the murder, as long as it didn't involve a lot of physical labor. "I'd say that I envied you, but I have a hunch there's a heck of a lot of work involved. After Doug died, I realized that life is too damn short to work hard."

"Most of it falls on Quill," said Meg loyally.

"And John and Meg, and Doreen and Kathleen . . ." Quill sipped her wine and yawned. "God, I'm tired. I usually have more energy."

Georgia shot her a shrewd glance. "It's been a tough couple of days. Exhausting work, discovering a body. Maybe I should make an early night of it and let you guys go to bed."

"Not before we thoroughly hash over who murdered Louisa Conway." Meg sipped at her predinner glass of wine. "I can't believe that this town's ignoring a murder. There must be something rotten in the state of Denmark.

Who in town do you suppose is guilty of crimes against the mini-mall? Nobody, of course,'' Meg answered herself. ''Conway's an idiot. A muckraker and a slime. Which means everybody in town who's invested in it has a motive.'' She took another swallow of the '87 Glenora Chardonnay and stuck her lip out at a belligerent angle. ''Including me. If the horrible Hedrick wants to get my kitchen closed, just let him try. I'll make a couple of headlines, all righty. Try 'Cook Kills Creep' on for size. But that still doesn't give us a clue as to who killed his mother.''

Georgia shook her head slightly. ''From what you tell me, Mr. Conway's brand of journalism might lie behind Louisa's murder, don't you think?''

''His mother didn't have much to do with the *Trumpet!*'' Quill offered.

''She bankrolled it, didn't she?'' Meg stretched out in her lounge chair. ''Maybe whoever killed Louisa thought the source of funds would dry up and then Conway would trumpet himself right out of town.''

''It'd be better to knock off Hedrick himself, wouldn't it?'' said Georgia. ''Seems to me that there's a lot more here than meets the eye.''

''You're probably right. But I've never liked to conduct an investigation on an empty stomach.'' Meg got to her feet. ''I vote we wait until after dinner. It'll take me just a minute to get the crab salad out of Quill's fridge and warm up the sourdough. And beans. We have these marvelous marinated green beans. I'm trying a new set of spices. You guys hold the investigation until I come back. Talk about something else.'' She stepped inside and closed the French doors behind her.

''You two make a habit of amateur investigation?''

Quill chuckled. ''In a way. Meg's pretty good at it, actually. When she gets back, ask her about our other—I guess you could call them—cases.''

''Ah!'' Georgia leaned back with a pleased sigh. ''What could be better? Gorgeous view, fabulous place. A bit of amateur detection to keep things interesting. And green beans à la Quilliam to come. Meg's a terrific cook. I sup-

pose you test out all her recipes before she tries them on
your lucky guests?''

"Oh, yes. One of the advantages.''

"Then how the hell do you stay so slim?'' Georgia patted her comfortably sized stomach. "After my husband
passed on seven years ago, I thought, well, I can starve
myself, get a face-lift, and trip around on stiletto heels trying to entice some sixty-five-year-old geezer into warming
the sheets at night. Or I could buy an electric blanket and
say the hell with it. I have three. Electric blankets, that is.''
She wriggled her eyebrows. "And, come to think of it,
there's been a couple of geezers, too. But to tell you the
truth, honey, at my age, a permanent male around the house
can be such a pain in the tail it's kind of a relief to be on
my own.''

"Did you have children?'' Quill asked diffidently.

"Douglas and I?'' Georgia's homely face clouded. "No.
One of my few regrets. He couldn't . . . that is, he could,
he was great at it if you want to know the absolute bottom-
line truth, there hasn't been a geezer yet that can even come
close, but I never got pregnant, and by the time we realized
that there might be something wrong, I was really kind of
past it, from a physical standpoint. It was the usual, low-
sperm-count kind of thing. And who knows? If we'd had
kids, the little bastards might have turned out god knows
how. But it would have been nice.'' She sighed, wistfully.
"Sometimes I think, if we'd had kids, I'd still have a little
bit of Doug. The curve of a cheek, a way of walking, that
would remind me of the kind of man he was. But life didn't
give us that. Gave us a lot of other things. But not that.
We had a hell of a good time together, except toward the
last, and who could have predicted that? I still miss him.''

So many cruel things, thought Quill, that age and disease
could do. She hoped for Georgia's sake that Douglas's
death had been merciful, although from the distress on her
face, it didn't look like it.

They sipped the wine in silence. Quill thought about children. Would a child of Myles's inherit his strong hands, or
the quiet, attentive way he had of listening? If Myles died,
would a son or daughter keep his spirit alive for her?

"I hadn't thought much beyond the first part," she said aloud. "Diapers and whatnot."

"About kids, you mean?" Georgia's smile was reassuring. "I've got nieces and nephews, and let me tell you, honey, the good stuff comes after the diapers part. There's a point where they get faces, you know? I'm here to tell you, as the most involved auntie of years past, present, and future, that all babies look alike. Then they hit three years old or so, and all of a sudden, there's the Nose." She patted her own rather prominent one. "And then the Chin. And they start to talk, and from being sort of soft, little, boring bundles that fit just right into the curve of your arm, they turn into people. Real ones. It's the damnedest thing, watching a kid grow up. You know that bit of life when you think things will always be like this? That part where any change is a big-time threat, because you're perfectly happy the way things are? That's a fantasy and kids are the best antidote I know for keeping things real. They change every day, in the most amazing, fundamental ways. And it keeps you straight, as a person. Makes you understand that life is hard, life is change, life is a battle. And the minute you sit down and try to grab the waves to keep the tide from going out, which is something we all want to do now and then, honey, here comes the kid, a living breathing agent for life assurance. Not insurance. Assurance."

"Jeez," said Meg, stepping through the French doors with a loaded tray. "The green beans à la Quilliam are going to be quite an anticlimax after that."

"Well, you asked us not to start the detective stuff until you got back." Georgia leaned forward. "God! That smells fantastic!"

Meg picked up a bean and handed it over. Georgia ate it, rolled her eyes, and said, "More! More!"

"What do you think, Quill?" Meg set the tray containing the beans, the crab salad, and a fresh loaf of sourdough bread on the wrought-iron table. Quill sampled the vegetable. "Rosemary. And garlic. I like it a lot."

Meg served with quick deft movements, then poured them all a second glass of the chardonnay. "I'll put the beans on the menu for the party tomorrow night."

Georgia swallowed a mouthful of crab salad. "Wow and more wow. That's it, guys. I'm moving in. I want to be a permanent guest. I'm absolutely serious. Do you have a rate schedule for the year?"

"We have one year-round resident," said Quill. "Mr. Stoker. Well, he paid for three months in advance, and he's talking about staying on after that. And we had to charge him the daily winter rates, which are a bit cheaper than the summer, but not all that much."

"No problem." Georgia stuffed a second forkful of crab salad into her mouth. "Doug left me pretty well fixed, bless his heart. Let's talk about being detectives, and about me becoming a permanent addition to the team." She stopped in midsentence, the remainder of the crab halfway to her mouth. "Unless you think I'd be a pain in the neck. I wouldn't, you know. I've got a lot friends who'd come to visit, and my needlepoint, and I make a religion of inertia."

"That's not it at all. We'd love it. It just seems so expensive, Georgia. There are a few lovely little houses in town you might like to look at."

"Do they have a cook in residence? Maid service? Great company? Not to mention a couple of at-home detectives?"

"Well, no," admitted Quill. "As a matter of fact, we'd love to have you as a permanent guest."

"Then let's talk about it. Not right this second. Later, after my head's a little clearer. Now, before we get to the case, let's talk about this party tomorrow night. Who's coming? Is it just for the Kiplings? Because you don't have to do it, you know. Everyone in the whole society is loaded to the gills, including me, and they need freebies about as much as a picnic needs ants. Food like this ain't cheap, I'll be bound. And that little *contretemps* yesterday afternoon was nothing. No need to apologize."

"We'll end up serving everybody at the Inn and a bunch of the townspeople, too," said Meg. "We always do. Quill invites anybody she thinks is lonely, or isn't getting enough food, or maybe a little depressed, and we'll be serving a hundred if we serve five. I'm not going all out, if that's what you're worried about, Georgia. We grow a lot of our own herbs and practically all the vegetables we serve. We bake our own bread. The only thing that'll cost is the wine, and we'll charge for that, and the sushi, and nobody except the Sakuras will eat that.''

"Cherry blossom," said Georgia, her mouth full.

"In the spring," said Meg helpfully.

"No. *Sakura* means 'cherry blossom' in Japanese."

"How do you know that?" asked Quill, fascinated.

"The Japanese are nuts for Kipling. Don't ask me why. Anyway, the society took a trip to Tokyo in April, and Lyle Fairbanks delivered a paper on the influence of Robert W. Service on Kipling's later work to the Rotary Club in Kyoto."

"There's a Rotary Club in Kyoto?" Meg buttered a piece of sourdough.

"The Japanese are nuts for Rotary, too."

"Robert W. Service?" asked Quill. " 'A bunch of the guys were whooping it up in the Malamute saloon'? That Robert W. Service?"

"That's the one! Lyle has a theory that he and Kipling knew each other in the late eighteen eighties. Kipling lived in Virginia for quite a while, you know, and Service was on the lecture circuit in the northeast in 1888 or some damn thing. I don't recall for sure. Can I have a little bit more of the potato thingy?"

"Dilled potato mousse," said Meg. "I like potatoes. I like potatoes almost as much as I like onions. When I die, if I come back as a vegetable, I want to come back as an onion."

"I wonder what Louisa Conway will come back as." Georgia helped herself to the mousse, took a sip of wine, and shouted suddenly, "My stomach is so happy! Sorry. Back to business. Well, I never met the lady, alive and breathing, that is, but from what I heard, she'll probably be back as an overripe mango." She looked up from the mousse, and her expression sobered. "I'm sorry. Doug always said I had a flapping lip, especially after a glass and a half of wine. This isn't a joke, is it? The poor lady's dead, and nobody seems to care. Now, how do we start this investigation?"

"John always says to follow the money," said Quill.

"And that's been true for two of our cases, at least."

"Sounds like a great idea to me. Does anyone know anything about these people? The name of their lawyers, or even what city they came from? I mean, from what I can gather, they've only been in town a few weeks, and nobody really had much to do with them."

"You have no idea how much we know about the Conways already," said Meg with a smug grin. "This is a small town. And a small town gossip mill is the amateur detective's best friend."

"So what does the town know about them?"

"The nonessential stuff is that Hedrick worked for the Department of Motor Vehicles," said Quill. "Before Louisa married money. And they've traveled quite a bit since Louisa inherited. Carlyle and Louisa were talking about the Côte d'Azur yesterday. The essential stuff is that Hedrick keeps all of his story notes in a little red book he calls his bible. That's what we want to take a look at. Then we need to make a list of everyone who was at the site to find out who had access to the hammer."

"Everyone?" said Georgia. "My God, the place was a zoo."

"It might not be that much of a hassle." Meg picked up a piece of sourdough, regarded it for a long moment, and put it down again. "The very first thing, I think, is to find out where the hammer came from." She shot a sidelong glance at Quill. "We used to have an in at the sheriff's department, and maybe we can revive that contact again."

"That gorgeous hunk?" said Georgia. "The one who's six-foot plus with the terrific tan and the steely gray eyes? This job's starting to sound more interesting by the minute. If I were thirty years younger and forty pounds thinner . . ." She looked at the meringue piled with strawberries and cream that Meg had made for dessert, chuckled, and dug in. "Forget that. Who's got the in?"

"Kathleen Kiddermeister," said Quill promptly. "Our head waitress. Her brother's the deputy."

"A-huh," said Georgia skeptically. She raised an inquiring eyebrow at Meg, who shook her head and smiled. "But how is it going to help to know where the hammer's from? I mean, don't you suppose it came from the site? Somebody just walked by and picked it up and hauled off and socked Louisa?''

''If we can pin down which of the carpenters missed it, then we can maybe get a better fix on who had the opportunity to pick it up,'' said Meg. ''Carpenters love their hammers—it's like Quill with her paintbrushes or me with my paring knife. And good hand tools are expensive. The guys either have them in their tool belts, in the trucks, or they're using them. I don't think pinning down the disappearance of the hammer is going to be as difficult as it sounds.''

''But what if somebody brought it with them?'' asked Georgia. ''Then we're talking premeditation, if I've got the term right.''

''And it doesn't have the feel of a premeditated murder, does it?'' asked Meg. ''So the first two questions are: Who was there? Who had access to the hammer? Then we can make up a list of suspects and take the next step.''

''And that is?'' asked Georgia eagerly.

''To link the preliminary list of suspects with Louisa.''

''How the heck can we do that? I mean, let's say we interrogate them one by one. The murderer's going to lie isn't he? Or she, as the case may be?''

Meg grinned. ''As I said, we have an in with the sheriff's department. Myles will be digging up all kinds of information. He can access computer records, subpoena lawyer's documents—like the will—find out if Hedrick's discovered any mini-scandals for real, or if it's just smoke. If Quill, that is, Kathleen, gets us the facts from the sheriff's department, we don't have to interrogate anyone. We do the legwork and put the facts together.''

''And that dishy sheriff is going to give you these facts?''

Meg shrugged. ''Most of this is a matter of record somewhere, isn't it? The facts are the facts, and most of them are available to anyone who wants to look for them. And Myles has always cooperated. Especially with Quill.''

Quill cleared her throat and folded her napkin carefully. ''If we're going to do this—and I'm not at all sure we should get involved, Meg—''

"Me, either," said Georgia frankly. "It's beginning to sound like a lot of work."

"But if we decide to do it, I think we should recruit Kathleen. She and Davy are pretty close. If she can get him over here for one of your meals, Meg, we can ply him with wine and get a data dump. Myles will go into Louisa's background with a fine-tooth comb. *If* there's a link in her past to anyone who was at the site this afternoon, Myles'll find it. Davy is his assistant—and he'll be able to keep us up-to-date."

"Myles doesn't tell Davy everything," said Meg. "It's far far better if you and Myles—"

"Meg! I know exactly what you're trying to do. It's not going to work. If Myles and I . . . I'll get to it, in my own good time. If we decide to get mixed up in Louisa Conway's murder, I want to handle this ourselves. I already have a list of people here in Hemlock Falls who seem worried over Hedrick's behavior. And we have a number of suspicions about the DeMarco Construction company. Why isn't anyone from the Falls working at the site? Why don't we ever see any of the workers in town for lunch, or to do a little drinking at the Croh Bar? We don't need Myles as much as we need to do a little legwork."

"Legwork," said Georgia dubiously. "There's that term again. Easy Rawlins does a lot of legwork. Spenser, too. Not to mention Travis McGee. Those guys all work out. We're not talking about a lot of exercise, are we? Can we just get the suspects here one by one and question them until they confess? Legwork sounds—tiring."

"Pooh!" said Meg airily. "It's a piece of cake."

"Meg's forgetting some of the more strenuous aspects of detective work, Georgia."

Meg grinned. "You mean like climbing into second-story windows and rolling under wire fences at two in the morning and that sort of legwork?"

"Yes," said Quill. "Not to mention being held at gunpoint, swallowing drugged drinks, and being attacked by guard dogs."

Meg patted Quill on the shoulder. "We survived all of that just fine. Not to worry. This one should be a piece of cake. Hedrick has plans to run articles exposing some scandal about the mini-mall, right? And Louisa funded the *Trumpet!* We've got a whole raft of possible motives if we look at this from the most obvious angle. That somebody wanted to stop Hedrick from publishing his lousy rag. It seems pretty likely to me that the murderer is right here in Hemlock Falls and has some connection to the opening of the mini-mall. So let's parcel out some assignments, here. Georgia, what if you volunteered to do something with the mall opening—you know, work on the Jell-O Architecture committee, or something. You're new in town, just sort of passing through, and nobody's going to get suspicious if you chatter away asking obvious questions. Quill's already got a plan to swipe the little red book. And once we get it, it's bound to be loaded with significant clues. Quill can handle the liaison work with the sheriff, starting tomorrow to find out about Louisa's nefarious past, and I—"

"Yes," said Quill. "And just what are you going to be doing while Georgia and I run around collecting clues?"

Meg waved her fork triumphantly in the air. "I will do the deduction! And another miscreant is brought to justice!"

"I," said Quill, quoting the notorious *New Yorker* cartoon of the little boy being enticed to eat his vegetables, "say it's spinach. And I say the hell with it."

Meg patted her sister affectionately on the knee. "Pooh! You're going to love it. The Snoop Sisters plus one ride again."

"Hmm," said Georgia. "It's beginning to sound like spinach to me, too."

"So?" Meg demanded "What's it going to be? I'll be busy tomorrow with the party arrangements. I think you should just sort of drop on by the sheriff's department, just in a casual way, you know, and Georgia and I—"

"No and no and no. No sheriff's department. No visits, casual or otherwise. Excuse me, Georgia, I hear the phone." Quill rose and stepped into her rooms. The air was cool and a little musty after the freshness of the Falls.

"Quill."

There would come a time, Quill thought, when the sound

of Myles's voice wouldn't catch her under the heart.

"How's the detective biz?" she asked lightly.

"We've got one of your guests here for questioning, and he doesn't speak English. Is there anyone traveling with him that does?"

"Not my Japanese guest! Myles, the man's the retired head of one of the largest multinational corporations in the world."

"That may be," said Myles dryly. "But he's got a rap sheet as long as your arm."

CHAPTER 7

"Thank God it's the chauffeur and not Mr. Sakura," said Quill in the darkness of her Oldsmobile. She signaled a left-hand turn and drew onto Main Street. They were on their way to the police station to rescue Mr. Motoyama. It was just after nine, and the last bits of daylight trailed on the horizon like the luminous wake of a ship. "If Myles arrested a billionaire industrialist for murder, we'd never hear the end of it. The media'd have a field day."

"It's bad enough that it's the chauffeur. Can't you see the *Trumpet!* headlines?" Meg pulled at her hair. "'Foreign Terrorist Checks In at Murder Inn. Sisters Sign In Killer!' And, in a discreet subheadline: 'Did He Register His Gun?!'"

"Sshush! Mr. Sakura understands more English than you think."

"Pooh!" Meg turned her head and raised her voice, "You okay, Mr. Sakura?"

A crisp, rather frigid voice behind them responded, "*Hai*."

"We'll straighten this out in no time," Quill assured him. A glance at the rearview mirror made her add hastily, "Mr. Motoyama should be out in time for the party tomorrow night. I hope you both will come."

"*Mo*toyama," said Mr. Sakura, firmly.

Meg settled back into her seat. "I can't believe Myles fell for this racist crap."

Quill was so startled she braked. "What the heck are you talking about?"

"It's pretty clear, isn't it?" asked Meg darkly. "Innocent foreigner in a small town lynched by paranoid citizens. The poor man doesn't even speak English. And there he is—alone, scared, petrified that the *gaijin* will string him up by his—"

Quill stepped on the accelerator with a jerk. "All Myles said is that he's pulled Motoyama . . . Mr. Motoyama . . . whatever . . . for questioning. He may have been a witness to something, Meg."

"Doreen heard through the grapevine that Mr. Motoyama attacked Louisa at the mini-mall project with a broom handle and chased her into the woods. On such evidence are the Billy Budds of this world strung up on the yardarm."

Quill, still stung at the wholly gratuitous insult to Myles, didn't answer.

"Louisa Conway wasn't killed with a broom handle, she was killed with a hammer," Meg continued, apparently unconscious of Quill's irritation. "Myles must have known that, but no, he attacks the most defenseless person around. An elderly citizen of a foreign country, eking out his poverty-stricken existence behind the wheel."

"That bozo O'Doyle, the well-known volunteer fireman and forensics expert, was the one who said it was a hammer. And I'll thank you very much not to impugn the reputation of one of the most honorable men I know."

Meg glanced at her out of the corner of her eye and hummed a fragment of "As Long As He Needs Me," which made Quill crosser than ever.

"It won't work, you know."

"What?" said Meg innocently.

"You know what. Trying to make me defend Myles. We've arrived, Mr. Sakura." Quill pulled into the municipal building parking lot, put the car into park, and turned off the ignition.

"Porice?"

"Yes. This is the police station."

"Sakura Kenji comes soon?"

"Yes. I spoke with him. Cornell University is less than twenty minutes from here. He'll be here very soon."

Mr. Sakura grunted doubtfully.

"So." Meg sighed "The great art critic arrives. Not that you'll want to talk about your work. Your former work, I should say. Now. About our true calling as detectives. Will you ask questions, and me take notes? Or vice versa? This is a great opportunity to pursue inquiries."

"Let's just forget the whole thing." Quill pushed the car door with barely enough force to keep it open. "I'm tired. I want to go home. And you're just thinking of ways to get me alone with Myles. I don't want to be alone with Myles."

"Heck, no. This little trip to the station house is right up your chivalric alley. Here we are, the Sisters, rushing off in the night to save—"

"Cut it out! I hate it when your imagination runs riot. Half the time you're in some twilight movie world."

"And which half would that be!?" demanded Meg with a grin. "Not the cooking half. Admit it's not the cooking half. I'm very realistic about that."

"Not the cooking half. You're very real world about cooking."

"You'd be bored without my imaginative contributions to our daily grind." Meg got out of the car with a Clint Eastwood slouch and whistled the opening bars of the theme from *A Fistful of Dollars*. Quill got out, slammed the driver's door shut, and opened the rear door for Mr. Sakura.

The parking lot was nearly deserted, except for a black-and-white police cruiser and Myles's Jeep Cherokee. Their footsteps echoed on the asphalt as Quill led the way to the station.

Quill, while not intimately familiar with the workings of multinational corporations, was braced for at least a hedge of lawyers, if not a planeloadful, appearing instantaneously like so many crew members beamed down from the starship *Enterprise*, The sheriff's office contained only Myles, his pinkly eager deputy Dave Kiddermeister, and a short, elderly Japanese with a fierce scowl: Mr. Motoyama himself.

The latter rose as they entered, prostrated himself on the floor before his employer and groveled. Mr. Sakura responded with a flood of furious, highly guttural Japanese and short, angry chopping motions of both hands.

"Good heavens," murmured Meg. "It's a good thing he doesn't have a sword."

Mr. Sakura finished his tirade. Motoyama rose and bowed. Mr. Sakura bowed back, and with an abrupt change of manner, turned to Quill and asked, "Porice chief?"

"Yes. Mr. Sakura, may I present Myles McHale?"

"*Konnichiwa*," said Mr. Sakura. "My aporogies for this . . ." He hesitated. "This benighted 'eathen."

Myles looked a little startled.

"Kipling," said a voice behind Quill. "My father is very fond of Kipling's poetry, and is, in fact, learning English by memorizing selected poems."

Quill turned to the tall Japanese who had come in unnoticed behind them. "Ken Sakura. I've been an admirer of your paintings for a long time. I'm delighted to meet you, although I'd hoped it'd be under less stressful circumstances."

"Wow," said Meg, under her breath, either in response to Sakura Kenji's eloquence or his looks, or perhaps, thought Quill, both at once. He was one of the most beautiful men she'd ever seen. Like many Northern Japanese, he had a compact, graceful swimmer's body. He dressed as most Cornell University professors did in summertime: blue work shirt rolled past his muscled forearms, chinos, and Docksiders.

"I can assure you, Ms. Quilliam," Sakura Kenji continued, "that my father's taste in the plastic arts is much less idiosyncratic than his taste in poetry. I told him, for example, that he would find your own work had the quality known to us as *shibui*."

Quill, out-of-proportion pleased, recognized the accolade for what it was with a violent blush, then made an effort to maintain her dignity with a skeptical frown.

"Except for the fondness for Kipling, his artistic taste is impeccable. I believe Kipling's chauvinism, his imperialism, his conviction that a selected race of men is destined to rule others, make the poet attractive to those of my father's generation." He smiled affectionately at his father, then took Quill's hand and held it a fraction longer than necessary.

"Well," said Quill helplessly. "Um. I'm delighted you came over to help with the translation effort. I'm sure this will be cleared up immediately. Sheriff McHale is just . . . is just . . ."

"Pursuing inquiries?"

"That's right," Myles interrupted equably. "You may be aware, Professor Sakura, of the events that took place here yesterday."

"So Miss Quilliam informed me when she called."

"Were you also aware of Mr. Motoyama's criminal record?" Myles leaned forward and read: "Three battery convictions, one assault, one vehicular intent to harm? All occurring on the same date?"

Ken Sakura's classic brow creased. He turned to his father. The conversation was rapid: courteous on the son's side; deprecatory on his father's.

"Sheriff McHale, there does appear to have been a prior incident." Ken hesitated. "My father says it was of no consequence,"

"Concerning?"

"Arising from Motoyama's war experiences. He's still somewhat resentful over the outcome."

"The war?" said Quill, bewildered. "Which war?"

"*The* war, Miss Quilliam. For Japanese of my father's generation, there is only one war."

"World War *Two*!" shrieked Meg. "Pooh! That was fifty years ago."

"My father is seventy-eight, Miss Quilliam, and Motoyama some years older. Motoyama associates certain English words with his experiences in an internment camp in the Pacific. The battery charges you refer to on his rap sheet, Sheriff, were brought by an elderly veteran of your Pacific campaign. The assault charges were made by a confederate of his who got in the way of the corncobs when the veteran ducked."

"Certain English words?" demanded Meg. "What kind

of words? You mean racial slurs? Mr. Motoyama threw corncobs at somebody because of racial slurs?''

Quill, with misgiving, recalled Hedrick's offensive characterization of John Raintree. Attitudes like that ran in the family. "And there weren't any corncobs handy yesterday," she said aloud, "but there were plenty of hammers."

Meg gave her a glance which somehow seemed to be approving and conspiratorial all at once. "So, Myles, Mr. Motoyama got in a fight with Louisa Conway? Over . . . um . . . certain English words?"

Myles, his attention caught by something beyond the office walls, didn't respond.

Dave Kiddermeister offered, a little diffidently, "It was Jell-O."

Mr. Motoyama stiffened, drew himself erect, and made a noise indicative of extreme displeasure.

Receiving no sign from his boss, Dave continued in a slightly more self-assured way, "And the fight wasn't with the deceased, it was with Mrs. Mayor."

"Adela Henry?" said Quill. "Mr. Motoyama got into a fight with Adela Henry over Jell-O?" The repetition of this (apparently) racially offensive word prompted another growl from Motoyama. Quill felt herself blush and said, "*Gomen na-sai*, Mr. Motoyama," which earned a reproving glare from Mr. Sakura.

Meg was scribbling notes on the back of a recipe card drawn from her pocket. "What was Mrs. Henry doing there?"

"Well, you know she's president of the ladies auxiliary," said Dave. "The auxiliary went to the mini-mall site with Harvey Bozzell to check out the location of the tent for the opening-day festivities. The ladies auxiliary's got this Jell-O architecture contest going—"

"Jell-O architecture?" said Ken Sakura.

"Yes. You know, buildings made out of Jell-O. Model buildings. Best buildings gets a cash money prize that's been put up by the Chamber, and the ladies auxiliary wanted to be sure ol' Harvey put the tent out of the sun, because it's August and bound to be hot and they don't want the exhibits to melt before the judging. They were thinking air-conditioning.''

"Buildings out of Jell-O?'' said Meg, her professional interest temporarily aroused. "Air-conditioning won't help much. You'd have to add sand to the gelatin, or something.''

"Anyhow, this bird Motoyama starts hollering and Mrs. Mayor hollers back and Motoyama grabs a broom handle and starts waving it around in what Mrs. Mayor calls a threatening manner—''

"Broom handle?'' asked Quill, bemused. "But what does this have to do with Louisa Conway?''

"Tae kwon do,'' said Meg, with an annoyingly superior air, "turns broom handles into lethal weapons. No, never mind, that's a Korean martial arts discipline. But I'm sure there's some Japanese equivalent. Why did you arrest Mr. Motoyama, Myles? Did Louisa Conway get into this argument over the Jell-O and start calling him names?''

"He hasn't been arrested for Louisa Conway's murder,'' said Myles. "Adela Henry swore out a complaint of battery against him.'' He turned his head suddenly, his attention drawn to the front door.

Ken Sakura leaned against the wall and folded his arms, his gaze direct and warm. Quill wanted to go home. "So this is really none of our business, Meg, now that Ken's here.'' She looked past Ken Sakura's left ear. "I really think it's time we were going.''

"It is *too* our business, Quill. Anything that affects the reputation of the Inn is our business. Myles, please pay attention to me. It is just typical of this town to accuse a non-English-speaking person of a different race of—''

"Quiet,'' said Myles. Meg stiffened in indignation. Myles rose from behind his desk, his eyes intent. In the silence Quill became aware of a low murmuring outside; the scrape and shuffle of many feet.

Myles was across the floor to the front door in three strides. He opened it to a parking lot suddenly packed with vehicles. The cars and trucks disgorged men, their faces shadowy in the uncertain light cast by sodium lights. The three Japanese became very still. Quill started after Myles and was stopped by Meg's urgent hand on her arm.

"Quill, it's a mob!" Her voice was astounded.

"It's a what?!"

"A mob. M-O-B. As in a large group of pissed-off citizens, mostly male, from the looks of it, ready to lynch somebody. Most likely poor Mr. Motoyama there, and all because he's Japanese. My God! I was just trying to snap you out of your lousy mood before. I couldn't have been right. A racist mob in Hemlock Falls!"

"That's absurd!" Quill protested.

"Sher'f!" came a shout from the parking lot. "Bring that Jap on out!" Myles jerked his head at Dave Kiddermeister, stepped outside, and shut the door behind him.

"My God," said Quill. "It *is* a mob." To her own amazement, she gulped. "You stay here, Meg, out of sight."

"Where the heck do you think you're going?"

"Out to help Myles."

"No, ma'am." Dave Kiddermeister, a little pale around his ears and nose, hooked his thumbs in his regulation leather belt. His attempt at official cool was somewhat undermined by his trembling chin. "Myles said to put you all in the lockup, just for safety."

"He said no such thing!" Meg glared at him. "Put the Sakuras in the lockup, if you want to, but we're going out there."

"No, ma'am, that's not part of riot-control procedure."

"The heck with riot-control procedure."

Quill pulled the door open and stepped outside, Meg at her heels. Myles looked very tall against the crowd of men facing him. He stood easily, balanced on the balls of his feet, hands at rest against his sides.

Meg began a nearly inaudible version of the theme from High Noon." 'Do not forsake me, oh, my darlin . . .' "

"Shut up," Quill hissed.

" 'On this our weddin' da-a-ay,' " Meg hummed, several decibels lower.

"Meg!" Quill's whisper was furious.

"You know I always sing when I'm nervous," Meg hissed back. "Besides, it diffuses the tension."

"Try giggling if you want to diffuse tension. What's wrong with a nervous giggle?"

"It makes me more nervous. And right now, I'm scared out of my tree." She resumed her tuneless hum.

"Well, gentlemen?" Myles didn't raise his voice, but it carried in the humid night air.

An ominous shifting of many feet, a low-voiced muttering: "We want that Jap."

Quill's bare arms prickled with gooseflesh.

"Elmer. Harland." Myles picked the men easily out of the crowd. "You men have some questions I can answer? Mayor? You have something to say, step out here in the light. Where I can see you."

There was a short, significant hesitation, followed by a sort of ripple in the thick of the crowd and subdued cries of "G'wan *out* there!"

"Leggo!"

"You chicken?"

"I'm *go*ing, durn it."

Elmer Henry's tubby figure emerged from the clustered group, the collar of his shirt rucked up around his neck.

"Adela sees that shirt, you'll get what for," Myles observed.

As always, the mention of his formidable wife's name made Elmer jump.

Myles smiled a little. "Now what's this in aid of, this meeting?"

"We demand to see that Jap." The anonymous voice came from somewhere behind a battered blue van.

Elmer directed a tremendous frown in the van's direction, then cleared his throat twice. "Yes, Sheriff. That Mr. Sakra? He as rich as they say?"

Myles nodded.

"Like, a billionaire?"

"So I'm told. You thinking of holding him for ransom?"

"Well, it's like this. We were having a little informal meetin' at the Croh Bar, just the fellas here, and we started talking about that mall project. And the unwanted publicity. Yes, unwanted publicity."

"From Mrs. Conway's death?"

"What? That? Yeah. That and other unwanted publicity. Of any kind. And we thought as how—"

The voice from beyond the blue van came in a belligerent shout: *"We wanna see—"*

"Pete," Myles interrupted. "Come out of there."

The van, Quill now realized, belonged to Peterson's Septic and Floor Covering. Petey Peterson himself, as broad as his cousin Harland, and as indefatigable as a rusty set of box springs, edged reluctantly into view.

"Ms. Quilliam?" Petey touched his billed John Deere hat. "Them terlits working okay?"

"Just fine," said Quill, a little huskily, "thank you."

Meg straightened herself to all five feet two of her inches and shouted suddenly, "So, Petey. You want to see Mr. Sakura? You and forty of your liquored-up buddies? Hah! Well, you can't, see? Before you do, you'll have to go through him"—she jerked her thumb at Myles—"and my sister. Got that?!"

"What about you?" Quill muttered.

"What d'you mean, what about me?"

"They just have to go through the two of us?"

"Yankee go home!" Meg shouted.

"Uh, Meg—" said Quill.

"You mean you already got to him?" said Petey a little desperately. "He bought your shares in the mini-mall project already? He don't wanna buy any more?"

Meg, who had swung into the "lookit that big hand move along" chorus of *High Noon* at the threatening level of a mosquito whine, stopped humming abruptly and said in a normal voice, "You want to make a deal with Mr. Sakura to buy out your shares of the mini-mall?"

"Yes, ma'am." Petey touched his hat in what was apparently a nervous reflex. "Rich as Jesus, this guy, right?"

"Croesus," Meg corrected. "This isn't a mob hunting justice?"

"A what, ma'am?"

"No attempts at lynching an innocent foreigner because of the color of his skin?"

"Ma'am?"

"You mean this is just a mob over a merger!?"

"Meg, darn it!" Quill cast an exasperated look at Myles, who jerked his thumb toward her Oldsmobile. "We're going home."

"Tell you what, Petey," said Mayor Henry. "Maybe we can talk to this Mr. Sakra at the party tomorrow night. Is he invited, too, Quill?"

"The party?" repeated Quill a little stupidly.

"Chamber's looking forward to it. Thing is, if he's gonna be there, we wait a bit to discuss bidness. That all right with you, Sher'f?"

"The Chamber's coming to the party?"

Meg started to laugh.

Quill looked at Myles out of the corner of her eye. "Meg. It's time to leave."

"Hoo!" Meg said.

"Meg!" Quill grabbed her sister firmly by the sleeve and pulled her through the crowd to her Oldsmobile. "Say goodbye, Meg."

"Goodbye, Meg!" Her face pink with suppressed giggles, Meg waved farewell, trailing a final "waaaaittt, waaaiit along . . ." as Quill squealed an illegal right turn at the red light.

"They're all going to think you're crazy," said Quill back in the kitchen. "Or drunk." She'd scooped up her phone messages from the front desk as they'd come in, and was separating them into two piles: return immediately and get-to-it-eventually.

"Well, I'm neither. Did you ever think about the total usefulness of country-western music, Quillie? I mean, there's a song for every emotional crisis known to the human heart. This is an *insight*."

"Who cares?" asked Quill callously. "There are three calls here from Hedrick Conway."

"Maybe he wants a date," said Meg flippantly. "Can you believe that Ken Sakura? Wow!"

Quill held Hedrick's messages over the get-to-it eventually file. "Oh, damn, I'd better call. It's probably about his poor mother." She crumpled the paper and went to the phone at Meg's recipe station.

"Ask him to the party tomorrow."

"Oh, right. With the entire Chamber of Commerce there, petrified he's going to expose some pathetic little secret? Not to mention the fact that he'd insult Mr. Sakura, or something. Besides, even Hedrick wouldn't show up at a party just two days after his mother died."

She dialed. He picked up with a careless "Yeah" on the third ring.

"Mr. Conway? This is Sarah Quilliam. I'd like to say how very sorry I am over your mother's...um... passing."

"She will be missed," he said, breathing through his nose. "Sadly missed."

"The...um...observances? They're scheduled soon?"

"The funeral, ya mean? You gotta talk to Carlyle. She handles all that."

"Well, if there's anything we can do, please let us know."

"About what?"

"About your mother's, um, passing."

"Oh. No. No. Casket. Grave. Not much to it. Although she will be missed."

There was a prolonged silence. Quill dropped the pink slips into the garbage bin. "I'm sorry to call so late, but I noticed that'd you left a couple of messages for me."

"Yeah. I did. About this party tomorrow night. I didn't get the time."

"The time?"

"Yeah. What time's the party going to be? I gotta arrange coverage. There's no telling what kind of news day it's going to be, so I can't promise I'll be there myself—people gotta get used to that, around here. They think they're gonna get my personal attention, they got another think coming. But Carlyle will be there with Sheriff McHale."

"Indeed," said Quill icily. "How nice."

"So when is it?"

"Seven," said Quill. "Seven o'clock."

"Dress?"

"Oh, is Carlyle planning on wearing clothes?" asked

Quill sweetly. "I mean, especially? It's white tie."

"White tie!" shrieked Meg.

Quill covered the receiver with one hand and glared at her.

"Got it," Hedrick said into her ear and hung up with the careless bang of a busy man.

"What!" Meg demanded. "White tie? Are you crazy? That's gloves and floor-length and colored stones."

"Huh," said Quill.

"She'll be so embarrassed, she'll go home," said Meg thoughtfully.

"Maybe."

"Even Hedrick will be embarrassed and go home. And how are we supposed to swipe the goods book if he's not there?"

"We'll create," said Quill, "a diversion."

"Like the diversion we had tonight? Thank God Myles stopped it."

"Stopped what?! A bunch of guys storming the sheriff's station over a business deal? You made a complete and utter bozo of yourself. And if it weren't for me, it would have been even more complete."

"You mean you didn't notice?"

"Notice what?"

"Quill, dammit. Marcos DeMarco was there with three of the guys from the site. In the shadows, behind Petey's van. Myles saw them, too. They had guns."

CHAPTER 8

"Meg said they had guns." Quill, behind the desk in her office, fiddled nervously with her paper cutter. The windows were open to the sweet summer air; lavender mingled with the scent of August lilies and the air was as soft as bathwater. It was just after nine o'clock. She and John were waiting for Doreen and Meg to start the weekly staff meeting.

"But you didn't see them?"

"I was so flipped out by her behavior that I wouldn't have seen Godzilla flattening the Town Hall."

"But as far as you know, the incident's closed. Nobody harmed the Sakuras, and Motoyama's out of jail."

"Mr. Motoyama is, yes. I think they're all back in the suite, including Ken—that is, Mr. Sakura."

"The art critic."

"It does not make a particle of difference to me what he is," said Quill.

John looked at her.

Quill had spent a restless night. She had dreamed her paints had been locked away and that she'd lost the key. She'd dreamed she was lost. She'd wakened to a bed without Myles, and wakened crying. "About the guns."

"I don't know about the guns. It's odd, certainly."

"Guns in the Falls. John. What's going on? Do you think there's something criminal about the mall project? Louisa was out there with a camera. What if she found out that . . ." She trailed off. Her mind was foggy. She was tired. She focused on the job at hand with an effort.

"What?"

"I don't know. I guess I'm worried about the investment. About the employees. We talked them all into subsidizing part of the project with payroll deductions. And Meg's savings, too. And mine, and yours, I guess. We'd been doing so well."

"We'd been doing very well. Which is why we put that three hundred thousand into the mini-mall. And which is why we're cash-short at the moment. We're watching expenses, remember? Now, I'd like to talk about this party tonight."

Quill, who'd forgotten to tell John about the mysterious increase in party attendance, said hastily, "I remember the days when three hundred thousand dollars seemed like a fortune. Six of my friends in SoHo could have lived on that for five years, each." She felt wistful. "And buy paints and canvas with it, too."

"Well, look forward to the time when you and Meg will be retired. That's your pension fund. Three hundred K may seem like a lot of money now, but it won't when you're ready to retire."

She reached across the desk and took his hand. "You're so good to us, John. We're feckless, Meg and I. Feckless. Without you, we'd be up the creek for certain."

"Without me, you might have invested that cash into certificates of deposit. Which is maybe where it should be."

"You're not *really* worried about the mini-mall investment, are you?"

He rose from the couch and went to the window. The buzz of the lawn mower reached them, one of the comforting sounds of summer. "Yeah," he said after a long moment. "I am."

"What makes *you* think that there could be something wrong with our investment? I know why I think that . . . but it's no more than a feeling. An intuition. Well, an intuition based partly on the fact that there's been a murder, and that the out-of-town construction crew was lurking around the sheriff's office with weapons last night. Myles always discounts intuition in an investigation. He says that you have to stick to facts. I have this horrible feeling that the mayor and Howie and Harvey are involved. All I've really got to go on is the reaction of some of the Chamber members to the latest edition of the *Trumpet!* Goodness knows I could be imagining it.''

John rubbed the back of his neck. ''I have to admit you've got a point. You know what's bothering me most? I don't know anyone from the work crews. The construction company that has the bid for completion is from New Jersey, so I'd expect the foreman and the supervisors to be from out of town—but they brought all the workers with them. Not one's from Hemlock Falls.''

''We didn't do a what-d'y-call it—background check on the low bidder, did we?''

''Of course we did. DeMarco seemed to check out. He posted a bond, his bank gave us the go-ahead, and he gave us photos and letters of reference from various jobs he said he'd done before. But we never personally talked to anyone who actually dealt with the company before. Letters and photos can be faked. And his bank's a small, privately owned one, which means he could have a lot of influence over the kind of information released to us.''

''But construction's going well. All the deadlines have been met. And the mall itself looks wonderful, John. I didn't look at progress yesterday, of course, because of the tragedy, but I'd been down to see it the week before— everyone who's invested has dropped by. It's terrific. It's beautiful. So, maybe I'm just imagining things.''

John shrugged. ''There was a murder. You didn't imagine that.''

''Yes,'' said Quill. ''Have you talked to Myles about this?''

''Myles talked to *me* about this. He's the one that noticed the work crew. He's been doing some checking on his own.''

''And?''

''It's inconclusive.''

''Inconclusive? What do you mean, inconclusive?''

''Quill, you know how he feels about you and Meg mixing into these kinds of things. You're both civilians.''

"You're a civilian, too!"

"That's true. But I don't spy on Inn guests, which is a misdemeanor, by the way—"

"It was surveillance!" said Quill. "On the Parker case. And we only did it once."

John grinned. "And I haven't hung out my shingle—if only metaphorically—as one half of a private detective team, and I don't go breaking and entering every chance I get."

"Now, wait just a second, John Raintree. You most certainly have contributed to the sort of mild bending of little laws that Meg and I occasionally—*occasionally*—engage in."

"I helped once. Under extreme provocation."

"I also know precisely what you're trying to do. You're trying to divert my attention from what Myles may or may not have found out about crimes at the mini-mall by laying down red herrings to make me forget it. Between you trying to keep me off this case, and Meg trying to keep me on it, I think I'm just going to go to Detroit."

"Detroit?"

"Detroit," said Quill firmly. "Nobody who knows the least little thing about me would ever dream that I would go to Detroit. Which means I couldn't be found, which would suit me just fine at the moment."

"That little depression hasn't lifted?"

"I am *not* depressed, thank you very much. Now. What's Myles discovered?"

John hesitated. "I really can't say, Quill."

"You 'can't say' to me!? Your partner in crime heretofore? And, dare I say it, your boss! If you don't deliver the goods, Raintree, you're fired."

"You can't fire me, I quit."

"Before you quit, give me at least a *hint* of what Myles has found out about DeMarco."

John shook his head.

"Does it have anything to do with any of the principal investors here in town?"

"Give it a rest, Quill."

"It just can't be anyone we know. Whatever it is. Almost

everyone we know has invested in the partnership. And they're either too honest or too smart to get involved in anything crooked. Howie Murchison is an old-fashioned kind of lawyer—honest, professional—and he's very smart. Now, admittedly, Elmer and Harvey aren't the most brilliant guys to come down the pike, but Harland Peterson is one of the shrewdest people in the village. He's made a fortune in farming, and you know how tough that is. And finally, Marge Schmidt, who is nobody's fool. Collectively, those five own more than sixty percent of the mall. And you're not going to tell me that any one of them is going to be involved in something crooked. I just won't believe it. It has to be this DeMarco. He's behaving very suspiciously, don't you think?''

''He's not behaving suspiciously at all, Quill. I've met him. You remember him. He stayed here at the Inn while we were getting the funding together last year.''

''I do remember him. He had a secretive sort of face,'' Quill mused. ''I remember thinking about it at the time.''

''Well, you never said a word to me, if you did.''

''It'd be just like Myles to keep interesting stuff about DeMarco under his hat. And let me hare off investigating some of my best friends, instead of focusing on the real culprit. I'll have to put DeMarco on my suspects list. If I do decide to investigate this, that is.''

''Quill! He isn't a culprit if there hasn't been any crime.''

''Murder isn't a crime?''

John groaned and put his head in his hands. ''Do me a favor, will you? Leave me out of any further discussions about this. And I'd really prefer that you not mention my name when you talk to Myles.'' He sat up. ''If you talk to Myles.''

''Maybe I won't and maybe I will,'' said Quill, struck by this opportunity for a little harmless blackmail. ''If I allude very carefully to this conversation and let him know that I know what you know, I might trick him.''

''No allusions, please. I gave him my word.''

''And you haven't told me a thing. What if I—''

''I mean it, Quill. Let's stick to business, okay? Now.

What about this free party this evening, for some of the richest people in America?''

"It's more than that. Meg sees the party tonight as a chance to find out if there's anything behind Hedrick's threats. We're going to create a diversion, and I'm going to get my hands on Hedrick's goods book. Now, about this diversion—''

"We're not going to have any trouble selecting a diversion," said John. "It'll be all our suppliers demanding payment, storming the back patio in a body like the cavalry driving my relatives to Canada."

"That was the Nez Percé."

"All AmerInds are brothers. Can we talk about business for a minute? Just how many people are coming tonight?"

"Well, there's twenty-four members of the Chamber, as nearly as I can tell, and the fifty guests we have staying here, and the sheriff's department, I guess, because Kathleen apparently invited Davy, who invited the rest of the deputies, and Myles is coming, and the Conways, so it's less than one hundred people, John. It can't cost all that much."

"So why has Meg brought in six extra kitchen staff from Cornell?"

"Six! Gosh. I don't have any idea."

"So there's extra labor. From the figures Meg gave me, I've estimated a cost of sixteen dollars a head."

"It's not too bad, is it? At least, not very. And it even includes the yellowfin tuna shipped in for the sushi, which is a million dollars a pound or something. She doesn't think many locals will eat it, so she probably didn't order very much."

"Thank God for that, at least. We're looking at a minimum two thousand out of pocket, Quill. How are we going to recoup a two-thousand-dollar loss this month? An unnecessary two-thousand-dollar loss, I might add. The Kiplings seem to be wealthy enough to afford their own party, and I'm not real sure I understand why we're in the middle of this whole thing. We can recoup some of the losses if we have a cash bar."

Quill sank a little lower in her chair, scratched her left

ankle, then pulled at her lower lip. "Well, they are our guests. Don't you think—"

John shook his head. "This is an inn, Quill. A profit-making business, supposedly."

"A cash bar seems so rude! The numbers have been good this quarter, haven't they?"

He smiled a little. "The numbers are never good enough."

"And of course, they are going to provide entertainment with their poetry reading." She added doubtfully, "Which will be good publicity."

"We hope."

"I hope so," said Quill seriously. "It'd be awful if everyone ignored their poetry. I'm so afraid it's going to be ridiculous. Although Doreen says the Kiplings are very demanding, except for Georgia, of course. I expect that comes from being rich. Anyway, they're much too nice a group of people to be publicly embarrassed. Georgia Hardwicke especially. Except that they've done this before, so maybe they don't care about being embarrassed. So I guess I'd have to say I don't want a cash bar."

John shook his head. "I like your logic. They're rich, but nice. If they were rich and rotten, you wouldn't object to a cash bar. But they're rich and basically pleasant. I will never understand your politics, Quill."

"We're here," announced Meg. She and Doreen came into the office and settled on the couch. "What are you two up to?"

"Staff meeting's up." Quill began to search for the agenda in the mass of papers on her desk.

"No, I mean what's up with you and John? John looks subdued. And you look . . ." Meg settled back, crossed her ankles, and regarded her sister though half-closed eyes. "Abashed. Wait. Wait. I'm applying my famous powers of deductive reasoning! It's the party, right?! John's bummed because you invited too many people to the party and it's going to cost too much!"

"I got a way you can save money," said Doreen grimly.

"You can leave my salary off the budget. And that-there profit-sharing, too. I quit."

"Oh, dear," said Quill. "Not again."

"You can save mine," said Meg. "*I* quit. I in no way want to be associated with the events this evening. It's not enough to say I'm dreading this party. I have a Foreboding. A Feeling. A Distinct Impression. Something awful's going to happen."

"I know why you want to quit, Meg. You're getting anxious over the food preparation. You always get anxious over the food preparation. And you always pull off something marvelous. What is it with you, Doreen?"

"That Stoker."

"I don't want to hear any more about Axminster Stoker. Not a word. Not a peep of complaint. What'd he do this time?" she added, reversing herself.

"He's follerin' me around."

"Following you around? If that's all he's doing, take it as a compliment."

"That ain't all he's doin'. He's stickin' his nose in. Like this-here party for example."

"How the heck did everyone get invited, anyway?" asked Quill plaintively. "We've got the whole town coming, for free. Poor John's in a swivit."

"I'm tellin' you, ain't I? It's that-there Axminster Stoker." Doreen folded her arms across her meager chest. "Said it's part of a customer satisfaction 'thank you' campaign, or some durn thing, and went around blatting to the whole town."

"You're kidding!"

"I don't kid about that boob."

"How many people do you think will show up?"

"We'd be safer figuring who ain't."

Quill looked at Meg. "Okay."

"Okay what?"

"Okay how come you're not swinging from the chandelier?"

"Because he told me about it. I've got extra help coming in from Cornell. And I've tripled the supplies order."

John made a noise like a tire losing air.

"Oh. Well. Good. So we're prepared. Except for the fact that we're going to be broke." She patted John's knee. He winced. She didn't blame him. It was more of a blow than a pat. Somewhere in the back of her mind, she knew she was being unreasonable, but she didn't care. "I'm so glad you guys saw fit to tell John and me, Meg. I mean, I'm only the manager here. And John, too. He's merely in charge of profits. Not to mention losses. John, why don't you quit, too? And me? I'll just go ahead and get that ticket to Detroit." She threw up her hands. "We agreed to control expenses this month. As a matter of fact, we agreed to talk to each other about what's happening, and do we ever? No. I set up these boring weekly meetings just so we can plan ahead, and look what happens. Do you know what I could be doing instead of wasting my time here? Do you?" She smacked her hand flat on the desk. "I could be painting! But I'm not! Because you guys just go ahead and arrange huge parties and order mountains of supplies for a free party for a bunch of people I don't even want to talk to. And I'm tired of it! There! You guys satisfied?"

"Jeez," said Meg. "Sorry."

"PMS," said Doreen.

John cleared his throat diffidently. "No offense, Quill, but you were the one that gave Axminster Stoker *carte blanche*. And he's the one that did all the inviting. And, kiddo, the party was your idea in the first place."

"Just . . . wait." Quill put both hands over her face. Outside, the lawn mower sputtered to a stop and started again. She wanted, suddenly, to be standing in front of her easel, her hair grayed with paint, her jeans smelling of turpentine. She took several long breaths. "Is that Brat of the Month award around anywhere? I'll wear it for a week, I promise."

Nobody said anything. Quill peeked at them, then lowered her hands to her lap. "I have been that bad, really?"

Doreen smoothed her apron. Meg whistled a few bars of "Who's Sorry Now."

John just looked sympathetic and said, "You'll get through this somehow."

"It's just—"

"We know," said John. "Take your time. We're all here. Quill, whatever you decide about what you're going to do. About Myles. About your work."

Quill blinked back a sudden sting of tears. "What I'm going to do is settle down and get to work. So. What's on the agenda this morning?" She found the memo she'd been searching for under the stapler. "Oh, dear. Employee satisfaction. Oh, dear again, I scheduled a lecture from—"

"Good morning," said Axminster Stoker. "I'm sorry I'm a bit late but someone"—he pointedly avoided Doreen—"asked the desk to suspend my wake-up call."

"Wasn't me, if that's what you're thinkin'," said Doreen belligerently. " 'Course if I'd bin a ree-ceptionist what temporarily lost her job on account of some meddling fool, I might forget stuff like that myself. Not sayin' I would, but I might."

"Well!" Axminster rubbed his hands together with a dry, papery sound. "Merely a process upset. Shall we get down to business? Sarah? You've passed around the pre-reading for today's little discussion on team building?"

"Um," said Quill. "I'm truly sorry. I forgot."

"But you do have the results of the Quality Circle problem-solving sessions with the *sous* chefs."

"My *sous* chefs?" asked Meg. "What were you doing messing with my *sous* chefs, Quill? Especially in the mood you've been in lately. They'll all quit, too, I'll bet. Just before the party."

"I haven't done a thing with your *sous* chefs, truly, Meg. I haven't done anything about the Quality Circles for a week."

"A whole week?!" Axminster's voice rose in what, in a more ebullient man, might have been a wail of despair.

Meg crossed her legs in satisfaction. "I *thought* things were going a little more smoothly than usual these past few days."

"Now, Meg, I'm sure we all appreciate Axminster's efforts on our behalf." Quill sighed. "It just takes so much time, Axminster."

A slight gleam of desperation appeared in Axminster's eye. "You'll recall from our meeting last week that you

were all assigned homework, *outside* your major compe-
tency areas, to hone your leadership skills. You were to
problem-solve with the maintenance people, Margaret.
Sarah was to meet—'' He broke off. ''Who's that in the
garden?''

Quill sat up straight. Ken Sakura walked in the rose gardens, the sun striking coally glints from his hair. He
stopped by the fish pond and sat on the stone bench, looking down at the koi. ''That's Ken Sakura.''

''Checked in with his pa last night to the extra bed in
the Shaker suite,'' said Doreen sourly. ''After they come
back from the sherr'fs.''

''Did Mr. Motoyama come with them?'' asked Meg in
mild interest.

''Yep. That Mr. Sakra senior was some kinda pissed off
at him, too.''

Quill, who was remembering Ken Sakura's essay on
''Energy in Art,'' said absently, ''It's Sakura, Doreen.
S-A-K-U-R-A.''

''You did say Sakura!'' Axminster interrupted, with excitement. ''A Japanese gentlemen? He isn't by any chance
related to Sakura Toshiro, the multibillionaire?''

''Yes,'' said Quill.

''Do you know who he is?!''

''Sakura Toshiro,'' said Quill. She realized she'd risen
part way out of her chair. That she was drawn to the garden
and the answers that might lie there. ''Managing director
of Sakura Indus—''

''Pardon me, pardon me, pardon me.'' Axminster raised
a hand shaking with excitement. ''He is *only* the inventor
of the KOP theory. He is *merely* a byword in the world of
key operating processes. That's all.''

''Goodness,'' said Quill feebly.

''My *God!*'' Axminster looked into the distance, his
khaki-colored eyes alight. ''My *God*. The master! Here in
Hemlock Falls. I must speak to him.''

''Not here,'' said Doreen laconically. ''Drove off with
that crazy Jap driver—''

''Doreen, darn it!'' Quill frowned at her. ''Please don't
use that term.''

"Well, chauffeur, then. And he ain't crazy, for real, I guess, although he drives like a sum-a-bitch."

"Can you arrange it, Sarah? A proper introduction? My Lord, he'll be fascinated with the improvements I've installed here at the Inn. Perhaps he would consent to observing a team in action—Wait! I have something even better. The results from the Do-It-Yourself reception team. No? I can see you all are not taken with that idea. Well, perhaps that wasn't quite the success we had anticipated. I know! He'll be at the customer celebration tonight, will he not?"

"Axminster, I've been meaning to ask you about that." Quill, conscious of an extreme impatience quite unlike her usual capable response to business problems, made a deliberate attempt to keep her voice from rising. "This party is going to cost us a great deal of money." She felt much better at the expressions of approval on John's, Meg's, and Doreen's faces. She felt effective. "We really *must* put a stop to—"

"Please! All of you. I have a great, very great favor to ask." Axminster stood in the center of Quill's Karastan carpet, to the right of the peach medallion, his hand upraised. "To my regret, I must ask you to please adjourn this meeting. I have factored in your disappointment. I am accountable. But I must have time to prepare a cogent, yet eloquent summary of my Hemlock Falls Strategic Plan in time to present to Mr. Sakura this evening. I'm sorry to disappoint you all. I have taken us off-line. But even the strictest interpretations of process control allow for exceptional events. This is clearly an exceptional event. Will you forgive me? Will you let me go?"

Quill thought: *I can go in the garden and ask him. He can help me paint again.*

"No problem here," said John.

"Hotcha," said Doreen, "I got real work to do."

"You bet," said Meg, rising with unflattering alacrity. She paused on her way out the door and wriggled her eyebrows at Quill. "You," she said, "stay away from my *sous* chefs. Take a little time off. We've got it all under control."

"Margaret! Hold on! We'll reconvene next week," said

Axminster. "Same start time, but we'll have to allow another two hours for a makeup session."

John, Doreen, and Meg turned to look at Quill as a unit. An accusing unit. In the garden Ken Sakura got up from the bench and walked out of sight, down the graveled path. "Axminster . . ." She stopped. Took a deep breath. Looked at her staff. Blew out with a sigh. "Let's talk about it later. Would you guys excuse me for a moment? Customer satisfaction survey, Axminster, very important." She stuck her head back in the door. "By the way. Meeting's adjourned."

She found him by the waterfall, watching the cascade of water through the branches of a willow curved over the gorge.

He turned with a welcoming smile.

"Mr. Motoyama's back?"

"The charges were dropped. Your sheriff arranged an apology between Motoyama and your mayor's wife. My father is impressed with Sheriff McHale. He finds him capable. For an American." His smile was infectious. "Motoyama should have been retired years ago—but it would have killed him, I think, to have no purpose in life."

"And that's important," said Quill. "A purpose."

He glanced at her. "It's all there is, don't you think? A worthy purpose, of course. Such as your work."

"I've been waiting to get a chance to speak to you. I appreciate what you said. The comment about *shibui*, last night, I mean."

"The 'essence of the beautiful,' *shibui*. Beauty itself. There's no real translation possible into English. Plato came close to describing the idea, and, I've always thought, so did your Transcendentalists. But it's a concept that's been submerged by commerce in current times. Not just here, but in my own country as well."

Quill watched the water fall with a sense of perfect understanding that made her very nervous, and completely inarticulate.

"Will your father stay with us long?"

"It depends. He's interested in your mini-mall project. A few of the men from the Chamber talked to him last night. He's asked me to help with translation. I've agreed.

I'm leaving tomorrow, since I'm needed back at Cornell, but I'll drop in every few days to see how I can help."

"I'd like to talk with you. About why . . ." She took a deep breath. "About why I haven't been painting." She waited, rubbing one thumb over the other. "It's an imposition, I know, but would you have any free time today?"

"Today? Today I have completely free. Motoyama has taken my father on a drive to the Finger Lakes. And I've admired your work—what I've seen so far. Shall we sit here, by the water? This grass is very appealing."

Quill settled next to him. Her arm brushed his shoulder. Aware that she was being quixotic, nervous about the inevitable, she demurred, "Isn't the mall a rather small project for someone like your father? I mean Sakura Industries is huge, isn't it?"

"He hasn't been active in the business for years, Sarah, since a small *contretemps* forced him to retire. A public brush with a woman, not my mother, which is something of an affront to decency in conservative Japan. The public nature of it, you understand, not the *affaire* itself. The minimall project is just a way of keeping his hand in." He seemed to accept, and understand, her evasiveness, and continued in a comfortable way, "This is a vacation trip for him. He went to see my children, of whom he's very fond, and then came here to see me. I thought he'd enjoy the Inn. It's serene. Quite lovely. Quite Japanese. And of course, the fact that he's staying here gave me a chance to meet you. Perhaps to see your work. I've seen it in New York, of course, but nothing that you've done since your last show."

The sound of falling water cradled Quill's silence.

"So, are you an artist that can talk about work in progress? Are you shy of supposed experts with reputations like mine? May I intrude on your pleasant life here, Sarah Quilliam?"

Quill caught his glance and held it. The sound of the water receded. She thought of all the things she had to do today: check on the preparations for goodness knew how many guests; make sure that the Kiplings had a stage for their presentation; review the reservations for the next month; not think about Myles.

"There are a few pieces," she mumbled. "I've packed them away. But we could . . . I'd like your opinion. Even," she added anxiously, "if you think they're not very good. You must promise to tell me the truth."

It'd been too many years since she'd talked about the balance of color and form, the transformation from perception to idea to canvas, the carrying forward of her voice as an artist. And he was easy to be with. With the rapid intuition of a passionate expert, he understood her sentences before they were completed. And her work, itself, that burden which she carried sometimes like a black dog on her back, sometimes like a treasured child, he saw what she was trying to do, when she succeeded and when she failed. And he talked about it. Not as Myles did, or Meg, with expressions of support ("It's . . . nice."), but with passion. Often with gratitude, once with astonishment—and twice with disapproval for the abuse of her gift.

"And that's all you did all day? Looked at your paintings?" Meg pursed her lips and sliced the yellowfin tuna with quick, delicate strokes of her sharpest kitchen knife.

"We had lunch in Ithaca. At Renee's. We had the most marvelous wine, Meg."

"So are you ready to work again?"

Quill moved the wooden mallet three inches to the right and back again.

"Or did you spend most of the day in the fetal position? Curled up and defensive—"

"Stop."

Meg rubbed one hand through her hair, leaving a bit of fish stuck over her left eyebrow. "I *should* make this sushi right on the patio, except that I'd die to have Mr. Sakura see me. Why the heck did I decide to do sushi for people who eat it every day of their lives and can tell good from bad, from C-minus?"

"Because you've got guts. No risk, no gain. You're an artist."

Meg shot her a shrewd glance. She deftly rolled a tablespoon of rice into a piece of seaweed. "So. About this investigation. You'll just have to lift that goods book from Hedrick's pants pocket all by yourself. I'm going to be stuck in here for hours.''

''I'll manage just fine.'' Meg's hair was standing up in short dark spikes, her usual response to the stress of preparations for a large party, and Quill added gently, ''It's not a big deal, you know. It's not like we're serving a gourmet club, or a New York crowd.''

''It's always a big deal. Have you thought about a diversion so Hedrick doesn't catch you committing a grade-one felony or whatever it is?''

''The Kiplings should provide enough. Dina told me that they've been distributing posters about their act all over town. Come to think of it, maybe that's another reason why we're getting all these uninvited guests. But I can't imagine that Georgia would let them do it. Or that the prospect of a thousand lines of Kipling's poetry in sixty minutes would attract anybody but Dookie Shuttleworth. Anyhow, the act is called The Kipling One Thousand! And I didn't totally forget my responsibilities, Meg. I asked Dina to take charge of the staging and the microphone and whatever before I went to lunch with Ken, and I checked with her when I got back when I went up to change for the party. She thinks it's going to be . . .'' Quill stopped, searching for a reassuring translation of Dina's expressed opinion that the Kiplings were crazy. ''Interesting.''

''As in 'oh, what an interesting baby' when it's the ugliest thing you've ever seen in your life? Hah!''

Quill decided to abandon this line of discussion. ''And I had an interesting talk with John this morning. About those guns. He's been concerned, too.''

''I knew something was up. What is it?''

''Myles has been checking up on the contractor for the mall, DeMarco. There's something suspicious going on.''

''Yeah? So maybe we'll find out why from that goods book.''

''Maybe.''

''I'm glad to see the old detective juices have started to . . . rats! What time is it?''

''Six forty-five.''

"Damn!"

"Are you wearing that for the party?"

"This? My shorts? My bandanna? And why not? You expect white tie? You expect me to go up and change *now*! Into a little summer something in gauze and cotton lace like that!" She waved the knife in Quill's direction. *"Now!? When I'm cooking?!"*

"Why don't I go check on the buffet?"

"Why don't you? *Bjorn!*" she shouted suddenly, over her shoulder. "You guys have that tapanade ready yet? Will you *get on the stick!*"

Quill escaped to the patio, where she found John and Nate the bartender supervising the placement of the bar.

"You look great," said John absently. "How's the chef?"

"The usual. Testy, cranky, and bossy."

"Glad to hear it. I've decided on a compromise for the drinks, Quill, if it's all right with you. Nate's selected five dozen cases of the Glenora chardonnays and chablis to circulate among the guests. If they want hard liquor, they'll pay the regular rates."

"Okay," said Quill meekly.

"I don't think we'll have too much of a problem with drunks. Myles and the deputies are guests," Nate said. "But you never know. Couple of the volunteer firemen can swill it down like anything, and they don't give a damn if they get arrested."

"They're coming, too?"

"That Mr. Stoker's been—"

"So I heard." She exchanged a rueful grin with John. "All we can do is our best."

"Halfway through, we run out, I'll bring up some of the Gallo," said Nate. "Kathleen knows who to give it to, so's no one will notice."

"You guys have covered everything," said Quill gratefully. "I didn't exactly mean to take time off today, but . . ."

John and Nate exchanged a look.

"That guy's an art critic?" Nate polished a glass with particular attention to the inside. "Saw him looking at your stuff this morning. Seemed to have an awful lot to say about it.'' He set the glass on the temporary bar and looked at her earnestly. ''Maybe I never told you, Quill, but I really like your paintings. I mean, it's . . . nice. You know what I mean? Some of it, it makes me happy to look at it. Some of the other—I don't know. Makes me kind of sad to look at. That picture that used to be in the lobby and that Mike put back up again? Makes me happy-sad. Just thought I'd let you know I really like it. Not that anyone had to tell me to tell you I really like it.''

''Thank you, Nate.''

''Thing is, John and I were thinking that we don't tell you how much we like your painting. So I don't know that you need to import some Jap—sorry, Japanese art critic to tell you the things we can tell you here.''

''Seemed to like your work,'' said John. ''And he's a fairly big noise in the art world, isn't he, Quill?''

''Myles likes your pictures, too.'' Nate started in on another glass. ''Told me so a couple of times.''

''How nice,'' said Quill through gritted teeth, ''to have the love and concern of the staff.'' Both men avoided looking at her. ''I appreciate the commentary, Nate. And John. But I'm standing here to tell you that my affairs are my affairs. I mean, not that I'm having an affair-affair, I mean affairs in the sense of—'' She stopped. ''Never *mind!*''

''What about a glass of that nice little Montrachet,'' Nate suggested. ''Smooth you right out.''

''I don't need smoothing out, thank you very much. What I need to do is take a look at the staging for the Kipling's show. Which I am going to do. Right now. Leaving you guys to gossip about me to your heart's content.''

The Kiplings milled around the French doors leading to the patio like lambs in search of a sheepdog. Quill counted backward from ten as she marched to meet them. Just once, she thought, it'd be nice to have a little life crisis all by herself, with people (unspecified) indifferent to her state of mind, and unsolicitous of her well being. Although, she admitted, to be fair, she wouldn't like it for long.

She half turned in her march across the floor to the Kiplings. Nate and John were staring after her with—what had

Meg called her expression this morning? Abashed. They had abashed looks on their faces. She stopped Kathleen Kiddermeister on the way to the bar with a tray of wine-glasses. "You're going to the bar? Would you do me a favor? Tell the guys I'm sorry I blew up at them. Tell them it's just *agita*. Tell them it's PMS."

"Nate and John? PMS? That's it? Got it." She gave Quill a nudge. "That Mr. Sakura's son? I saw you two today. Wow! You introduced him to Myles?"

"They are the closest of friends. True buddies. Brothers under the skin."

"O-*kay*. Just asking a simple little question. Uh, Quill. I know I told you before, at least, I'm pretty sure I have, but that iris painting that used to hang in the Tavern bar, over the fireplace? It's . . ."

"Nice?" supplied Quill helpfully.

"Yeah! That's it. Nice!" She hitched the tray to one hand and used the other to pat Quill on the shoulder. "John told us we should appreciate you more. Meg, too—told us, I mean."

"Thanks."

"And we do. That Georgia Hardwicke's calling you. See what she's got on? That dress is *really* nice."

"You look gorgeous!" Georgia Hardwicke boomed across the floor. "Nettled, but gorgeous. What's the problem, sweetie?" With the Fairbanks, Miss Kent, and Jerzey Paulovich trailing, she swept toward Quill in a blaze of teal green and gold thread and enveloped her in a hug. Quill hugged her fiercely back. Georgia, with her cheerful, matter-of-fact approach to life crises, was just the person she wanted to see.

Quill said into her ear, "Listen, before we're engulfed here, do you want to come up to my room after the party? I have to talk to somebody, and you're just about perfect."

"As soon as it's over." Georgia released her, gave her a wink, and said loudly, "Well, here we all are. What do you think?"

"You're dressed like Victorians!" Quill was delighted. "You all look terrific!"

"It's authentic evening dress," said Miss Kent proudly.

"The Victorians, as you know, had a sense of decorum and order lacking in today's present fashions. Georgia's turban and satins distinguish her as a widow of substance. My lace cap and black taffeta state clearly I am an unmarried lady of certain means and *une age certaine* and Mrs. Fairbanks is quite obviously a married belle. The color of her over-skirt was quite popular in the 1880s—it's called *feuille morte*."

"Dead leaves?" Quill smiled. "It sounds lovely in French."

"Our men, of course, don't have the colorful options open to them that we ladies do. But they are quite correct in crisp black and white. Except for Jerzey's waistcoat. We've never been able to do a thing about Jerzey's waist-coats. He claims that the Polish aristocracy is of a tradition older than the Empire's—and who's to say he is not cor-rect? When one thinks of the Mongols! Well. I shall not bore you with the historical details. Do you think," she asked a little anxiously, "that there will be sufficient num-bers in the audience?"

Quill eyed Jerzey's crimson brocade. "I think the bro-cade's lovely. And we hope for a very good turnout. Is the stage satisfactory?"

"Miked and ready to go!" boomed Lyle Fairbanks. "We'll start in fifteen minutes, run for an hour, with a ten-minute intermission, and then circulate among the guests, in costume of course, to answer any questions they might have about the poet. One wouldn't, by any chance, have notified the—ah—press?"

Carlyle Conway came onto the patio from the lawn, wearing a black slip. Quill squinted. No, it wasn't a slip. You couldn't really call it a dress, either, except that it did cover her stomach and rear end. But that was about it. If the earrings brushing her shoulders were diamonds, she could buy the mini-mall three times over—and the Inn, as well. Hedrick shambled along beside her, carrying a cam-era. She didn't see Myles.

"One did, sort of," said Quill, in response to Lyle's disingenuous question. "But one isn't sure what the coverage will be like. That's our local newspaperman over there.''

"Who's the tart with him?" asked Miss Kent with a delicate air.

Quill smiled at her. "His sister."

"Tell them we shall be available for interviews immediately after the show," said Lyle with an expansive gesture. "Friends?" to his cohorts. "Shall we circulate?"

"As soon as I circulate to the ladies', dear." Georgia winked at Quill. "Bit of tummy trouble. I'll see you later, will I? After the show."

Carlyle and Hedrick headed straight for the bar. Quill pushed herself in their direction, stopping to greet people as the patio began to fill up. By the time she reached them, Myles had come in from the dining room entrance. That, and the affable but distancing sort of way he greeted the Conways, made Quill wonder if she'd been jumping to conclusions. Then she wondered why she was bothering to jump to conclusions, since she didn't care.

"Hello, Myles. Ken Sakura said that the business over Mr. Motoyama was settled peacefully."

"I like that dress," he said. "You should wear lace more often."

"It's just the most useful fabric," said Carlyle, wriggling her way past a goggling volunteer fireman, his indignant-looking wife, and two gaping deacons from Dookie Shuttleworth's church to join them. "Lace hides all kinds of flaws, don't you think so, Sarah? That sort of crepeyness at the neck that creeps in after thirty-five. Or so I'm told."

"We were all very sorry to hear about your mother," Quill said a little stiffly. "If there's anything we can do, please let us know."

"Poor Mamma." Carlyle's eyes filled with tears. She took a hefty swig of champagne. "A party animal like her would have loved this." She examined the glass with a critical eye. "Wouldn't have liked the champagne, though. Tastes flat."

"Press room?" demanded Hedrick.

"Excuse me?" Quill eyed his sports jacket. There was a notebook-sized bulge at the breast pocket.

"Place for this reporter to sit, take notes, that kind of thing. Places like this usually have a press room all set up, with special food for the reporters."

"Who in the world are all these people?" Carlyle frowned, then stretched her hand over the bar to Nate for a refill. "You have anything a little less provincial back there?"

Nate raised his eyebrows. Quill shook her head slightly, then caught Myles's eye. He grinned.

"Sorry, ma'am. We're out."

"You might find the hors d'oeuvres less provincial, Carlyle," said Quill. "How do you feel about sushi? Lo-cal, in case you want to take off a few pounds, and really quite delicious. It's not to everyone's taste, of course, but a woman with your experience might find it just the ticket."

Carlyle smoothed her throat with one red-tipped nail. "Myles, what do you think?" She drew her finger down to the top of her cleavage. "Mamma always told me men didn't like a skinny woman. A question of geometry, she always said. 'Curves, Cay' "—she flicked an eye in Quill's direction—" 'rather than angles.' You want to escort me over to the sushi tray? I see the two Japanese gentlemen appear to be enjoying it."

"That's the one, Cay." Hedrick scooped a fistful of tapanade from a passing waiter's tray and tossed the toast triangles into his mouth one by one. "The old guy. Worth a bundle."

"As though that mattered, Heddie." Speculation narrowed her eyes. "But the fish looks wonderful."

"Do try it," urged Quill. "And Hedrick, we don't have a press room, but I did set up the possibility of an interview for you. Why don't we see if we can get Mr. Fairbanks aside for a moment? He'd love to tell you about his performance for this interview."

"An exclusive," warned Hedrick. "Stories that show up in the *Trumpet!* don't get covered by other newspapers."

"I haven't said a word to anyone," Quill promised. "We'll find somewhere you can take off your coat and be comfortable. Myles? If you'll excuse us? Why don't you help Miss Conway to some sushi."

The look of alarm in his face, she thought, as she led Hedrick through the crowd, was more than satisfying.

"There's such a great view from the gazebo, Hedrick, and it's well away from the noise of the party. Shall I take you down there to wait while I find Lyle Fairbanks? You can sit and listen to the Falls, maybe take off your jacket, and perhaps write down a few questions about the Kiplings."

"Sure," said Hedrick unenthusiastically. "You got some food to take with me?"

"Certainly. Shall I get you a plate, or would you like to select it yourself? There's a bit of a buffet, over by Carlyle."

"Raw fish? It's not this reporter's cup of tea. But I'll do it." He sighed, martyred. "Don't go off."

"I'll be right here," Quill promised.

Hedrick slouched his way over to the buffet table, whispered into his sister's ear, grabbed a fistful of food, which he dropped on a plate, and shambled back.

"Carlyle is having a whee of a time," Quill observed. "Although a bit of food seems to have slipped down the front of her dress."

Carlyle, the slip dress having attracted the attention of the mayor, the Sakuras, Petey Peterson, and a short, muscular man Quill recognized as the mysterious contractor Marco DeMarco (whose presence Quill couldn't account for, unless Axminster Stoker had decided to inflict his Total Quality Management theories on the construction business, too), wriggled her shoulders, tossed the jeweled earrings, and retrieved the bit of fish from her décolletage.

"Huh," said Hedrick. "She usually gets someone to help her. This is a pretty dead burg."

"Help her get food out of her dress?" said Quill, too amazed to think of a polite way to phrase the question.

"Yeah." He chuckled. "Old party trick. Ma used to do it, too. Watch what she does now."

Carlyle tossed the bit of fish into the air, swallowed it . . . and died.

CHAPTER 9

Why Andy Bishop, Meg's lover and Hemlock Falls' only physician, wasn't at the party, Quill didn't know. But he told her, later, nothing could have saved Carlyle once she'd ingested the poison. At the time, watching it, Quill was stretched to breaking point, waiting for help, and helpless.

It wasn't a pretty death, or an easy one. The worst was her terrified eyes. Carlyle's eyes were to haunt Quill's dreams for years. The poison was merciless in its attack, trailing agony and awareness in its wake. DeMarco and Myles, the strongest men there, held Carlyle down, until whatever had poisoned her became stronger than all three of them. The convulsions tore her hands and feet from their grip, arcing her body backward until her head touched her heels. At the end, a terrible rictus stretched her mouth wide, exposing the perfect teeth in the grin of a year-old corpse.

And it took forever.

"Twenty-seven minutes," said Quill, on her balcony, after the body had been taken and the guests had gone home.

Georgia sighed. "Who timed it, for goodness' sake?"

"Myles. It's automatic, I guess."

Meg, silent, refilled her brandy glass, and lit a forbidden cigarette.

"I am glad I didn't see it," said Georgia forcefully. "Doesn't sound like this detective stuff is as much fun as

I thought. So what do we do now?''

"Forget it," said Quill. "Leave it to the experts."

"Forget it? Do you know who is in my kitchen right now?" Meg demanded huskily. She stubbed the cigarette out and threw it over the balcony. "Right *now*? A forensics team. A real one. Going over that damn tuna. They've closed me down, Quill."

"It's just until they've bagged everything and sent it off to the lab."

"What are we going to do about breakfast? Lunch? About all the people who'll check out? What about Hedrick? What his newspaper doesn't do to the reputation of this Inn, his lawyers will."

"But what could have killed her?" said Georgia. "There's no food poisoning that acts like that, is there? I mean, there's no way that it could be your cooking, Meg. Hell, you can keep on feeding me, and I'll sit outside with a sign around my neck. 'Get well-nourished here.' '' She patted her ample stomach and tried a chuckle that died in the silence. Below them the sounds of the evidence team grimly at work in the kitchen floated across the air.

"Andy did say food poisoning doesn't act so quickly," said Quill. "Botulism takes thirty-six to seventy-two hours. Salmonella six to twenty-four."

"Fugu is that fast," said Meg.

"Fugu?" Georgia set her brandy glass on the table with a click. "I know what that is. From the Kipling's trip to Japan. It's a poisonous fish liver."

"And it's a neurotoxin. One of the deadliest." Meg kicked the table leg.

"That doesn't make sense," said Quill. "How in the world could the liver of a Japanese fish get into your sushi?"

"In the tuna," said Meg glumly. "I told you. That's why those idiots underneath us are going through my kitchen."

"You mean to tell me you can't tell fugu liver from tuna filets?"

"Well, of course I can. But it might have gotten mixed

up in the shipment, somehow, and been removed, leaving a few drops of fluid. Even a little touch is deadly. It's nasty stuff.''

"That seems truly unlikely.''

"The alternative doesn't make sense either, does it?'' asked Georgia. "That someone carried it with him—or her—and deliberately introduced it into the sushi.''

"If it was the sushi,'' said Quill absently.

"What else could it have been other than the sushi!'' Meg's voice was thick with tears. "And I made it.'' Quill put her hand out and closed it over her sister's wrist. "I suppose we should be celebrating the fact that I didn't kill half the population of Hemlock Falls.''

"Maybe somebody wanted to bump off the 'voluptuous slut.' '' Georgia's chuckle sounded again, a little more confidence in it.

"The what?!''

"I told Georgia that's what I was thinking about her,'' said Quill. "I felt awful about it.''

"Confession's good for the soul,'' said Georgia comfortably. "And I told you then and I'll tell you now, the fact that she may have been murdered doesn't change her character. As a matter of fact, it's probably why she was murdered: her character.''

"Murder!'' said Meg with scorn. "It's a pretty damn inefficient way of murder. There is no guarantee that Carlyle herself was going to eat that sushi. I prepared it in advance—which you're not supposed to do, but I was too nervous to do it in front of Mr. Sakura and his son—and it was sitting out on the buffet for at least twenty minutes before Carlyle popped it into her mouth. And several other people had tried it before that. I counted. I made three dozen pieces, and there were twenty-two left on the platter. I found six half-eaten pieces in the potted rose-bushes by the lounge chairs. Some of them were wrapped in napkins. They all had bites taken out of them.''

"People trying it on a dare, I suppose,'' said Georgia. "Did you turn those over to the police for testing?''

"Yeah.'' Meg ran her hands through her hair. "I just don't understand it.''

"Let's do this the logical way," suggested Georgia. "Who served her the sushi?"

"Somebody said she picked it off the tray herself." Quill shuddered. "That was a long twenty-seven minutes. Half the crowd was asking questions and the other half . . ."

"The other half, what?" asked Georgia.

"Just watching."

"Oh, God. People."

"Somebody else—one of the men—said that she didn't eat it right away. She held it for a while, toying with it, then flipped it into the air. DeMarco said she was trying to catch it with her mouth. It slipped down the front of her dress. I was watching from across the room with her brother, and I saw her dig it out and try again. She caught it the second time."

"She didn't drop it on the floor, and maybe someone picked it up for her?" Georgia suggested.

"Nope. Not that I saw, at least. Maybe someone else would know."

"And nobody handed it to her."

"That's what they said."

"Could she have picked it up from a separate plate? Was it off the platter that everyone else ate from?"

"Georgia, I don't know! I assume so."

"Sorry, sorry. Just trying to get to the bottom of this. I can't believe it's Meg's fault. I mean, it has to be deliberate. With her mother murdered not one day ago? There's a pattern here, ladies."

Quill sensed Meg's muscles relax a little.

"That's true, isn't it?" Meg said. "And nobody's accusing me of smacking Louisa over the head with a hammer and throwing her into the river to drown."

"They most certainly are not." Georgia was empathetic. "Now. I think we should make a list of the people who were both in Louisa's vicinity and near Carlyle at the time she ate that stuff."

"I still don't see how the poison could have gotten on her piece, and not on other pieces," said Meg stubbornly.

"Maybe someone had a squirt gun. Or a teeny-tiny

dart in a blowgun. Maybe someone next to her poisoned her at the same time she ate the fish. So it might not have been the sushi at all. Did you see anyone touch her, Quill?"

"I wasn't paying close attention," Quill said. "But there were a lot of guys standing around her. And she was the sort of person who invited touching."

"Now we're cooking with gas." Georgia heaved herself to her feet. "You have a pencil and paper around here?"

"Sure. Near the phone in the living room."

"I'll be right back." She stumped heavily into the living room, closing the French doors behind her.

Meg looked at Quill. "Teeny-tiny blowgun?"

"She's pretty neat, isn't she?"

Meg nodded.

"She's right, you know, Meg. It probably wasn't the sushi."

Meg's face lightened.

"Here we are, ladies. Now." Georgia returned and settled herself with a groan in her chair. "Who was within spitting distance of the late, unlamented deceased?"

"Spitting distance?" said Quill doubtfully. "Wait a second." She closed her eyes, imagining that she was going to paint the scene. Carlyle stood in the center of a group of admiring men, the thin black strap of her dress slipping off one tanned shoulder. Marco DeMarco stood nearest; to his left were Elmer Henry and Pete Peterson. To Carlyle's right was Sakura Toshiro, and behind him, a faithful shadow, Mr. Motoyama, a tray with a hot towel in his hands. The other figures were faceless. Quill opened her eyes. "I can't see everything."

"Draw it," suggested Georgia.

"Draw it?"

"You're an artist. Your fingers will remember what your brain doesn't. Draw it."

"I need my sketch pad."

"I'll get it." Meg darted inside and was back in a few seconds. "I've got the graphite pencil, too."

"Great. Now here's Carlyle, and yes, of course, Jerzey

Paulovich." Quill set the scene in a few quick strokes. "And here—good grief. Harvey Bozzel. And Howie. And Marge Schmidt. And Lila Fairbanks."

"And who are Harvey, Marge, and Howie when they're at home?" asked Georgia.

"Howie's town attorney. Harvey's our local advertising guy. Marge is one of the richest women in Hemlock Falls."

Georgia took the drawing pad and cocked her head. "Then she can afford not to wear a bowling jacket to a posh party. Big women like me should pay attention to clothes."

"Marge always wears a bowling jacket."

"Avid bowler, is she?"

"Well, no," Quill admitted. "She just likes bowling jackets."

"I love Hemlock Falls! Go on, Quill. Are these people connected in any way?"

"Oh, yes, all of them are. With the mini-mall project."

"Well, well, well, well, well. Now we're getting somewhere, ladies. And who among this group was at the mini-mall site two days ago when Louisa died?"

Frowning, Quill flipped to a new page in the sketch pad and wrote the names down. "Everyone except DeMarco. I think Myles told me he was in San Francisco checking on a shipment of leach-line piping."

"Next question, ladies, would seem to be, who'd have access to fugu?"

"The Sakuras," said Meg. "Naturally."

"Why would Mr. Sakura want to dispose of Carlyle? He hadn't even met her before this evening, had he? You might as well suggest that *I* had a motive."

"The mini-mall project?" Meg suggested. "You said he was interested in it, Quill."

"The mini-mall project is too small, unless it turns out to be the site of a proposed government installation or a silver mine, and worth millions. And I really doubt that, don't you?" said Quill. "Ken told me his father was interested in buying it as a sort of hobby. That would give Mr. Sakura a motive if he thought the stories in the

Trumpet! might wreck the mall's success, but it's a really, really weak one. The motives are much stronger for the people who want to sell it to him.''

''Your mayor?''

''And Harvey. And Marge. They're all big investors,'' said Meg. ''But then, we are, too, which puts us right back to suspecting me and my kitchen.''

''It doesn't!'' said Georgia forcefully. ''Put that right out of your head. Neither you nor Quill was near the lady when she bought the farm.''

''Bought the farm?'' said Quill, bemused. ''You know something . . .'' She trailed off. She sketched a tall, shambling blond male in a badly fitting sports coat. ''Hedrick went over to the buffet to get a plate of food while I waited to take him down to the gazebo.''

''The gazebo?'' Meg smiled. ''So you *did* decide on seduction to get his jacket off.''

''I did not! I was hunting for Lyle Fairbanks. I thought that he and the Kiplings would be pleased to have a newspaper article about the group, and I was setting up an interview. I figured it was a safe topic, since even Hedrick couldn't write a nasty article about a fan group for a poet.''

''Hedrick,'' mused Georgia. ''Look at all the money he'd inherit with his mother and sister gone.''

''Great minds think alike. It's remotely possible that he could have carried the poison in his jacket—it was bulging with all sorts of stuff, by the way.''

''Did you get the goods book?'' asked Meg.

''No, Meg, with a woman dying at my feet, I did not have time to rifle her brother's pockets for the goods book. Anyway, he could have carried the poison over, dropped it on her sushi while no one was looking, and skittered back to me with no one the wiser. There was an awful crowd around her.''

''So we add Horrible Hedrick to the suspect list.'' Meg's color was returning, and the animation was back in her face. ''Okay. I like this.'' She turned to Georgia. ''What do we do next?''

''We're getting closer to who—but we're just guessing

as to the means. Fugu seems very unlikely to me. It could have been something else entirely. Cyanide.''

''No bitter almond smell, though,'' said Quill. ''I always thought that cyanide poisoning was accompanied by a smell of bitter almonds.''

''The 'how' is important,'' Georgia said decisively, ''because it has an impact on the 'who.' ''

The phone rang inside Quill's rooms. She got up, took the call, and came back. Meg looked at her face. ''What?!''

''That was Andy. He's sending in a preliminary cause of death. By a naturally occurring neurotoxin ingested through the fish.''

Meg closed her eyes. ''Did he ask to speak to me?''

''His preliminary guess is that it was on the sushi. He's sent all of it off to be tested. It'll take a few weeks. So we're back to square one. And Meggie, we're going to have to keep the kitchen closed for a few days. Just until a sweep for the poison is made.''

''He didn't ask to speak to me.''

''I think he's afraid you'd be upset with him, Meg.''

''Of course I'm upset with him! I'm thoroughly pissed off. I know he's just doing his job. Any of us here would have done the same thing. *But he could have told me himself.*''

''You know men and how they hate fuss,'' said Georgia. ''They just refuse to understand that if you *do* understand you still need to be able to whack them around a little bit.''

''Makes sense to me,'' said Meg.

''Try telling any of 'em that. Doug was the same way. Rather leave town for a few days than talk it out.''

''Myles, too,'' said Quill, suddenly aware that this was a small part of her whole anxiety about their possible future together. ''There's too much that men refuse to discuss.''

''It's genetic.'' Georgia was firm. ''Probably accompanies testosterone in the endocrine system.''

''Or Andy could just be putting his job first, and me second,'' said Meg, with a touch of bitterness.

"I don't believe it," said Georgia. "It's just a preliminary, right? He's being careful. All those medical guys are too careful. It was not your cooking, Meg. Andy, bless his heart, and not that I've ever met him, loves you too much to be personally present when he causes you pain. Everything is going to be all right. I feel it in my bones. And believe me, at my size, the feeling has to be pretty strong to get all the way to my bones."

"Maybe, maybe not," said Meg. "Earlier today you mentioned something about quitting?" She hummed a few bars of "Detroit City" in an angry way and tossed off her brandy. Her lips were tight. "That's it for me. I'm going to bed."

"There's one good thing about the big kitchen being closed," said Georgia. "It's going to give us lots of time to conduct a proper investigation. We'll get this cleared up, Meg, see if we won't." She heaved herself to her feet. "I'll see you two in the morning? At breakfast? They aren't going to stop you cooking for an old friend, are they?"

"Nope," said Meg. "Both Quill and I have kitchenettes in our rooms. Why don't we meet in mine, about eight o'clock tomorrow morning? What would you like for breakfast? You can have anything you want."

Georgia grinned. "Just as long as it's tuna. Pancakes. Casserole. Soufflé. Whatever. Solidarity forever!"

"So here's the plan," said Quill after she and Meg had escorted Georgia to the door. "We quit. We buy a little house on the beach. You, Georgia, and I retire. And there will be *no men* allowed except twice a week for, you know—"

"Sex," said Meg with a small grin.

"That. And conversation. There is something about the masculine point of view that adds to life, when you keep it on impersonal topics, like the lack of a national health-care plan. It's just when emotion gets in the way that you have to watch the backs of their heads receding into the distance. I mean, can you imagine Myles, or Andy, offering Georgia's kind of support?"

"Andy's just doing his job," said Meg. "Did he think I'd be angry with him? Did he say anything at all?"

"Call him when you get to your room and ask him yourself."

"Why shouldn't he call me?"

"Because he's a man."

"Aristotle wouldn't like this train of logic."

"It is somewhat circular," Quill agreed. "I'm going to call Myles."

"You're kidding."

"I just learned something."

"What?"

"I'm not sure. Something about women having hearts, and men having souls, with no voice to express them. I haven't worked it out yet."

"When you do?"

"Yes?"

"Don't tell me. I know I'm not going to understand a word of it." She stopped on her way out the door, her gray eyes direct and clear. "Tell Myles hello for me, when you see him."

"I'll do that."

Quill went out on the balcony to clear the wrought-iron table of glasses and retrieve the brandy bottle. The moon was a silver thumbnail in a quiet sky. A small animal rustled in the herb garden. The scent of crushed thyme curled though the breeze from the river nearby. She lit the citronella candles, left the French doors open, then rinsed the glasses in the sink and put them in the dishwasher. She went back outside and leaned over the railing. The kitchen was dark. A car door slammed in the parking lot. The car motor started up and drove away. Footsteps sounded in the gravel path near the kitchen. Quill leaned out and called, "Hello?"

"I saw your light." Myles's voice was tentative. "You're still up?"

"It's hard to sleep," Quill admitted. "Will you come up?"

Myles was quiet, his body a large shadow in the thin moonlight. "Are you sure?" The uncertainty in his voice warmed her (although a part of her admitted it could have been the brandy).

"Yes. Very sure."

"Any other man," said Quill drowsily, several hours later, "would have thrown a rock at my window and said something inspired." She adjusted her head against his chest; she could hear his heart beating.

"I can't remember all of it."

"All of what?"

" 'What light through yonder window breaks? T'is the east and Juliet is the sun. Arise, fair sun and kill the envious moon . . .' and that's it."

"But it occurred to you. Love and homicide, even in Shakespeare."

"Particularly in Shakespeare. The man was a great psychologist."

Quill was silent a moment, working this out. "I'm not sure what you mean."

"I'm never sure what *you* mean, Quill." He grasped her by the shoulders and pulled her upright. He was very dark against the unbleached muslin of her headboard.

"Can't you say it?" she asked gently.

"Can't I say it? Can't *you* say it?"

"This conversation is ridiculous. If it is a conversation." She pulled away and got out of bed.

He rubbed both hands over his face. "All right. Here goes. I love you."

"I love you too, Myles." And she did.

"And this is where we were three months ago." There was an unfamiliar note of impatience in his voice. He swung his legs over the side of the bed and looked at the floor. "Isn't it?"

"Yes."

"Until I asked you to get married and start a family."

"Yes."

"And you said, as nearly as I can understand it, that you already had a family."

"I did?" said Quill, startled. "I guess I did."

His face was dark. A vein pulsed in his forehead. "I

still don't understand what you meant. Have you changed your mind?''

He knows, thought Quill. He knows I haven't changed my mind. She cleared her throat. "No. I haven't changed my mind."

"Then what is this? What is this?"

"I haven't seen you like this before, Myles, what—"

"What was the last hour about, Sarah?" He was impassive, except for the vein in his forehead.

Quill watched it, fascinated. "I just missed you."

He picked up the lamp sitting on the night stand and threw it at the wall. It hit base first, and shattered. "Then what the *hell* are you doing?"

"What I was going to say"—Quill's voice was tight with anger—"was that, yes, I have a family, and my work, Myles, my work. I'm a painter, Myles, or I was, and no, I don't know if there's room in it for you. I don't know where you would fit, Myles. And now you've started smashing my furniture. And now I don't know a damn thing. And we're back where we started. Or where we ended. So just leave, please, but before you do"—she marched toward the bathroom, the only place in her small suite where she didn't have to look at him—"pick up that lamp."

She sat in the bathtub and cried a little, into a towel, and when he didn't knock at the door, and she heard him leave, she went back to bed and cried into the pillowcase that still smelled like the back of his head.

"So that was the crash I heard last night." Meg swirled the hollandaise in her copper sauté pan and plied the whisk with energy.

"He picked it up, though. Did you talk to Andy?"

"He called, yeah. Last night."

"Everything okay there?"

"Seems to be. We're going to Syracuse for a couple of days, as soon as this is over."

"What did he say about the case?"

"Not a lot. We agreed not to talk about it."

"Everyone else in town is going to be talking about

it.'' Quill moved restlessly around the room. The essential differences between the two of them was nowhere more in evidence than in their rooms. From childhood, Meg had been a collector, and she liked chaos. Cookbooks, magazines, and kitchen equipment catalogs spilled out her bookcases and lay stacked on her windowsills. She'd chosen bright, sunny colors for her drapes and furniture: pinks and oranges with touches of a vivid spring green. Quill could never imagine Meg in anything but sunlight.

"You heard about the emergency Chamber meeting this morning?" Meg pulled the crumpets from the toaster oven and set them on three plates, slipped the poached eggs on top, and poured out hollandaise in a thin stream.

"Yes. This town has more emergency meetings. Did *you* hear that it's going to be held in Marge's diner?"

"No! Nobody wants to eat here?! That does it! Let's sell the damn place. Maybe Mr. Sakura will buy it.''

"As a matter of fact, the mayor was very disappointed it couldn't be held here. But Myles thought that the less activity around the area where the death occurred the better. But I don't think we have to worry about people checking out, or refusing to come to the Inn to eat. You remember our first murder? And how we thought it would empty the Inn? And instead, everybody stayed out of some perverse interest?''

"That's a lot different from people thinking I'm poisoning them in my kitchen.''

"Nobody thinks that.''

"Did you ask Myles how the investigation's going? How soon we can reopen? Whether or not he thinks it was murder by persons unknown—or murder by *me*!''

"I didn't have an opportunity to bring it up.''

"Hmm.'' Meg glanced her sidelong. "Could you drain that spinach for me, please?''

Quill ran the spinach through the colander.

"So, what was the argument about?''

"What are you going to do with the spinach? I thought you were making eggs Hollandaise.''

"It's eggs Florentine. There's no ham. And stop ducking the issue, Quill."

"It wasn't about anything." Frustrated, Quill slammed the spinach on the counter, leaving a green trail of water on the floor. Meg bent and wiped it up without comment. "I caught him just as he was leaving the kitchen last night. And he came up, as I told you. . . ."

"And you had a lovely reunion, and then what?"

"He wanted to know if I'd changed my mind."

"And you said what?"

"I started to explain that I hadn't really, and then he threw the lamp against the wall!"

"Quill. Let's get this straight. Three months ago you tell the poor man you don't want to marry him, or bear his children, or have anything to do with him as a human being, but he's fine as a sex partner."

"Now, wait just a minute!"

"No. You wait. And last night you'd had a glass of brandy to settle your nerves after that awful business and it was a warm summer's night, and we had some good female bonding going and there's Myles crunching his way powerfully across the gravel and *you* holler the equivalent of 'hey, sailor' and after you've had your wicked way with him, you say, sorry, I didn't really mean what you thought I meant, and you're surprised when he throws a mere lamp against the wall?"

"When you put it like that, it sounds sort of mean."

"Sounds mean? It stinks! If a guy had done that to you, you would have thrown him against the wall."

"A sailor, maybe," Quill said between giggles. "Not the sheriff."

"Well, I think you owe the poor man an apology. Honestly, Quill. You kicked him right in the ego."

"Coo-ee!" said Georgia, knocking as she opened the front door and came in. "Looks like you've recovered from the little setback last night, ladies. Sorry I'm late, but!" She paused dramatically. She was wearing yet another bright caftan, this one red, white, and blue with silver stars embroidered at the *V*. "I have discovered a Vital Clue!"

"Before eight-thirty in the morning?" said Meg. "Good work. What is it?"

"You'd both better sit down. This is big. This is really big. This is bigger than I am."

"Well, let's sit at the breakfast table," Meg suggested. "We can eat while you tell us." She pulled out one of the bentwood chairs at her kitchen table and waved Georgia to sit. "So, what have you got?"

Georgia settled herself, her expression sober. "This." With a curiously restrained gesture after her exuberant entrance, she withdrew a small notebook from her sleeve.

"The goods book!" Quill picked it up. "My goodness! Where did you get it?"

"This morning. I got up early. That brandy hadn't set too well on my stomach. As a matter of fact, I'd been a little queasy all day yesterday, nothing to do with your cooking, Meg, just a spastic colon that hits now and then. Anyway, I couldn't sleep, so I got up this morning at a simply ungodly hour—six, for Pete's sake—and went down to sit in the gazebo. By the way, you'll be delighted to know that I called Adela Henry, the mayor's wife, and offered to help carry Jell-O buildings to the tent tomorrow, so that's set. I figured I could catch any town gossip that they might not let you in on, Quill. Anyhow, back to the gazebo—that guest—the skinny one that looks like he's been ironed?"

"Axminster Stoker," said Quill, paging through the book.

"He was out jogging. Well, he jogged right past me and yelled over his shoulder that I'd dropped something over the edge of the railing. So I found it in the sweet peas."

"Myles and his men didn't search down there, did they?" said Meg. "Here. Let me see."

Quill handed it over and asked Georgia, "Did you read it?"

"Are you kidding? Of course I read it. Hedrick Conway's that slobby blond man, isn't he? I saw him last night talking to you. Well, he may be a sloppy dresser, but he's a very organized note taker. There's a lot of garbage in there, Quill. Your manager, John Raintree? I didn't know he'd been involved in a murder case a few years back. . . . ''

"Yes," said Quill, tight-lipped.

"And did you know that somebody named Miriam Doncaster . . ."

"Our town librarian," Quill said.

". . . is having an affair with a fellow named Howie M.?"

"Howie Murchison?!" shrieked Meg. "No!"

"He's town attorney," said Quill. "What else did you find?"

"Well, there's a lot of background stuff on you, Quill. I had no idea you were so famous. And Meg . . . there was a little about your husband's accident. My dear, I'm so sorry—but none of that's important—at least, not to our investigation. Look here." She took the book out of Meg's hands and flipped to the back. The three of them bent their heads over the table.

"It's a lot of stuff about a chemical called neurobenzine," said Meg after a moment.

"Used in printing . . . guess what?" said Georgia.

"Newspapers?" hazarded Quill.

"And guess what it is?"

Meg and Quill looked at her.

"A neurotoxin. A deadly neurotoxin."

"No!" they chorused.

"See? There's a lot of stuff here about the EPA regulations on disposing of it. And see this here?"

Quill read aloud: " 'Hi. Haz.' that must mean highly hazardous. 'Contact with skin, soft tissues. Symp: anoxia.' That's oxygen deprivation, right? 'Convulsions. Death within minutes. Anecdotes.' Anecdotes? He must mean antidotes. 'None.' "

"Oh, my God," said Meg. "He killed his own mother and sister. Oh, good grief. How awful. I'd better give Andy a call. And Quill, Myles should know about this. No, you won't want to call him. I will."

"Wait a minute." Quill, paging through the 'goods' book, found a few sentences which cast her relationship with Myles in a highly unflattering light. The reference was listed under 'Poss. Stories.' and a putative headline noted:

'Innkeep Trades Sex For Freedom! Sheriff's Girlfriend Avoids Plumbing Prosecution!''

"Those damn toilets," Quill muttered.

"You found that, huh?" said Georgia.

"Yes."

"There's more, of course. The guy's a creep. With a mind like a sewer. But that's not the only thing. There's a list of New Jersey phone numbers written under DeMarco's name, and in several pages following that—look for yourselves."

"You're kidding!" Meg ran her hands excitedly through her hair. Georgia paged through the book and displayed the page triumphantly.

"That settles it. We have to turn this over to Myles."

"No," Meg said. "If Hedrick knows the book's been turned over to the police, he's going to take steps to destroy evidence."

"We can't suppress this, Meg," Quill protested. "What if he kills somebody else?"

"I want my kitchen open, Quill. Soon. We can solve these murders ourselves. And we don't have to go through official channels like Myles and Andy do. We can be a lot quicker."

"And a lot more illegal," Quill muttered. "It'd be quicker if we gave the police this book, wouldn't it? I'm just afraid Hedrick will kill someone else."

"What if we suppress it just for a little while? And as for more murders, it looks to me like Hedrick's run out of relatives."

Georgia shouted with laughter. "Sorry. I don't know why I think that's so funny. Let's work backward from what we know." She held up one finger. "First, it's pretty clear that Hedrick's none-too-subtle threats to disclose something nefarious about the mini-mall operation have everyone in town upset. So upset that they're looking to Mr. Sakura to buy them out. Yes?"

"That's right," said Quill. "But there's a slight discrepancy in what we know, here. When Sakura Toshiro checked in, he showed me a letter from Elmer Henry, inviting him to tour the mini-mall site when he arrived here in Hemlock

Falls, with an eye toward purchase. Ken Sakura claims that his father discovered the investment opportunity the day before yesterday, when the group of men arrived at the sheriff's office to talk to him directly about it. So which is it? Second, if Elmer had been in contact with an investor, why didn't any of the other investors know about it? And if it was supposed to be a secret, why did Mr. Sakura show me the letter?''

"So we need an explanation of what that's all about," said Georgia. "Let's make a list, and we can assign activities to the best investigator." She dug a spiral notebook out of her capacious purse. "Okay, that's question number one. What's next?''

"Who is Marco DeMarco, and why is Myles investigating him? John claims that it's very odd that there are no local people employed at the construction site. Hedrick''— she tapped the goods book—"clearly has been following the same trail. So someone needs to call these numbers in New Jersey and do a little digging. Is DeMarco involved in something crooked? What kind of reputation does his construction company have? He's got to be a prime suspect in the murders. Maybe he's knocking off the Conways one by one to keep a story from being written.''

"Investigate DeMarco," Georgia wrote, speaking aloud. "Let me tackle that one, will you? Sitting and making phone calls is my idea of how to do legwork. And while I'm at it, I can do a little background digging on Hedrick, as well.''

"Our restaurant's nearly ready, but DeMarco would expect me to want to take a look myself," said Quill. "It'd be really easy for me to drift on down to the mall site and ask him a few questions myself.''

"If it's DeMarco behind the murders, Hedrick's next in line to be killed, isn't he?" said Meg. "Which, I admit it, gives us the more reason to turn this book over to Myles, Quill." She paged through it. "Sheesh! How did he *get* all this stuff?! Here's something about poor Marge's affair with Gil Gilmeister. Now, that was a sad thing. I'll tell you what I'm curious about. Who's nasty enough to dump all this ancient dirt into the lap of a newspaperman?''

''Beats me.'' Georgia, eyeing the cooling eggs Florentine with a wistful look, said in an abstracted tone, ''Meg.'' She rolled her eyes pathetically. ''Those lovely, lovely eggs are getting cold!''

''Oh, rats. There's grapefruit, too. Hang on.'' She bounced to the counter, served the eggs, and began peeling grapefruit. Georgia tucked her napkin into the *V* of her caftan and began to eat.

Quill picked up the red notebook and said thoughtfully, ''The final suspect is, of course, Hedrick himself. And the notes about the neurobenzine are very suggestive. Very.''

Georgia swallowed and nodded. ''Hedrick gets my vote as the murderer. He's got the best motive of all. All that cash.''

''We don't know that for sure, do we?'' asked Meg. ''There's been talk . . . but there's always talk. Have you ever noticed how people want to believe that other people are rich? They nod at you in this significant way and say something like, 'Oh, yes, *she's* doing all right,' based on no evidence whatsoever.''

''Men especially,'' said Georgia. ''No, thanks, honey, no grapefruit. I don't want to ruin my record for highest amount of healthy food *not* consumed in a day. As a matter of fact, those crumpets are wonderful. Could I have one plain, with just a bit of jam? Well. I can maybe help there, too. As you know, I'm loaded. I've got a couple of banker friends who can maybe help us out. It'll take a few days to get the info back.''

''Do we have a few days?'' asked Meg. ''There's a much shorter way. There's an emergency Chamber meeting this morning, and Howie Murchison will be there. He handled the Conway closing on the Nickerson building. Quill can pin him to the wall about Hedrick's finances. Believe me, those baby hazel eyes and curly red hair of hers conceal a steely mind. Howie'll talk, and not even know he's talking. And there's the local OSHA office.''

''The local OSHA office?'' Georgia stopped with a crumpet halfway to her mouth.

''They can tell us where Hedrick is likely to buy neu-

robenzine, what it's used for, how much is on hand. They'll
have copies of the MSHS.''

"And what's that when it's at home?"

"Materials safety handling sheet," said Meg offhand-
edly,

"She's showing off," said Quill. "We had a case last
year . . . anyway, Meg, I don't know what the local OSHA
office could tell us that Andy couldn't. Why don't you put
him, in your own inimitable way, onto neurobenzene as a
possible murder weapon. Without letting him know how
we know, of course.''

"I can't do that unless I know what the heck it is, can
I? I mean, how do I introduce it casually into a conversation? 'Andrew. Speaking of neurobenzine . . . or Andrew, I
was wondering a lot about the properties of neurobenzine.' ''

"Meg, you can do it more subtly than that."

"Okay, okay! I'll try my wiles on Andrew. Are you going to try your wiles on Howie to see if Hedrick really does
have any cash?"

"Sure. But I'll bet that Gee will have better luck with
the bankers. Howie takes confidentiality stuff seriously."

"And what do we do about this?" Georgia tapped the
red notebook.

"We copy it," said Meg smugly, "on the office copier.
And we put it back where you found it, Georgia. Myles's
men had the chance to discover it last night. They'll have
a chance again today, if Hedrick doesn't come looking for
it first. So we are not interfering with an investigation at
all.''

Quill frowned. "And if Myles doesn't find it before Hedrick?"

"We'll give the copy to him. This is Monday, right?
How much time do we need to pursue our leads and solve
the murder?"

Quill threw up her hands. "How the heck should I know?
A couple of days to answer the question we've raised. You
know Myles's resources—he'll probably solve this before
we do anyway.''

"Hah!" said Meg. "But we are going to give him a run

for his money. If we don't turn up anything significant by Friday, I vote we give the goods book copy to him then."

"Agreed. Georgia?"

"Fine with me!" She spread a third crumpet with blueberry jam. "Just as long as I continue to get to play the Nero Wolfe part, and not the Archie Goodwin part. Wolfe never left his house, he ate terrific food, and somebody else did all the running around. Archie?" She wiggled her eyebrows at Quill. "When you get back from the Chamber meeting, report. And Fritz, this crumpet?" She burped. "Satisfactory."

Quill picked up the red notebook. "Shall we reconvene after the Chamber meeting at Marge's diner? It's for lunch, so why don't we meet in my office about three o'clock and compare notes. In the meantime, I'll copy this off, then put it back where you found it, Georgia. Are you going to make those phone calls?"

"Wrote 'em down and will do."

"I've got to go down to the sheriff's office and give Deputy Dave a statement about how I prepared last night's dinner," said Meg. "I'll bring some of that sour cream pastry with me. If Myles isn't there, maybe I can drop tidbits into Dave's mouth like Bathsheba with the grapes and charm him into letting me know what's going on at the official end. Quill? You'll put that copy in the safe?"

Quill, reading, answered her absently. "Sure. If you think we need to take precautions."

"Georgia? Did anyone see you pick the book up this morning?"

"Just that little fellow, Stoker."

"Well, act ignorant if he asks you anything. And Quill? Quill!"

Quill, her hands icy, had come to the end of the goods book.

Meg nudged her. "Make sure no one sees you slip the book back into the sweet peas. I think we should be careful."

Quill looked up. Her voice was distant to her own ears. "You didn't get all the way through this, Gee, did you?"

"No. Wanted to bring it up to you guys. Why?"

"Hedrick's been trying to find evidence that the mall's been built over a toxic waste dump. There's a note here: 'Check DeMarco Toxic Waste Disposal, Inc. Relative?' And another set of notes from an OSHA Materials Safety Handling Sheet. About mercury poisoning."

"Oh, my God," said Meg. "Oh, no! If it's true, this is even worse than the murders!"

"Then you've lost all your money," said Georgia soberly. "And so has half the town."

"It's worse than that. Don't you see," said Meg, perfectly white. "If it's true, that mall will be killing people. Lots of people. Just like the Love Canal in Niagara Falls. It took years for them to stop the dumping. And in all that time people died, and died and died."

CHAPTER 10

"Let me see that." Georgia grabbed the note book and frowned. "This is ridiculous, Quill. DeMarco with a brother in toxic waste disposal? I don't think so." She threw it onto the breakfast table. "More muckraking."

"It doesn't say brother. The note says 'relative.' It might be a father or an uncle or a sister."

"Didn't you say DeMarco was from New Jersey? I've been to New Jersey. It's filled with Italians. And De-Marco's a common enough Italian name."

"Do you think it's true?" Georgia shook her head in disgust. "I've seen and heard what this little newspaper of Hedrick's is doing to the Falls. It's my guess that the little bugger is thinking of going big time. Creating more of those stories in which the adjective *alleged* is in little tiny type and the noun *coverup* in huge letters on the front page."

"It would explain a lot," said Quill soberly. "Except that I haven't had a chance to tell you about the guns, Gee."

"The *guns*!"

When Quill explained the near riot that Meg had quelled with off-key renditions of movie theme songs, she threw back her head and laughed so hard her whole body shook. "Oh, my." She wiped her eyes. "I'm sorry. It isn't funny. From what you've said, it could have a real disaster. But, oh, I wish I'd seen it!"

"I've changed my mind," Meg said. "We've got to turn this over to Myles."

"He'll take it public," Quill warned. "You know him, Meg. He'll call in the DEC and the EPA, and if Gee's right, Hedrick will have exactly what he wants."

"Quill's right, Meg. It seems to me that you have a very delicate situation here. If there's any truth at all to these allegations Hedrick's alluded to in this notebook, your little town's in trouble."

"It'd explain the mayor's nervousness," said Quill. "It makes no sense at all that he'd contacted Mr. Sakura to buy out the mall unless he'd discovered . . . this." She set the notebook on the table. "Everyone's excited about this project. Why sell out? Unless there's a rumor about toxic waste disposal that's making the rounds, and frightening people. It frightens me, that's for sure."

"We would have heard about it. And if not us, then John," Meg said. "We're investors, too."

"Would you?" Georgia asked shrewdly. "Quill said herself that you two wouldn't participate in a coverup for one minute. And neither would John. If most of your investors have their life savings tied up in this, it'd make a great deal of sense to sell what they could and get out, and let Mr. Sakura handle the hassle with the EPA and the DEC. What you two should think about, or rather the three of us, is whether or not there's anything in this. I still think it's just another sleazy idea of Hedrick's to sell newspapers."

"Louisa was killed at the excavation site for the septic tank," said Quill. "And she had a camera around her neck. The film had been removed. What if she found cylinders containing mercury under the tank? And DeMarco saw her, hit her with the hammer, and dumped her body in the river? It would explain the boldness of the crime, too. I mean, the woman was killed in broad daylight, in an area where fifty or more people were potential witnesses."

"You're going to go down there, aren't you?" said Meg.

"I think one of us should. It'd be unusual for you to take the time from the kitchen to go visit the site, but it's totally logical for me to be there to check on the progress of the boutique restaurant. And we have to find out what we can, Meg, before we turn this over to Myles. I agree with you. It wouldn't be right to sit on it for long. But what if Georgia's right, and there's nothing to this but Hedrick's vivid imagination?''

"Even if it isn't true, it doesn't mean that DeMarco didn't find it easier to knock Louisa and Carlyle off than deal with a fraudulent claim that the place is a toxic dump,'' Meg warned. "It could be dangerous to be alone with him. Why don't you take John with you?''

"He's in Syracuse, checking on the delivery of the kitchen unit. He's due back at the Chamber meeting at noon. I don't think we should hang around waiting to see if everyone in town begins to develop central nervous system disorders. I think I should go look right now. Besides, the fewer people who know about this, the better.''

"Hey, I'll go with you,'' Georgia said.

"No.'' Quill grinned at her. "You hate legwork. You said so yourself. And running like heck from DeMarco and his revolver-wielding minions could be real legwork. I'll just go down there, poke around in an innocent way, and see if I can pick up enough sinister vibrations to justify blowing the whistle on the whole project.''

"Quill, I don't like this.'' Meg ran both her hands through her hair.

"I promise you, Meg. I'm not going to do anything silly. I'll admire the progress on the mall, bat my eyelashes, and see if I can discover whether the septic tank was set before or after Louisa visited the site. If it was after, the probability that she found something suspicious in the hole is higher. I'll also ask DeMarco directly if he knows of anyone to handle our toxic waste. If he gives me the name of his uncle Frankie, we've got another reason to turn the goods book over to Myles.''

"And I'll include a background check on DeMarco Disposal in my phone calls this morning,'' said Georgia.

"I might as well leave right now, then.'' Quill got up.

"Sounds reasonable,'' Meg admitted. "Just as long as you remember not to go in the basement.''

"The basement?'' said Georgia.

"All those gothic novels we read when we were kids," Quill explained. "The dumb heroine *always* went into the basement. Alone. At two in the morning. With the homicidal first wife lurking near the freezer with an ax. Meg, I'll be very careful to run like heck at the first sign of suspicious behavior."

"I'll just bet. Quill? If you don't call here by eleven thirty, I'm going to get Myles and those Norwegian cousins of Harland Peterson's and come out to get you."

"Deal," said Quill, and went to change her clothes into something more appropriate to sleuthing than shorts and a cotton T-shirt.

Quill drove through the summer morning. She'd copied the goods book, tucked the copy in the office safe, then dropped the original unobtrusively among the sweet peas by the gazebo. There had been no sign of Hedrick. She let her mind drift for the few miles it took to get to the mini-mall site. The less she concentrated on the possibilities ahead (kidnapping? being whacked in the head with a hammer? maybe it wasn't mercury but plutonium packed in Baggies, and she'd fry like a potato in hot fat?), the cooler she could be. As fond as she was of fictional detectives who welcomed the rough stuff, she much preferred a more civilized approach to bringing miscreants to justice, like policemen and courtrooms.

The countryside was drenched in green, and the air sweet with the smell of cut grass and ripe corn. She and Meg had chosen this spot at a time when Meg had been recently widowed and Quill dried up as an artist. The decision had been made in haste, but neither had truly regretted it. The town and its surrounding countryside were too beautiful for regrets.

Hemlock Falls was located in the middle of the path of glaciers which had moved through the region tens of thousands of years before. Farther south, toward New York itself, the countryside recalled the English Cotswolds in spring and summer, with gentle hills, meadow-covered, and stands of ash and birch. Central New York was harder country. Granite poked its rocky knuckles through the soil,

leaving land too thin for intensive farming. The glacier's
chief legacy here was water, for which Quill felt a passionate affinity. It fell in clear ribbons from the lips of
gorges; wound in streams through grasses thick with clover,
timothy, and red fescue; and formed an occasional ribbon
wide enough to be called a river.

It was on such a river—the Taughannock—that the
Hemlock Falls Investment Group (Ltd.) had selected the
site for its mini-mall. Harvey Bozzell (Bozzell: The Agency
That ADS Value!) had named it The Mall At The Falls,
even though the nearest real waterfall was three miles up-
stream near Trumansburg, in a rare burst of professional
reticence.

In far too short a time the familiar and soothing land-
scape gave way to construction and Quill approached the
mall with increasing trepidation. The sounds of Carlyle's
death, the memory of her face, were a rising accompani-
ment to the distant hum of tractors cutting hay and the
occasional birdsong.

Quill parked the Olds on the newly asphalted parking
lot, turned off the ignition, and thought hard for a moment.
How would she know what she was looking for when she
saw it? She really doubted that if DeMarco was dumping,
it was in canisters labeled ILLEGAL DISPOSAL. On the other
hand, neither Carlyle nor Louisa Conway appeared to be
the sort of women who would know more than Quill would
about building sites, much less toxic waste disposal. If the
late Mr. Conway had made his fortune in construction, then
it was remotely possible that Louisa had been a forewoman
on a job site, but somehow, recalling the creamy skin, the
lazy, sensual bodies of both women, Quill didn't think so.
Louisa'd probably picked him up in line at a bank. She
made a mental note—"Find out how Conway made his
fortune"—and decided that if either Louisa or Carlyle had
come across something at the mall that was suspicious—
and been killed for it—Quill could figure it out, too.

Except if that were true, wouldn't one or more of the
other investors in the project have noticed it? The thought
of a vast village-wide conspiracy flashed through her head,
and she shivered in the heat. Louisa had been killed near

the site of the leach fields, a spot which didn't particularly interest anyone, unless they'd been tipped off to a problem, as Louisa may have been. No one else would have been especially interested, except Petey Peterson, out of professional curiosity, and he'd have been the first to cry an alarm, since he'd been vociferous about his failure to get the contract to install the leach field.

She got out of the car and surveyed the new mall.

Like the village itself, the mall had an American Colonial air, with white clapboard storefronts, cobblestone paving in the open-air atrium, and flower-filled planters painted black. At forty thousand square feet the mini-mall had been designed to accommodate six small retail stores, the Inn's boutique restaurant, and a McDonald's. The six stores and the two restaurants formed a horseshoe around a small paved court. The mall entrance had four thick pine doors, ten feet high, with a span of sixteen feet. They were painted in a cross between robin's egg and teal blue with Paramount Exterior Latex Paint, obtained at cost from the local Paramount Paint factory.

The large doors were open to the warm summer air. Quill passed a hand-lettered sign that read: GRAND OPENING !!! with a date two days away in bright red paint. Beneath it, someone had taped an old *New Yorker* cartoon that read "Watch this space" and featured a hill with three empty crosses on it. Quill stopped and looked at the cartoon with a frown.

"Can I help you?"

"Mr. DeMarco."

"It's Sarah Quilliam, isn't it?" Marco DeMarco was unmistakably a construction boss. His skin was deeply weathered. His eyes were a bright blue in a nest of wrinkles. His hair was graying, but showed traces of brown. Quill liked the way he looked; a thick-set, barrel-chested body that spoke of years of hard, manual labor. His face was expressive, his eyes were watchful. He reminded her a little of someone; she couldn't recall who.

"Ignore that cartoon. It's just a little employee humor. Some of the boys think I'm driving them a little hard. I'm not sure how to thank you for the party last night."

"Oh, it was nothing, really."

"No. I mean I'm genuinely not sure how to thank you. I've never been to a celebration that ended quite like that before." His tone was wry, and slightly apologetic. "It must have been quite a shock for you and your sister. I understand they've closed the kitchen temporarily."

"It should be open soon."

"I sure hope you didn't lose much business. My guess is that everyone pretty much sticks around to see what happens next. People." He shook his head. "You can always count on the bastards to do the wrong thing. Well, have you come to check on the progress of the restaurant? We're ahead of schedule, thank God. Your plumbing's not hooked up, but almost all the wiring's done, and the fixtures are in place. Your kitchen's scheduled to arrive any time now. I've got a crew ready to install it as soon as the truck delivers it."

"I wish Meg and I'd had your crew on the Inn remodeling." Quill crossed the courtyard at his side. "I've never heard of a construction project that was *ahead* of schedule."

"You acted as GC on your remodeling yourself? General contractor," he added, with a hint of impatience.

"Oh. Yes. It was a mess," said Quill. Establish rapport with the suspect—it was a maxim she recalled from somewhere. Or was that hostage-taking? "I mean, everybody was wonderful, but it seemed impossible to keep to a schedule. I used," she added casually, "local firms, of course. But then I was going to do business here, so I thought it'd be better to keep the business in the village. The locals tend to talk too much, if you know what I mean."

"Smart."

They stopped in front of the new restaurant. Quill sighed.

"Got a problem?"

"Oh, no. Not all all. It's beautiful. It's overwhelming, as a matter of fact. This is a new venture for us, you know. Every time I see it, I get cold feet. I tend not to think about it much when I'm not in front of it. My business manager takes care of all the details and he's just terrific. But I'm standing here thinking—''

"What have I done? Buyer's remorse? Don't worry. It's going to work out just fine. People will come here to eat just because of the design. And once they taste your sister's food? No problem.''

"Do you like the design?" asked Quill wistfully. "I wanted to sustain the associations to the Inn—which is quite historic, you know—and I think it's lovely, but then, I did the sketch myself. I wanted to suggest pre-Colonial without being too . . .''

"Kitschy?''

"Exactly. You don't think it's too kitschy, do you?''

"I think it's great. The brickwork on the open hearth is a real nice design. Real nice. And I like bricks for flooring, although the mason cussed a bit laying it.''

"So did the mason with the Inn remodeling. Of course, that was mainly a restoration job, with all that cobblestone, and that was a trick, getting the old to blend with the new. I had to go out of town for that job. I used a Guy Jones, out of Syracuse? He's a Welshman. We have some excellent masons here in town, though. Where did your worker come from? I'd like to meet him and thank him for doing such a wonderful job.''

"He's been done for a few days. Sent him on back.''

"To where?''

The bright blue eyes narrowed. "To another job.''

"I see," said Quill, looking at the hammering, nailing, and sawing going on frantically around her with what she hoped was an air of convincing surprise, "that *you* decided not to use any local workers. Smart," she echoed his comment.

"As you've discovered," he said in a rather dry way, "Part-timers and jobbers can lead to a lot of disruption. And when you've got a penalty for not making deadline, as I do, you use the guys you can count on.''

"You've got a penalty if you run over the opening date?''

"Yeah. The lawyer you've got on the contract end of things?''

"Howie Murchison."

"Right. Like most lawyers, a real bastard. Pardon the expression. Nailed my back to the wall on this one. If I don't make the deadline, I pay a penalty of six hundred bucks a day."

"You're kidding!"

"Not about money I don't kid. I'll tell you something, though, there's a guy I want on my side in a fight."

"Howie?" Quill, who usually didn't think much about Howie at all, began to see the balding, bespectacled town justice in a different light. "We're a small town," she added proudly, "but that doesn't mean we're small town, if you know what I mean."

"You sure got some big-time murders."

"Yes." Carlyle Conway's dead face rose before her mind's eye. "The sheriff hasn't said anything official, has he?"

"McHale? If he had, fat chance the bastard'd tell me. There's another one for you, Miss Quilliam. Like Murchison. Not much gets past that one." He shook his head. "Changed my mind about small towns, I'll tell you that."

"Sheriff McHale is retired from the New York City police department," said Quill. "He had quite a career there, I understand."

"That a fact?" DeMarco rubbed his hand thoughtfully along his lower jaw. "Wish I'd known."

"Excuse me?"

"Nothing. Look. We're having a few problems with the septic, and I want to get on over there to take a look. You look around all you want. Anything I can do for you, just let me know."

"I wouldn't mind seeing the septic tank."

"The septic tank?"

"You may have heard. We're having some problems with the plumbing at the Inn. There was an article about it in yesterday's *Trumpet!*"

"Come again?"

"Our local newspaper. Anyway. I'd be really grateful for any plumbing advice you could give me. And . . .

um . . . we have another small problem I thought you might help us with?''

"Yeah?" He looked at his watch. "My engineer might have some time. I really don't."

"If you don't mind, it's something a little private."

His glance flickered over her. She'd decided that jeans and a tank top would be the best uniform for detecting toxic waste in a hostile environment. She'd lost a little weight in the past few months, and she was suddenly aware that her stomach was exposed. She pulled self-consciously at the tank top. "You know my sister and I run the Inn at Hemlock Falls."

"Yep."

"And we, um, well, we run into problems with the DEC, the EPA—you must know how difficult it can be dealing with the government on issues of, um, disposal of certain substances."

"What kind of substances?" His glance was unfriendly. Quill, who'd thought this question out beforehand, was ready. "Gasoline."

"Oh, shit. Don't tell me you have buried tanks?"

"We think so. The Inn's quite old, and it's had a great many owners. We're pretty sure at one time in the thirties and forties they had pumps put back."

"And you think you've got contaminated soil? Shit," he said again. "That's a tough one. You're looking at a quarter million, maybe three hundred thousand in removal expense."

"I am?" said Quill, genuinely astonished, and extremely glad there were no gasoline tanks buried at the Inn.

"Oh, yeah." He placed a hand on her shoulder. Quill jumped. "I'm really sorry. The EPA regs will kill you."

"You don't know of any way we could dispose of it for less than that? The EPA doesn't know anything, and I'd surely hate for them to find out."

"Best advice I can give you is ignore it. What they don't know won't hurt them."

"Couldn't we just dig up the tanks and put them somewhere else?"

"Ms. Quilliam, you seem like a nice little lady to me. I

have to tell you, if you did decide to get some fly-by-nighter to take those tanks up for you, I sure don't want to know about it." There was a faint, very faint, look of contempt on his face. "I can tell you this, if you won't take offense where none is meant. There's too many people with the kind of attitude you've got. Let it be someone else's problem. The earth, Ms. Quilliam, is everyone's problem. You've heard of the Sierra Club? I'm a charter member. It's a . . fine organization, and I can give you some literature on . . ."

Quill (who contributed faithfully to the Audubon Society every year) thought it was just her luck to hit the only green construction company in Central New York.

She apologized, which stemmed the flow, then, in dogged pursuit of the requirement to at least take a look at the place where Louisa died, asked DeMarco if his engineer could give her advice on septic systems. With DeMarco's admonitions in her ears, they left the mall by way of the service entrance and walked over a field gouged and rutted by the passage of heavy equipment. A bulldozer and a backhoe were running at full speed. The noise, which had been mere background inside the mall, was astonishing, and DeMarco's lecture petered out.

"We're getting sod in tomorrow!" DeMarco shouted at her. "All this'll be green by Wednesday. Eugene! Hi!" He waved energetically at the backhoe driver, a scrawny, hollow-chested man in his late thirties. "Pray for rain!"

"What?!"

"Pray for"—Eugene flipped a lever, and the dozer and backhoe cut off simultaneously—"*rain*!"

"Not for a few days yet, Marco. I want to wait to get this covered up, and rain, it'll slosh it up." He climbed down from the backhoe and nodded abruptly at Quill, his eyes sly and a little curious. "We've got a hairline crack at the other end. Happened when it was sunk, I think."

"Shit," said DeMarco. "Sorry, Miss Quilliam."

"A hairline crack?" said Quill. "That's not good, I take it."

"Show ya, if you like. It's this big pit over here." Eugene flicked his eyes over her jeans and tank top with genuine appreciation. Quill followed them to the lip of a huge pit. The hole was three-quarters filled with half of a giant concrete tank. The top lay upside down in the dirt on the far side of the hole. "Can't put the top on right yet, Marco. We're testing the tank with water. If it goes all the way through, the tanks got to be patched. It's going to take a couple of days to dry, and we're not going to have the plumbing up and running in time for the opening-day ceremonies, Marco. If it doesn't, no sweat. Either way, we have to keep the top off so the cement patch will dry, so no rain, please."

"Going to run into some regulatory problem if we don't put the top on, quick. Some kid could fall in."

"What is this thing, exactly?" asked Quill.

"Five-thousand-gallon sewage tank, ma'am." Eugene grinned. His teeth were in terrible shape. "You interested in sewage?"

Quill considered several responses to this. Whatever was going on here, and it was getting increasingly unlikely that it was illegal dumping of toxic waste, she still had to find out. "Passionately," she said and batted her eyelashes.

Eugene the engineer had clearly been marked from birth as a man dedicated to sewers. "First thing," he explained, his rather muddy brown eyes alight, "is the location. You got to have gravel and sand, not clay. Clay does things to drainage you don't want to think about. You don't have gravel and sand, you got to bring in."

"And did you draw in sand and gravel here?" asked Quill.

"Here? In this kind of glaciated soil? Heck, no. Beautiful gravel. Fantastic sand. No sweat at all. Perc test was beautiful, just beautiful."

"Perc test?" asked Quill, thinking of coffee.

"The percolation test," DeMarco supplied. "You dig test holes, pour in a couple of gallons of water, and time the absorption rate."

"Six minute holes," said Eugene with pride. "Now the field itself, out here,"—he swept an arm in an expansive wave—"is where your PVC pipes go. The sewage comes from along the gray line from the building, into the holes

along the top of the cover of the holding tank, and through
a four-inch pipe into the tank itself. The concrete tank's in
two pieces, like you see.''

"The tank's awfully large," ventured Quill.

"Tricky to place. But the bottom half went into the hole
just as nice. Can't understand why the darn thing cracked.
Marco's real picky about his suppliers. Can't afford any
trouble. Well, concrete's a mystery.''

"When did you set it?''

"Three days ago, just before that woman was murdered.
And they sequestered the site temporarily. The crack and
that business with that woman drowning set us back a couple of days while the police were here.''

"You were there that day?" Quill asked, her eyes
opened to their widest extent.

"Day the tank was set? Wouldn't have been anywhere
else. Dang, I wish I knew why we got that crack.''

"Did you see it, Mr. DeMarco?''

"Me? Nope. I was in San Francisco, sizing up another
job. Came back here soon as I heard what happened.''

"The guys were as careful as a mother with a baby,''
said Eugene, a slight flush along his cheekbones.

"Aw, I know that, Eugene. You boys do good work. I
came back because of the accident. God knows what the
family's going to do. We're insured and all, but you just
never know what the hell kind of bug the survivors are
going to get up their ass . . . begging your pardon, Miss
Quilliam. I've talked to our lawyers, and it doesn't look as
though anyone could hold us liable, but Jesus, these days
with juries you never know. Woman gets cracked on the
head around a construction site, all kinds of crap jumps out
of the bushes.''

"Well, she sure as hell didn't come near the tank when
it was set. Not that her head could have caused that crack
anyhow,'' Eugene added generously. "Not enough
weight.'' He stared doubtfully into the pit.

Quill, mindful of Howie's list of the spread of criminal
activities engaged in by contractors, impulsively decided to
try another tack. "Perhaps there wasn't enough concrete in
the concrete? You know, maybe the numbers of bags per

square inch was short, or whatever?''

The silence was deadly.

"You can't possibly mean what I think you mean,'' said DeMarco, his eyes icy.

"In paint, you know,'' said Quill feebly.

"Paint? What the hell's an accusation of my shorting the concrete got to do with paint?'' DeMarco's tan darkened to an ugly red. "I've been in business—good, honest, straightforward business—for twenty years, Miss Quilliam.''

"You mean it is a bad thing not to have enough concrete?'' Quill, perjuring her feminist principles without a qualm, tried to look guileless. "I'm an artist, you know. I paint pictures. And if my paints aren't mixed just right, they crack when they dry. I'm truly sorry. I seem to have offended you both.''

DeMarco clipped his words as though he was biting the heads off cigars, or chickens. "I defy anyone, at any time, to find a damn thing wrong with my concrete. You bring any inspector in here that you want. You bring the Feds, the state, the town, and test this concrete.''

"I'm sure it's excellent concrete.''

"Damn straight.''

There was an ugly silence.

"My, um, septic system?'' said Quill eventually.

"Right.'' DeMarco shot a fulminating glance at his watch. "Gotta go, Eugene. Fill her in, will you? Unless she's trying to find out if we're cheating on that, too.''

"C'mon, now, Marco. The little lady was just asking. Probably got as tough a boss as I do.'' Eugene winked at her.

"Uh-huh. Catch you later, Eugene. Ms. Quilliam.'' He tugged at his billed cap and stalked off, his ears still red.

"How come the guys at the Inn put someone as pretty as you in charge of the drains, anyhow?''

"You were telling me, Eugene,'' said Quill, "about how the sewage comes from the gray line and then through these holes?''

"Yeah. Drains on down. Sits for a bit. Bacterial action breaks down the sewage. When the level gets high enough, the overflow goes into the outlet pipes and out into the field, where capillary action diffuses it into the air.''

"This has been very helpful,'' said Quill. "We've got some problems at the Inn, as you know. But everything's perfectly clear to me now.''

"What kind of problems?'' asked Eugene.

"The toilets back up.''

"How long's it been since you had her pumped out?''

"Oh. I don't know that we have had it pumped out,'' said Quill vaguely. "I just didn't realize how important it was unless it didn't work.''

"Well, that's it, you see.'' Eugene was confiding. "People just ignore sewers. One of the most important things in life, isn't it? Making sure the toilets work good? People take it for granted, neglect it, until it's too late and then bam!'' He flicked his fingers upward. "You got trouble. And then what they do? They blame you because they didn't get routine maintenance on a perfectly good system.'' He shook his head once in disgust. "I could tell you stories. Anyway, you get your tank pumped out. If the toilets still don't work, you look for a plug in the pipe.''

"A plug in the pipe.''

"Yessir—uh, ma'am that is, a plug in the pipe. One time I got a troubleshooting call on a system. A fox was trapped in the input valve. Couldn't get nothing into that tank from the gray line. Little sucker's head was jammed right up against the end.''

"How did the poor thing get in there?''

"Sucker must have been pretty determined. Vet thought maybe it was rabid. Squeezed itself right down into that hole. Fact. Toilets didn't work for three days while we got that cover off of her and pulled that fox out. Look, you want some coffee? Tell me about your plumbing problem? I got a little time, while we test for the leak, maybe I can come on up and take a look.''

"That would be very, very kind of you, Eugene. But you're a professional, and I couldn't possibly impose on you. We seemed to have solved the problem. Temporarily at least. But I'd love a cup of coffee. Maybe you could give me some suggestions on preventive maintenance.''

"Sure thing."

Quill received what she was sure was excellent, although irrelevant, advice on the frequency of pumping the tank (yearly, given her usage), the cost of a replacement system, the virtues of sewers (None. He was a leach field man all the way), and desirability of plastic pipe over iron. The coffee, from a much battered Mr. Coffee located in the trailer the men used as construction headquarters, was strong, sweet, and curiously comforting.

"My goodness," said Quill, after Eugene had exhausted his opinions on artificial bacteria for rapid decomposition. "Eugene? I couldn't help but overhear that you were around the day Mrs. Conway was killed."

"Oh, yeah. Jeez. Quite something, wasn't it." He moved a little closer.

"Terrible," Quill agreed. "And then her daughter, last evening."

"Yeah! I heard that! Man!" He put a tentative hand on her knee. He smelled of damp earth. Quill was perched precariously on an orange plastic chair; she edged back as unobtrusively as possible. His eyes were eager. "You saw it?"

"No. No, I didn't. I was in the kitchen seeing to an order."

"I thought you worked up at the Inn. A waitress, are you?"

"That, and in charge of the plumbing system," said Quill amiably. "Anyway, by the time I got there, the ambulance had come to take the body away. I'm sorry," she lied, "to have missed it. I don't suppose you were, um, in on it, here. That day her mother was killed?"

"Well." He drew a deep breath. "Not really. No, I can't say as I saw anything. Although I did see her, of course, before she went into the woods. And I saw the argument with that Japanese fella. Crazy around here, Wednesday. Crazy vibrations." He grinned. "Maybe that's what cracked my tank."

"But you noticed Mrs. Conway."

"Hell, who wouldn't of, looking like that."

"Was she around here very long?"

"Mmm. Sheriff asked me the same thing. She was taking pictures, I remember that. Quite a lot of them."

"Of anything in particular?" asked Quill. Her heart went a little faster and she set the coffee mug on the metal drafting table.

"People more than things, really. She took a picture of that Japanese guy, which he didn't like by a long shot, and that big shot who's his boss. He was here looking for Marco, and was some kind of teed off when he wasn't here."

"Mr. Sakura was looking for Mr. DeMarco?"

"Yeah. Marc said he's some kind of big shot—or was—he's retired now. So instead of being worth maybe a billion dollars, he's worth half a billion."

"And she took other pictures?"

"Of the hole, here, for the tank. And some of the guys on the big wheels."

"Pardon?"

"The backhoes and the dozers. And then a bunch of other people came up in a van, and she was taking pictures of them and that one guy, yeah, I remember that one guy. Jeez!"

"She got into an argument with him?"

"Heck no, I did. Little short son of a bitch looked like he had a ramrod up his ass. Oh. Sorry. Anyway, I complained to Marc. 'That's just Stoke,' he said. Doesn't mean any harm."

"You must have run into Mr. Stoker."

"Wanted to know if I had some kind paperwork for how often I finished my work on time. What is he, from the government?" Eugene snorted. "I'm telling you, those sons of guns from the inspection offices, they'll drive a good man to drink in no time. I . . . hey!" He gave a patently artificial start of surprise. "Speaking of drink. You wouldn't want to stop by a little place I found in town for a drink, say, after quitting time here?"

"Gene. Thanks. But I have to work this evening."

"You do, hah? Tough boss?"

"Really tough. You know how it is."

"I do. It's why I went into business as a consulting engineer. You ought to think about, miss . . . I didn't get your name. Marc out there gets kind of forgetful about those things.''

''My name's Sarah.'' She stood up carefully in the confined space and extended her hand. ''I really enjoyed our talk. It's been tremendously helpful. I'll definitely know what to do when my toilets back up again.''

''We could pace off the leach field if you wanted to get an idea of how much space your boss would need for a good new system. You'd be amazed at how those new bacteria save on line space.''

''I would love to.'' Quill looked at her watch. ''But it's lunchtime, and I have get to the Hemlock Hometown Diner by twelve o'clock.''

He held her hand warmly. ''You're not carrying two jobs, are you? Being a waitress at that Inn's got to be tough enough.''

Quill disengaged herself and stood up. The trailer was very small, and she brushed against him inadvertently.

''Boy, Eugene, doesn't everyone have more than one job?''

''Guess that's the brush-off,'' he said. ''Can't say as I blame you folks. Course, you might have the wrong idea about me. I never served hard time, myself.''

''Hard time?''

''Just a little fiddling with some checks. Some of the guys on the big wheels, you want to stay away from them. Couple of assaults, one or two rapes.''

''You mean the work crew's made up of ex-cons?''

''You didn't know?'' His muddy brown eyes were sly. ''Sure thing. That's why Marco there can get us so cheap.'' He opened the door to the outside with an elaborate regard for the space between them.

''It's not that, Eugene.'' Quill, flustered, eased herself down the rickety metal steps. ''I'd be glad to go out for a drink with you. It's just that I'm already involved. . . . ''

Eugene slammed the door shut. Quill, thoughtful over this new piece of evidence, drove slowly down the hill to the emergency Chamber of Commerce meeting.

CHAPTER 11

"You see any sign of Hedrick Conway yet?" Elmer Henry directed a depressed whisper fragrant with meat loaf into Quill's left ear. They were crowded into Marge Schmidt's and Betty Hall's Hemlock Hometown Diner! (Fine Food and Fast) with twenty of the thirty-six members of the Chamber of Commerce. Elmer glanced from side to side and added with an attempt at his usual ebullience, "I told'm one o'clock. Said all we was going to have was lunch, and he said he didn't have time to eat but wanted to address the Chamber, that's what he said, address the Chamber at this emergency meeting, so I said fine, after lunch then, one o'clock. But we got a couple of things I want to talk about before he gets here."

Quill, wondering if Hedrick had discovered that the work crew at the mall site was composed of—what should she call them, the formerly incarcerated?—nodded in an abstracted way.

"Mr. Big Bucks couldn't be here in time for lunch?" demanded Marge Schmidt. "I ordered the Blue Plate for 'im, and he'd better fork over the three ninety-eight like the rest of you done. What is he, cash-short paying for all them funerals?"

"Cash-short?" said Mayor Henry with a short, scornful laugh. "Oh, he can afford to pay for lunches he don't eat, I guess. No skin off the Conway nose, no sir. Got money to burn, Hedrick does. That's what he said to me, anyways, last night. By the way, Quill, good party, except for the murder of course.''

There was a murmur of agreement and a general atmosphere of "thanks." John Raintree, on Quill's left, gave her a nudge and a wink.

"Anyways," the mayor resumed with gloomy relish, "he goes and tells me the family motto. 'Just send me the bill, Al,' he says to me. 'That's the Conway motto, just send me the bill.' ''

"Bill for what?" asked Marge with a disapproving air. She repeated, "All them funerals?" Marge, whose build rivaled that of one of the smaller sumo wrestlers, and whose jaw was remarkable for its resemblance to the rockier promontories of Hemlock Gorge, was impressive in disapproval. And as senior partner in her diner and one of the wealthier citizens in town, there was nothing like fiscal improvidence to incur her contempt. "And why'd he call you 'Al?' Your name's Elmer."

"Not 'Al'—'El.' Calls Harvey Bozzel 'Har,' Esther West 'Es.' Probably call you 'Mar.' ''

"I'd like to see him try," said Marge with a notable air of belligerence. Then back to the issue, "Bill for what?"

"I suppose the sheriff'll be 'Sher' or 'Sherry,' '' said Elmer, not looking at Quill. "Cain't see Myles puttin' up with that."

"Quill don't give a hang what Hedrick Conway calls Sheriff McHale," said Marge with all the subtlety of the Sherman tank she resembled. "Least not anymore." Quill, who had wrongly assumed for months that public interest in her love life would cease to be a topic of interest after a suitable period, cut a piece of lemon pie carefully apart with her fork and said nothing. " 'Course maybe Miriam Doncaster was right and she did see you two over to the Hilton in Syracuse last week." Marge stopped in midsentence, her little eyes narrowed to thoughtful slits. "On the other hand, what I shoulda asked is what Miriam was doing in the Hilton Bar and Lounge at one o'clock in the morning on a Saturday, anyways." She leveled her gaze at Quill. "She with Howie Murchison over there, or what?"

Howie, absorbed in a sheaf of papers, looked nearsightedly around at the sound of his name.

"No," said Quill. Both Elmer and Marge looked at her with smug grins. "I mean 'no,' I have no idea who Miriam was with because I wasn't there."

"Oh," said Elmer, somewhat crestfallen. "I wonder who it was, then. Miriam was sure it was Myles. And a redhead like you, Quill. Or maybe she didn't say it was Myles. Maybe she said it was somebody else. Who were you with at the Hilton, Quill?"

"I wasn't at the Hilton with anybody," said Quill between her teeth. Quill, her feelings a little hurt that she'd put her life in jeopardy (well, it *could* have been in jeopardy) wasn't in much of a mood for the mayor's heavy-handed jocularity. She took two deep slow breaths, then said as amiably as she could, "Shouldn't we get the meeting started, Mayor? If you want to discuss the murders with the Chamber of Commerce members before Hedrick gets here, there isn't much time. It's twelve-thirty."

"Murders?" Elmer blinked rapidly. "Oh. That. Myles is takin' care of that, isn't he? No, we got something a little more urgent."

Quill, not sure that anything was more important than solving the murders, said, "If you could tell everyone why Hedrick wants to address the meeting, it might be helpful. Then we can all be prepared."

"Right, right." Elmer lumbered to his feet and whacked the mahogany gavel against its rest. There was none of the usual settling down; the silence was instant and complete. "We got a problem here, folks."

"I'll say." Harvey Bozzel leaned back in his chair, his hands behind his head. "You realize the opening-day ceremonies for the mall are the day after tomorrow. The plans are going well, very well, I want to assure you folks about that, but I'm calling for action, folks, action!" He got to his feet, ready to pace impressively up and down, considered the crowded dimensions of Marge and Betty's dining area, and sat down again. "We've got to put our eyes to the ground and our shoulders to the wheel—"

"Not now, Harve." The mayor mopped the back of his neck with a large checked handkerchief. Quill listened intently, and with some distress, to the ferocity of their conversation.

"Yes, now!" Harvey said in an urgent undertone. "This other can wait! Until afterward. This mall opening is one of my biggest projects." He broke off, a little teary-eyed, and raised his voice. "We've got to put our noses to the grindstone!"

Quill, whose minutes pad was sticking slightly to the Formica top of Marge's table, sketched a hunched-over Harvey with his eye on the ground, his shoulder to the wheel, and his nose to the grindstone.

"Siddown!" the mayor hissed in a violent whisper. "We talked about this alread—I mean, I'm gonna talk to them, okay? So just shut up."

Harvey sank back into his seat, his face red.

The mayor rose, and with uncharacteristic hesitancy said, "Now, folks, I got some good news for you. Harvey and Howie here know all about it already, and I know I got their support. We got a chance to get out of—that is, to sell the shares in the mini-mall to a very good buyer. A very good buyer. One of the top men in his field. But he's put a time limit on the offer which is five o'clock tomorrow. I think we ought to discuss it before that Conway fella gets here."

The room erupted into loud noise, overrode by Esther West, whose correspondence course in Projecting for the Stage had clearly paid off. "Sell our shares in the mall? Why should we do that?"

"I got my reasons," said Elmer. "Now, we don't aim to make a lot on this sale—"

"When you and Howie and Harvey put this deal together, you told us we'd make eight to twelve percent on our investment," Esther said firmly. "Now why in heck should we give it all up?"

Howie Murchison drummed his fingers quietly on the table. Harvey ran his finger around the collar of his neatly pressed striped shirt. Elmer swallowed hard. "I don't know that I care to say, at this point. What I got to say is that we have a tentative offer from Mr. Sakra."

"Now, Howie here and I have looked this tentative offer over good. And it seems pretty decent to me."

Elmer named a figure. The room erupted again. Quill began to sketch a volcano with Chamber members tumbling out of the top and the mayor writhing at the bottom in hot lava.

"That's barely what we put into it!" shouted Norm Pasquale, the high school principal. "We'd make less than four percent on our investment. I could have made more money at Mark Anthony's bank!"

"Three and a half percent more, to be precise," said Mark Anthony Jefferson, vice president of the Hemlock Savings and Loan. "Our savings rates have always been competitive. I hate to say I told you so, but—"

"You're still miffed because we didn't go local for the financing," said Marge. "Go on, Mayor."

"Howie here's horsed up a short summary of what Mr. Sakra's offering," said Elmer. "And I think you want to take a look at it. He's gonna pass this prospectus around." He raised his voice over the tumult. "And you all *put this stuff away* the minute that newspaper fella shows up, you got it? Because that muckraking son of a gun is gonna be here any minute, and if he gets ahold of this, we'll all be in the soup. Now, quiet! Howie? You want to take over here?"

Quill turned to John. "Do you have any idea what's going on?"

John scanned the short paragraph handed to him and waited a moment before replying. "I'm not sure, but if what I think has happened has in fact happened, we'd better sell out."

"But our restaurant!"

"This offer provides for the leasing of retail space. We can keep the restaurant. What's interesting is that the lease is for a very short period of time. Put it together, Quill."

"Put what together?!" Quill demanded. "I don't have the least idea what's going on."

"Shh!" said Marge fiercely. "We got company."

The diner (a former launderette) had two large glass windows and a glass door fronting Main Street. Everyone watched as Hedrick Conway pulled his Cadillac under the PARK HERE AND DIE! sign Marge had installed to keep access to the front door clear. He unfolded himself from behind the wheel, stood on the sidewalk and tugged at his sports coat, then looked up to see the entire Chamber staring at him through the glass. Quill, out of some obscure impulse toward courtesy, felt compelled to wave. He looked behind him, then up and down the street, and raised one pale hand in a half-hearted response. He shambled through the front door and into the diner.

"Have a seat, Conway." Marge extended her foot and hooked an empty chair. Hedrick sat down and hunched forward, his large hands dangling between his knees.

"Sorry about your ma," said Elmer, rather diffidently, "and my condolences on your sister."

"Has the sheriff found out anything yet?" asked Esther. Hedrick opened his mouth and closed it with a mutter.

"Nice car," offered Harvey. "You get it locally?"

Marge rolled her eyes.

"Is there something we can do for you, Mr. Conway?" said Quill. "Do you need any assistance with the, um, observances?"

"You're kind of stuck on funerals, aren't you?" Except for purplish smudges under his eyes, Hedrick looked much the same as he had the day before, and the day before that. Quill began to consider seriously the possibility that Hedrick had killed his own mother and sister, if only because he seemed so unaffected. "I came to cover the Chamber meeting, of course. Wanted to get some comments on this new mall coming into town."

"Opening ceremonies are scheduled for three o'clock, tomorrow," said Harvey briskly. "And I'll be happy to give you a quote on that, Hed."

"*Hed*," thought Quill, bemused. "*Hed?!*"

Harvey spoke with the gravity suitable to the occasion. "Some of the stuff we want to keep off the record until the big day, of course, but I can tell you, in strictest confidence, that we've extended an invitation to Helena Houndswood, the star of stage, screen, and TV—"

"That bitch?" Marge threw her head back and hooted like a diesel truck on a downward slope. "Harve, you got about as much chance of that ol' girl showing her face in this town again as a snowball in hell."

"We've extended an invitation," repeated Harvey stubbornly.

"That's not the mall I was talking about." Hedrick, a light in his eye Quill didn't like at all, flipped slowly through his book. "Acting on information received, this reporter discovered that plans for a new outlet mall on Route fifteen have been finalized this morning."

Marge sat forward with a sudden thump. Her gimlet eyes narrowed.

"Bingo," said John under his breath. "I thought so."

"A new *outlet* mall? Our mall isn't an outlet mall," said Esther. "Our mall's a mini-mall. A collection of small but select shopping opportunities for discriminating shoppers. You said so yourself, Harvey. You mean there's another mall going up? If there's another mall going up . . . There can't be another mall going up. There's no way our little mall could compete with another mall!"

"That's right." Hedrick's loose, rather wet lips stretched in a grin. "Got the list of investors right here."

"So!" the mayor interrupted heartily. "We appreciate this information, Mr. Conway. I expect that we'll be able to read all about it in that fine paper of yours. Harvey, maybe you want to take Mr. Conway outside and give him a few—"

"Wait just a goddamned minute." Marge folded her arms underneath her substantial bosom. "Who's on that investment list, Conway?"

"You'll read all about it in the next issue of the *Trumpet!* This reporter can't divulge his sources. You're not going to catch me giving away a scoop, like some." His eye drifted toward Elmer and away again. "So what's your comment on this new mall, Mayor?"

"I'd absolutely have to study this situation to see how it affects the people of this good town before I could commit myself," said the mayor. "But I can tell you this. Any new enterprise that brings new faces and taxes to our fine village is to be welcomed. Unless, of course, it adversely affects jobs and raises taxes in the area. Which it won't. I don't think. But if it does, I'm against it."

" 'Mayor Sees New Mall as Threat,' " Hedrick spoke as

he wrote. "Murchison? What about you? You lawyers always have something to say."

"No comment," said Howie tightly.

" 'Town Justice Invokes the Fifth.' "

"Now, wait just a goddamned minute, Conway!"

"Bozzel? You've anything to say?"

"I think we'd do better to take a meeting over at your place, Hed. Folks, if you'll just excuse us, we'll go off-line with this." Harvey placed a hand on Hedrick's shoulder and propelled him to the front door. Hedrick turned to face them once before they left. Quill's pen, busy with her cartoon drawings, stilled. She'd never seen such malevolence on a human face before.

"Jeez," said Meg. She, Quill, and Georgia were eating a late supper in the dining room. The room was dominated by floor-to-ceiling mullioned windows looking out over the Falls, and a huge cherry sideboard along the long wall facing the foyer entrance. Quill had taken a chance with the color scheme; the wallpaper border was cherry maroon mixed with sunshine yellow and celadon green; the carpet was a soft, light mauve; the tablecloths a deep pink. It shouldn't have worked, but it did. Meg sighed and swallowed a bite of lemon chicken. "So it's not a toxic waste dump, but it's a waste. There's no way our poor little mall can survive the competition."

"Mr. Sakura's offer isn't generous, but it's fair," said Quill. "At least that's what John says. And Meg, no one can compete with your cooking. You've made the Inn a success, and the boutique will be a success, too, no matter where it is."

They'd turned more than forty walk-ins away for dinner; curiosity seekers, Quill suspected, since there was a discreet sign, plainly lettered, on the front door that read, KITCHEN UNDERGOING REMODELING—PLEASE COME AGAIN, a feat of tactful prose by Georgia. "So the mayor let the cat out of the bag. Then what happened?"

"Elmer called a breakfast meeting of the investors for tomorrow morning, to give everyone a chance to go over the prospectus. Then he and Howie hustled out of there."

"Did you get a chance to talk this over with John?"

"Meg, the poor guy's going crazy getting the boutique restaurant ready to open. We've all been too busy to even think about this, this afternoon."

"There must be something I can do to help," said Georgia. "I mean, this is a big deal for you guys, a new venture."

"Quill is actually very well organized." Meg smiled at her sister. "Sorry, that sounded as though people don't expect you to be organized, but if you weren't, how would you do all that has to be done to run the Inn? Actually, all the upfront stuff was planned months ago, Georgia. We issued invitations to the opening in early June, got a good acceptance rate, ordered flowers, china, equipment, prepared the staff, all that stuff well in advance. Making sure that everything is delivered on time and put in place is something John does—which is why he's busy now and we're not. At least, not more than usual, when my poor kitchen's closed because of your boyfriend."

"Myles is not my boyfriend. People don't have boyfriends anymore."

"Then what do they have?"

"An insignificant other?" Georgia flung both her hands out. "Sorry. Sorry. Give me another glass of that super white wine, and I won't be rude, I swear."

"Because your good friend and buddy, then, closed my *kitchen*! Anyhow, all we can do now about the opening is worry, and there's absolutely no use in doing that. What we can worry about are these murders. Quill, do you think Eugene was serious? That the work crew at the mall is made up of . . . of . . ."

"The recently incarcerated?" Quill suggested, rather pleased with the political correctness of this phrase. "It sounded like the truth to me."

"New evidence, then." Meg put her elbows on the table with a smug air. "And Georgia, you've been grinning like a cat in cream since we started dinner. You've got something, too, don't you?"

"You don't think it could be the chicken marinated in plum sauce?"

Meg smiled. "Could be."

"Or the second bottle of wine?"

Meg burped. "Nope."

"Well, you're right. I've got something. Something big. But I want to save it. Let's see what you guys have, first, then we'll see how my stuff fits in."

"Okay by me." Meg took a healthy swig of her wine and began to tick off each point on a finger. "We have two murders, linked by the victims' familial and professional relationship."

"Gawd," Georgia interrupted, "You're pretty good at this. That was so . . ."

"Succinct?" said Quill. "Direct? Unambiguous? You ought to see her cook." She drained her glass.

"The murders occurred a month after the Conways moved into town and announced their intention of taking over the *Gazette*. Louisa's murder occurred on the third day of the publication of the first issue of the *Trumpet!*, Carlyle's on the very day of the second issue of the *Trumpet!*"

"Maybe the murderer hadn't seen it until Thursday?" Georgia suggested.

"Wait," said Meg. "We're simply listing facts, here. We'll extrapolate later."

"Then I definitely need another helping of this fantastic dessert. And another glass of wine."

"It's new," said Meg, momentarily diverted. "Strawberries, rhubarb, and raspberry tart. You're the first to try it."

"It's fantastic." She helped herself to a third tart from the dish in front of them. "Okay, the engine's stoked. What's second?"

"Louisa was killed from a blow to the head with the classic blunt instrument."

"How blunt is a hammer, anyway?" Quill mused, aware that four glasses of the Italian white she'd drunk were making her extremely mellow. "Some hammers aren't blunt at all. A tack hammer, for example."

"Never mind. Anyway, her body was dumped in the river, presumably—and I'll allow myself a little extrapolation here—by someone *not* familiar with Hemlock Falls."

"Not familiar?" echoed Georgia. "Why do you say that?"

"Because anyone from around here knows the current in the river. We all swim in it, or if we don't swim in it, we at least understand how it flows. Anyone from Hemlock Falls . . ."

"You're repeating yourself," reproved Quill, and hiccuped.

". . . would know if you tossed a corpse in the river, it wouldn't be carried away by the water's flow. It'd stick around. We've got a lazy river in these parts."

"Hmm," said Quill, "I hadn't thought of it, but you could be right."

"Could be? I am," said Meg with innocent satisfaction, "rarely wrong. When was the last time I was wrong, Quillie?"

"September first, 1993," Quill replied promptly.

"September . . . oh! Ha-Ha."

"What?" Georgia demanded.

"An ill-fated foray into blintzes. On September second, I repented."

"But, Meg, what if the murderer didn't care if the body was discovered?" asked Georgia.

"All murderers care if the corpse is discovered."

Quill offered the fact that Carlyle Conway's death rather negated that.

"In this instance," said Meg, "the murderer clearly wanted to plant the murder on me." She brooded for a moment. "And it may come to that."

"Meg, for heaven's sake. You haven't heard from Andy yet. We don't even know—"

"Wait. I haven't finished my succinct, direct, and unambiguous summary of the facts." Meg swallowed her third glass of Pinot Grigio with a flourish and poured a fourth. Quill peered at her rather dubiously. "When I, with all that time on my hands this afternoon because Evil Forces have closed my kitchen . . . evil forces . . ." Quill took the glass from Meg's hand, got up, and placed it on the sideboard, then poured her a cup of coffee. Meg gave her a sunny smile, got up, retrieved her wine, and sipped it. "I wrote down who was at the mini-mall site. Then I wrote down who was near Carlyle at the party, and I compared the two." She hiccuped, and articulated carefully, "I excepted, of course, ourselves and the citizens of Hemlock Falls. And here it is." She produced the list with a flourish from her shorts pocket and spread it on the table.

"Sakura Toshiro, Mr. Motoyama, Marcos DeMarco, Hedrick Conway, Axminster Stoker, Jerzey Paulovich," Quill read.

Georgia frowned. "The suspect list is wider than that. Even buying the theory that no one from the Falls would throw a body in the river, which I guess I do, there's the rest of the Kiplings, including me, not to mention the criminal construction crew. All of us were around when the murders occurred."

"The recently incarcerated have paid their debt to society," said Meg mournfully. "And besides, the only one from the site in both places was Marco DeMarco."

"He wasn't at the site," said Quill. "I told you that. He was in San Francisco. I think you've had a little too much wine." She considered this. "I think I've had a little too much wine."

"Deee-Marco in San Francisco? Oh, dang." Meg frowned, then brightened. "He could have had an agent?"

"True. But then, so could have any number of the guests at the party. And that includes the forty-eight or so current residents of the Inn."

"But none of them were near Carlyle on the fatal night, except DeMarco," said Meg. "And Andy told me that whatever it was that she ate, symptoms would have appeared within seconds. Seconds. Which means that it had to be someone in that circle of guys around her."

"Motive," said Georgia. "Since we're being succinct, direct, and unambiguous, let's talk about motive. Why would any of these six want to kill Louisa and Carlyle?"

"DeMarco might want to keep everyone from knowing that there were ex-cons at the site," said Quill. "But I doubt it. I mean, who would care?"

"Lots of people, I should think," said Meg, on whom the wine appeared to be having a sentimental effect.

"You're such a nice liberal, Quill, but it obscures your mind."

"Obscures my *mind*?"

"Think about it. How would Mrs. Elmer Henry feel if she knew that the 'formerly incarcerated' were loose and running around Hemlock Falls? What about Esther West, bless her heart? Or any of the ladies in the Society for the Advancement of Jell-O Architecture, for that matter?"

"Or even us, if you want to be fair about it," said Quill wryly. "Wouldn't be all that good for the reputation of the Inn, would it?"

"Probably not," Georgia agreed. "It would certainly distress Miss Kent."

"So we should add ourselves to the suspect list, Meg."

"Except that *we* know that a body thrown in the . . ."

"Okay, okay. Drink your coffee."

"Motive," said Georgia, again, with firmness.

"Obviously we are clueless as to motive, at this point"—Meg scowled—"which brings me to the second reason we should discount the murderer being from Hemlock Falls. If Elmer, Harvey, and Howie knew about the discount mall going up on Route fifteen—"

"We don't know that for certain, do we?" Quill protested. "I mean, not only do I have a hard time believing any one of those three would actually kill somebody, I can't think that they'd knowingly—"

"Screw their friends?" interrupted Georgia cynically. "C'mon, honey. You know what people are like where money's involved."

"No, I don't," said Quill, with unaccustomed firmness. "I know what some people are like over money, but not the mayor. And not Howie. DeMarco told me today that Howie's a fine lawyer, and there's a man that should know. Howie could have gone to a big city practice any time these past years, but he didn't. He chose to stay here."

"Here," echoed Meg.

"Sentimentality," said Georgia, attempting the word twice, "is a surefire way to torpedo an investigation, in my view." She laid her fork on her plate. "What about this Harvey Bee. No. Bossy. No. Bozzel?"

"Harvey . . ." began Quill.

"Harvey," said Meg.

They looked at each other.

"Harvey," said Meg, again, "could very easily be tempted by cash. But he has such a loose lip that everyone would know about it within days. I mean, he's in advertising, for goodness' sake."

"That's true of Elmer, too," said Quill. "He's a small-town politician. Neither one of them could keep a secret to save their little souls."

"Aha," said Georgia. "Now we're getting somewhere." She hitched herself forward. "I've listened to you talk about the people in the Falls for a couple of days now. And I've seen how you all relate to each other. I like it, by the way, which is one reason why I very well may decide to settle here, but that's another story. Anyway, let's look at motive like this. The discount mall project must have been in the works for how long—several months?"

"It took almost a year to get the mini-mall project up and rolling," said Quill.

"What was the period of time from project approval to the pros-pec-tus? The offer to invest?"

"Eight months or so?"

"And from the pros-what's-it to the raising of the actual money?"

"Not very long at all," said Meg. "Howie had a lot of people he wanted to approach. I'd say it took a couple of weeks."

"So it's likely that the offer for investment in the discount mall has been out—what—two weeks? Three?"

"About the same time that the Conways took over the *Gazette* and turned it into the *Trumpet!*" said Quill slowly.

"But—" Meg stopped herself. "Nothing. Never mind. I think I've had too much wine. Go on, Georgia."

"I can't. I was just using deductive reasoning."

All three of them found this incredibly funny. Bent over with laughter, Meg shoved her chair back, went to the coffee stand, and brought back the second bottle of wine. Quill split it between the three glasses.

"Oh, dear." Meg wiped her eye with her sleeve. "So.

Are you ready to spill the beans?''

"You mean the grape?''

"I mean the sushi! Oh! God! That was awful, wasn't it?'' Meg covered her mouth and rolled her eyes.

Quill coughed and tried to sober up. "What Meg wants to know is . . . what did your bankers tell you about the Conways?''

"A-hum!'' Georgia's laughter shook the small table, rattling the glasses. "Ladies. Sit back. Listen up. Get this.'' She leaned forward and said in the loudest whisper Quill had ever heard, "Now that his ma and his sister have bought the farm—''

"Kicked the bucket,'' improvised Meg.

"Fell off the roof!'' said Quill.

"Fell off the roof?'' Meg swayed in her chair. "Quill, what kind of metaphor is that?''

"Listen, ladies!'' Georgia stamped her foot. It made an impressive thump. "Mr. Conway is the sole inheritor of—''

"Half a billion?'' Meg sat up straight.

"The sole inheritor of . . . nothing! He's broke!''

"That sorry piece of liver pâté?!'' shouted Meg.

"That sausage!'' cried Quill.

"That pork *roast* . . . !''

"I like pork roast!'' Georgia said. "Don't make him a pork roast!''

". . . is broke?! He has no motive? Aagh! I can't stand it!''

"Oh, dear.'' Quill balled her napkin and wiped each eye in turn. "This isn't funny. This just isn't funny. What about Louisa's supposedly rich husband, Georgia? I thought he died and left her tons.''

"If Louisa had it, it's gone now.'' Georgia looked smug. "I found out something else, too. Hedrick and Carlyle are the offspring of a first marriage, the origins of which, my attorney tells me, are lost in the mists of time. Louisa herself has a bit of a checkered past. One of those women that turns up in the pages of *Town & Country* magazine in the background at parties which are definitely on the fringe, or shows up in the racing news at the Saratoga sales in August, hanging on the arm of an ersatz Italian prince. Mr. Conway senior—after a marriage of some three years to our Louisa—died under very suspicious circumstances at his home in Boca Raton."

"What sort of suspicious circumstances?"

Georgia looked smug. "Food poisoning. From an unidentified neurotoxin. In the *hors d'oeuvres*."

Quill opened her mouth and closed it. The wine suddenly seemed an encumbrance.

Meg ran both hands through her hair. "So. Hedrick's a real suspect, Georgia. What do you think we should do next?"

"With a little bit of luck, I think we can nail him the day after tomorrow. At the opening-day ceremonies for the mini-mall."

"How?" Meg's breath was soft and whiny. Quill pushed her gently back into her seat.

"Ssst! Sit back and look innocent." Georgia rearranged her draperies around her ample shoulders and waved to someone behind Quill. "Whooee! Here we are!"

"Innocent? I'm not guilty," muttered Meg. "Who said I was guilty?"

Quill turned in her seat. "Myles!" She flushed, painfully, the warmth rising from her neck to her hairline. Andy Bishop, Hemlock Falls's best (and only) internist, was right behind him. Myles crossed the soft carpet noiselessly, his eyes casual; Quill knew that twenty-four hours from now, he would be able to give a complete description of what he saw, down to the number of wine bottles and the color of Georgia's hair bow.

"We've got some information on what killed Carlyle Conway," he said. "May I join you?"

CHAPTER 12

"Did I do it?" asked Meg.

Andy pulled a chair next to her and sat down. He was just above medium height, with a sinewy jogger's body. He'd recently taken to wearing glasses; the light from the chandelier reflected off the lenses, and Quill was unable to read his expression. He put his arm around Meg's shoulder. "I told you from the beginning you didn't do it."

Myles's glance flickered over the wineglass. "No. You didn't. It wasn't the sushi."

"Neurobenzine," said Quill. "I knew it!" She exchanged significant looks with Georgia.

"Neurobenzine?" Andy turned in surprise. "Where'd the heck did you get that idea?"

"Just a thought," said Quill airily. "I was reading up on neurotoxins the other day"—she ignored Georgia's stifled snort of laughter—"and thought perhaps that could have been it. You know—it's used in printing. Like newspapers."

"Forty years ago it may have been," said Andy. He pushed his glasses into place with a forefinger. "But Carlyle Conway didn't die of it, that's for sure. It's highly corrosive. If she'd gotten that on her breasts, I would have seen it right away. That would have been an even more unpleasant death than the one she suffered."

"Not neurobenzine?" Two thoughts flashed through Quill's mind: the first, disappointment that a perfectly good number-one suspect seemed to have been moved down the list to number two or three; the second, that she didn't feel quite as guilty about not turning the goods book over to Myles right away. "What was it then?"

Myles didn't say anything for a moment.

"You don't mind?" asked Andy, with raised brows. "It was the neurotoxin derived from fugu, Meg, but—"

"Shit!" Meg turned pale.

Andy covered her hands with his. "But it wasn't in the sushi, Meg. It was between her breasts."

"Between her breasts?!"

Andy nodded. "It'd been wiped on."

"Wiped on! Are you serious?"

"That's what it looks like."

"But how?" The taut, unhappy look had vanished from Meg's face.

"Someone wearing surgical gloves is my guess. I'm not sure. It's ingenious, I have to admit."

"Good grief," said Quill. "It must have been Hedrick!"

"Oh?" Myles drew a chair up beside Quill and sank easily into it.

"He's the only one who knew her. He told me she had this party trick, he called it. She'd flip an hors d'ouevre in the air and let it fall between her breasts, then take it out and flip it into her mouth." She looked at Myles. "Is that a sexy sort of thing to do?"

"Under the right circumstances." A grin flickered behind his eyes. "But the killer didn't necessarily have to count on the party trick. Andy's checking with a toxicologist in San Francisco to determine the interval for the absorption rate. We don't have a good idea of when the first symptoms appeared. We were hoping you could help. I take it you were in the kitchen, Meg. So Quill—do you remember precisely when you saw her arrive?"

"Yes. I do. It was just before seven o'clock. I was standing with you, Georgia, and the Kiplings. She came in with Hedrick."

"Did you notice any unsteadiness in her gait?" asked Andy. "Did she seem unstable?"

Georgia and Quill looked at each other at precisely the same moment. Georgia went *ahum!* to conceal a laugh.

"Look, sweetie," she said to Myles. "The woman was wearing stiletto heels and swinging that pair of hooters like the ladies my youngest nephew used to call street sweepers. Of *course* she had an unsteady gait."

"You went over to greet her, then?"

"I went to the little girl's room. By the time I'd gotten out of there, the trouble'd started. I have to say, it was one of the worst sights I've ever had in front of me. And there wasn't a damn thing I could do to help the poor woman." Quill squeezed her hand sympathetically. "But you, Quill, went over to the bar to say hi, right?"

"Yes. But she seemed perfectly fine to me. Normal. I'd only met her once before."

"Do you recall anything unusual at all?" asked Andy.

"What was unusual was that either Hedrick or his sister was there at all," said Meg. "I mean, good grief, their mother had been brutally murdered the day before, and the two of them invite themselves to our party and show up ready to have a whee of a good time. That's what I think is unusual. Did you talk to the Horrible Hedrick? What did he say, Myles?"

"I didn't ask him why he had the gracelessness to attend a party within a day of their mother's death. They're living in the apartment over the newspaper offices, and they left there at about six-fifty. It took them a few minutes to come up the drive. Hedrick let Carlyle off at the entrance while he parked the car around back. She didn't go through the foyer, apparently, but walked around the side of the Inn and entered the patio through the gardens. Which is odd. It's a longer route. We're checking to see if she met anyone on her way in. And when she got to the bar, she said the champagne was flat."

"It wasn't," said Quill indignantly.

"Which may have been the first indication that she was in trouble."

"The symptoms of fugu poisoning are a diminution in the sense of taste, numb lips, convulsions, paralysis, followed by death," said Andy. "Eyewitness accounts, including yours, Quill, and Myles himself, indicate that she may have been wiped with the poison on her way into the

Inn. It's possible that she was exposed to it earlier, but
Hedrick claims the two of them spent an hour getting ready
for the party—and I know that the interval between expo-
sure and symptoms would have been less than that, even
with the poison absorbed through the skin of the breast
initially.''

"Who could have access to such a thing?" asked Georgia. "I mean, the obvious choice is the Sakuras. It's a Japanese poison that comes from Japan."

Myles grunted.

"But then the question is why? They hadn't met her
before, had they?"

"I don't know that geography is as important as knowl-
edge of the drug itself," said Myles. "Although it's certainly relevant. The fish is available in certain stores in San
Francisco, Los Angeles, and, of course, overseas."

"So you're looking for a sophisticated world traveler,"
said Georgia. "All of the Kiplings are well-traveled. Including me."

"Marco DeMarco had just come back from San Francisco," said Quill. "He told me so himself."

"And poor old Axminster Stoker toured the country a
lot before he settled down with us," said Meg. "I know
'Frisco and L.A. were on his itinerary."

"So we're no closer to a solution," said Quill, frustrated.
"I still vote for Hedrick. Georgia, did your lawyers find
out what happened to all that money Louisa was supposed
to have? I mean, he's the likeliest suspect here."

"Your lawyers?" asked Myles politely. "I take it you
all have been pursuing inquiries on your own?"

"Sort of," said Meg.

"In a way," said Georgia.

"Nothing major," said Quill.

Myles looked stern.

"Jeez." Meg ran her hands through her hair and left it
sticking up in spikes over her ears. "Let me get you guys
some fugu-free coffee."

"Decaf for you, kiddo," Andy ordered. Meg nodded
meekly.

Quill met Georgia's large brown eyes. "Yes, *sir, doctor sir!*" Georgia muttered.

"What?" said Meg.

"Nothing," said Quill. "We're just amazed to see you in love . . ."

". . . in thrall," Georgia contributed.

". . . to the doc, that's all."

"Shut up," said Meg amiably, bringing down two fresh cups from the sideboard, and hesitating over the dessert plates. "You guys want tarts? There's more than enough for everyone. I'm going to have another."

Andy raised his eyebrows and patted his flat stomach. Meg looked dubiously at her own slim middle, then left the dessert plates on the shelf.

"*Oof! Hah!*" trumpeted Georgia, suddenly, striking the wineglass with a fork. "*Oog Hah! (clink)*"

"What the heck, Gee?" Meg, caught between a scowl and a laugh, sat next to Andy and grabbed his hand.

"Thaaat's the sound of the meeen, working on the ch-a-a-ain, gay-ang-ang!" sang Georgia, in a surprisingly lovely (and loud) alto. "That's the so-oo-u-nd of the me-en working on the chain. Gang."

"Jeez! Is that supposed to be some sort of political comment?"

"Not *some* sort. A *direct* sort, honey. You want to eat, eat."

Meg grabbed a fork and speared a tart from the plate. "There. Solidarity forever."

"Yes!" Georgia shot her fist in the air.

"About those lawyers, Mrs. Hardwicke," said Myles, a hint of impatience in his voice.

"My Gawd, look at the time! It's bed for me." Georgia winked at Quill. "Coward that I am, I don't want to stick around and be interrogated by your sheriff. You tell him. That's the way Nero Wolfe works, isn't it? He had Archie cooperate with Lieutenant Cramer. She'll cooperate." She pinched Myles's cheek and trundled out of the dining room, swaying like a two-wheeled cart with a heavy load.

"Me, too," said Meg. Andy got up and held her chair. She looked up at him with a smile that sent a pang through

Quill. "See you at breakfast, sis."

After they left, the silence in the dining room was profound.

"Andy and Meg seem to be getting along."

"Yes." Quill folded her napkin into a neat triangle. "What do you think of Georgia?"

He smiled.

"Myles, I want to apologize for last night."

"I owe you an apology for losing my temper."

"You had reason, I suppose." Quill's throat was full. Cautiously, as if she were very careful about it, he wouldn't see, she unfolded the napkin and pressed it under each eye in turn.

"I've been thinking. What would you say if we gave us another year or so. Let things go on the way they were before I became"—he stopped, searching for the right word—"insistent."

"Do you mean it?"

"I mean it."

"The, um, business of children? That's important to you."

"You're important to me."

Quill bit her lips hard and concentrated on the pile of crumbs Georgia had left beside her plate, pushing them into a pyramid with her finger. "Okay," she said finally.

"Okay."

Neither of them spoke for a moment.

"I had to go to Ithaca today to pick up the results on the autopsy. I stopped at the art store. Here. I brought you this." He reached into the breast pocket of his sports coat and brought out a camel's hair artist brush with an ebony handle. It was an elegant one that Quill had longed for, and never had the heart to purchase. "You told me it'd be a waste, not to use a brush like that."

"Oh, yes. It would." She took it. The curve in the center fit between her thumb and forefinger with a feeling of much-loved music.

"I talked to Ken Sakura today." Quill stared at him. Myles, who'd never, in all the time she'd known him, failed to meet her look directly, lowered his eyes. "He teaches at

Cornell. He agreed to see if he could bypass some paper-work and let me audit a couple of classes.''

"Art appreciation?" she said, astounded. "But, Myles, you need to take all kinds of courses before you get to art appreciation."

"Art history, first. I told him I wanted to understand how you fit in the mainstream of current painters. He started to tell me . . .''

"He did? What'd he say?"

". . . and I stopped him. I wanted to discover that myself. And I want to understand. So that the next time you use this"—he touched the ebony-handled brush gently—" I could say, 'yes' or 'no' instead of—what was the jargon term I used before? You know, that specialized, in-the-know artists and critics-only language that you artists use?''

"Nice?"

"Nice. That was it. Nice. I swear to you, Quill, I will never again tell you that a piece of work you've done is nice."

"Oh, Myles." Quill shook her head. "That's so nice of you, Myles. It's so *nice!*"

"Idiot," said Myles. "Let's go to bed."

Quill woke to the sunlight crossing her muslin sheets, and the sound of Myles whistling in the shower. She stretched. The bedside clock said eight-thirty. The paint-brush lay on the nightstand, sunlight catching the swell of the ebony handle. She sat up and took it in her hand. She swung out of bed and walked barefoot to the French doors overlooking the herb garden.

Could she do all three? Art? The Inn? Myles and a family?

She closed her eyes, and the Inn rose before her mind's eye in all its sprawling, untidy, hodgepodge glory. Quill had a set of photographs taken in the days when the Inn had been a way station on the Underground Railroad. Even in faded brown and white, the copper roof, dark shingles, and fieldstone patios were impressive among the rich gardens. They would be that way for another three hundred years. And the guests would continue to come, like Georgia Hardwicke, who'd cheerfully abandoned the Kiplings, for weeks at a time, and even, Quill thought, like Axminster Stoker, who like English gentlemen of the past century, had taken rooms and lived in hotels for the rest of their lives.

The Inn had healed Meg, at a time when Quill thought her sister would never recover from the grief. And Quill had found a refuge, too, at a time when her art, quick to bloom, had become repetitive and stale.

She felt, rather than heard, Myles come across the carpet.

"Are you contemplating the greatness of your work?" His voice was teasing.

"More like Ozymandias," said Quill ruefully. "It's all changing, Myles, isn't it? Meg's recovered from Colin's death, and in love again. That's part of what you're willing to wait for, isn't it? She'll marry Andy, and things will change for me."

"I'm sure there's an appropriate quote about how the more things change the more they remain the same, but I can't think of it."

"You've never thought about giving up police work and maybe becoming an Innkeeper?" Even as she said it, she knew it was wrong. She turned to face him. "Wash that from your mind. Erase it. We're equal."

"But separate." He stood several feet away and made no move to touch her. "Would you want me to paint?"

"Of course I would!"

"Think about it, Quill. Would you want me to paint? Can any relationship stand the world judging the two of us on exactly the same ground?"

"It's not a competition, Myles."

"*Competition* is the wrong word. It's a matter of the part of your gut that's you. Not me. Not someone else. You."

A breeze stirred the muslin drapes at the window. She heard the familiar slide-stump that meant Doreen was hauling the paper cans out to the burn shed. A scent of crushed thyme came to her.

"I faithfully promise to shoot you, if you ever decide to paint. Now, Myles, about this investigation. Oh, my lord."

She clapped her hand over her mouth. "That's why! All these years! You haven't wanted me to help! I never realized."

"Jesus Christ, Quill. The reason I don't want you involved is because it's usually dangerous, and I don't want my attention diverted from solving a problem. The other reason I don't want you involved is because you might inadvertently withhold evidence . . ."

Quill, with a guilty start, recalled the copy of the goods book in the office safe.

". . . or worse yet, destroy it. No, dear heart, I am not worried about you supplanting me as sheriff."

He meant it. "Why?" asked Quill. "Is it because I'm a lousy detective?"

"Nope. Actually, between the two of you, you and your sister aren't bad. Dave's a good deputy, but he doesn't have anywhere near your intuition about people, or your intelligence, for that matter. All good investigation relies on teamwork. I don't want you involved, Quill, because you don't have any training, and I don't want you hurt."

"I can take care of myself. And I could learn. Will you teach me, then?"

"Within the limits allowed by law, I might. And if you promise to stay away from the rough stuff, absolutely."

"Myles, you're a fogey. You're forty-six years old and the sexiest man I've ever met, but you're a fogey."

"Right. Now." He sat down on the bed and began to pull on his socks. His chest was tanned, and the muscles rippled under the dark skin. "First rule is turn it over."

"Turn what over?"

"Whatever it is that you've got. Georgia found out something, didn't she? I want to hear it. And if there's anything else, I want that, too."

Quill went to her bureau drawer and pulled out the goods book.

"We found it yesterday morning."

He thumbed through it and set it aside.

"You aren't angry?"

"Next."

"Myles, there are all kinds of clues in there—"

"Hedrick Conway didn't do it. What else have you got?"

"Hedrick is the best suspect we've got!" Quill summarized the results of Georgia's inquiries, ending with Georgia's discovery of the death of Hedrick's stepfather.

"The Conway case? Can't say as it rings any sort of bell at all." Myles stood up to put his trousers on. Quill watched him with what she recognized as doting admiration. "I can check with a few of the guys I know in Florida. She's sure there was an indictment? A trial? Does Hedrick have a record? Damn. I'm slipping. I should have checked it myself."

"She didn't say there was a trial, no. Myles, do you think it's Hedrick? It has to be Hedrick. He's positively inhuman about the deaths of his family. I mean, he hasn't said a word!"

"There could be a very good reason for that. And you may have given it to me just now. No, I don't think Hedrick killed his mother and his sister. But the business about his stepfather is a loose end. And I'll tie it up today."

"But Hedrick must be the only one with a motive. And what happened to all that money! Maybe there wasn't any money. Nothing else makes any sense, does it? I mean, the scandal behind the mini-mall turns out to be that a significant competitor is going up a few miles away. Although I don't know for sure, it's pretty obvious that Elmer, Howie, and Harvey Bozzel have all invested money in it . . . although where Harvey gets that kind of money is anybody's guess."

"Say that again?"

"The fact that a new mall is going up isn't a motive for murder. It's maybe a motive for Elmer not getting reelected if people find out he he—"

"No. About Harvey."

"Well, where would Harvey get the money to invest in the new mall? He didn't have enough to buy shares in our mall, remember?"

"Damn. I'm losing my grip." He buckled his belt thoughtfully, then grinned. "It's your fault, Quill. I should have picked that up, too."

"Were you very depressed after we broke up?" she asked shyly.

"Guess so."

"Meg said I was horrible. Doreen said I was horrible. Oh, Myles. I've been such a jerk! Look at me! I never cry! And here I am, a leaky faucet."

"Ssh. Quiet." He came over. Held her. Kissed the top of her head. "It's over. The tough part. We'll just have to be careful from now on. Now, is there anything else?"

Quill, who was beginning to think she should decide to carry a handkerchief as a permanent accessory, rubbed her face on the sheet. "Just a few more things. You know that the reason Marco DeMarco has been so secretive is that his work crews are all ex-convicts."

"Yep. Next."

"You knew that?"

"I've known it for a while. Had a talk with DeMarco soon after he started the project."

"And you never told me!"

"I would have, except for a couple of things. First, you would have been down at the site feeding them soup and making sure that nobody was discriminating against their rights."

"Myles!"

"Second, I didn't want anyone in town deciding that the usual crimes and misdemeanors in a place like the Falls were the fault of DeMarco's work crew. I've got the records of all the men he's had working for him, and I've kept an eye out."

"I wouldn't have said a word."

"Your behavior would have said a lot. And finally, dear heart, for the past four months we haven't exactly been communicating."

"Oh. That's true." She bit her finger. "So if it isn't Hedrick, and it isn't anyone in town because all the secrets about the mini-mall seem to be secrets that no one would murder for, then who is it? I'm still betting on Hedrick. Unless, Myles, is it someone on the construction crew? With a grudge against the Conways?"

"It's possible."

"Who *is* your chief suspect, then!?"

"There are five people I want to keep my eye on in particular. Paulovich, Fairbanks, Motoyama, and De-Marco. I'd like you to talk to your employees and see if any one of those men was seen walking with Carlyle Conway the night of the murder. Be discreet. Be quiet. But be complete."

"That's four names you gave me. Who's the fifth?"

"Axminster Stoker."

"Axminster Stoker?! The man couldn't hurt a fly. If anything, he's in danger of being knocked off himself, by Doreen. I can't believe he killed two people he's never even met!"

"How do you know he's never met them? And why do you think he's incapable of murder? Where does your opinion come from? It's based on what evidence? That you like him? That you find him inoffensive? Do I need to tell you that some of our worst murderers have been quiet, inoffensive people who the neighbors say could never have hurt a fly?"

"No. No. You're right. I'm sorry. Just the facts, ma'am, all right? So I'll include Mr. Stoker. You want me to question them?"

"No, dammit. I don't want you confronting a potential killer. I want you to talk to the staff. See who could have bumped into Carlyle, literally, since Andy's sure that someone put on a surgical glove and wiped the poison between her breasts a few minutes before she tried the trick with the sushi."

"Why do you suspect these five?"

"Stoker worked for the pharmaceutical company that Conway's fortune came from."

"He didn't!"

"It's how he found out about the Inn. You're attached to the Golden Pillars Travel Company, right? And they offer packaged tours to corporations; yours is one of them. When Stoker decided to retire, he very efficiently went through the list of vacation spots the company offered its employees. He's an efficient man."

"He never indicated in any way that he'd met any of the Conways before!"

"I doubt that he knew the Conway women, or Hedrick himself. The company's huge, and people like Stoker never met the principal stockholders. But it's a lead, and we've got damn few leads at this point."

"And DeMarco?"

Myles wandered into her kitchen and began to make coffee. "Now, there's a guy who might knock a couple of people off as a warning to Hedrick not to print something about the mall. That's a strong possibility. And I don't want you going near him, understand?"

"I'm far readier to believe that DeMarco is involved than Axminster."

Myles flipped the coffeemaker on. "I can't argue with that. But the second rule about an investigation, Quill, is to follow every lead. Sometimes the trail starts with the tip of a fingernail. As a matter of fact, there was a murder solved years ago that began with the tip of a finger, literally."

"Ugh! So DeMarco's a strong contender."

"The strongest to date."

"And Mr. Paulovich?"

"Mr. Paulovich knows something he's not telling me. It's no more than that. There could be a number of reasons for it. But I don't like it. He's lying about it, whatever it is, and until I find out, he's on the list."

"What about Lyle Fairbanks?"

Myles removed the coffeepot from the hot plate, and stuck his cup under the filter before the pot was full. "Do you want some of this?"

"I'll wait a bit, thanks. Lyle Fairbanks?"

"He's not a suspect as much as he is a potential source. And unlike those others you can talk to him directly. Just be discreet and unobvious. I want a list of where the Kiplings have been in the last three years, and the dates when each of the members joined. We'll cross-match that with similar information from Hedrick, and from DeMarco. See if I can come up with some idea of when their paths crossed." He gulped the coffee. "That's it."

"Mr. Motoyama?"

"I'll handle him."

"But I could talk to Ken."

"Exactly." He smiled. "Even my tolerance has its limits. Quill. I want you to call me as soon as you get anything. And listen, you're to keep this to yourself, understand? It's important. Do you promise?"

"I promise. But, Myles—"

"I've got to go." He kissed her. "Dinner tonight?"

"Yes. Wait. Myles. Will the kitchen be open?"

"Up to Andy. He's in charge of forensics. I'm through with it."

"If it's open, I'll meet you at the usual time. I'll be busy."

"Ten-thirty, then, unless I hear from you." The door closed behind him.

Quill went downstairs to find that the kitchen was open and the dining room empty, and Meg crossly banging her copper pots with a wooden ladle.

"What's wrong?"

"They moved all my *stuff*! Poking around in here!" She slammed the Cuisinart to one side of the butcher block counter and glowered. "And we're open tonight and two of the *sous* chefs called in with bogus excuses, and nobody who's supposed to be here for the morning shift has shown up, so I'm going to be short-staffed on top of everything else! *Go away!*"

"Don't you want to hear about Myles?"

"Any fool could have predicted that last night," said Meg loftily.

"Myles doesn't think Hedrick did it."

"So?"

"So he's not upset about the goods book. As a matter of fact"—Quill pulled at her lower lip—"he didn't seem to think much of my investigative efforts at all. He assigned me to the sort of thing he'd assign a junior investigator."

"Go investigate where my underchefs are, will you? I can't cook tonight without them."

"I'm sure they'll turn up."

"If you're so sure, then *find them!*"

"You got it, sis," said Quill with a fair imitation of

Humphrey Bogart. She went through the swinging doors into the dining room, and from there to the foyer. It was going to be a good day. She could feel it. Meg in that kind of mood always cooked superbly. People were starting to arrive for the opening of the mini-mall. They'd eat at the Inn. Meg's legendary fame would spread. She had some really interesting detective work to do. And Myles . . . Quill smiled to herself. There was Myles. Who was going to be very surprised at the quality of her investigation. She crossed into the foyer and saw that the Chinese vases either side of the mahogany desk were filled with giant dahlias. Quill felt the impulse to dance across the floor. Dina was sitting behind the reception desk, winding up a phone conversation. Quill waited until she'd hung up the receiver.

"Finally, Quill! Things are getting back to normal! We've got a third of the dining room filled already for lunch, and six reservations for dinner! And it's not even nine-thirty." Dina's face was flushed, and she picked nervously at the phone cord.

"Any messages?"

"Lots. John called in from the site. The kitchen came. He's going to be there all day making sure it gets in right. He took his PC with him, so I think he said to tell you he'll have the quarterly numbers by this afternoon. And he wants to know about Mr. Sakura."

"What about Mr. Sakura?"

"He said, 'Offer?' " Dina wound the phone cord around her wrist, pulled the phone off the receiver, and said, "Gosh! Sorry!"

Quill paged through the pink slips. "What's this next message?"

"It's from Mr. Stoker."

"I see that. It says 'will deliver results from A.M. employee meeting, one o'clock.' What's that all about?"

Dina shrugged and began erasing an entry into the bookings ledger with careful strokes. Then she rewrote it.

"Dina? What's going on?"

"Maybe you should find Mr. Stoker and ask him."

"Well, I needed to see him anyway. I'll just get my notepad and go find him. Where is he?"

Dina had emptied the contents of her purse on the desk and was intent on sorting through the various gum wrappers, blushers, lipsticks, and Cornell Student Parking stubs that littered the top. "Huh?"

"I said, do you know where he is?"

"Yeah."

"Well?"

"Oh. You want me to tell you where he is? He's in the gazebo. With . . ." she trailed off in a mutter.

"With whom?"

Dina opened her checkbook, looked at it, and sighed.

"Dina!"

"Yes'm? Gee, I'm not sure who he's with. Anything else?"

"Meg said that some of the staff haven't shown up for work. Would you check the roster and make a few calls?"

"Some of them may be at the gazebo," Dina said with an air of sudden enlightenment.

"They're where?"

"They're at the gazebo. With Mr. Stoker. Everybody but me. I told them," said Dina, "that I would never betray you. Never. Besides. I didn't invest in the mall anyhow."

A suspicion of trouble sped across Quill's mind. "Oh, my goodness." She swallowed, then said again, "Oh, my goodness."

"Actually, I think you'd better get out there," Dina said pointedly, now that the secret was out.

Of course. The news of the discount mall would have spread like wildfire. And everybody in the Inn had cheerfully signed for weekly payroll deductions to make up the amount that she and John had invested in the mini-mall on their behalf. Quill had a cowardly desire to hide in her office.

"Are they, um, expecting me at this meeting? Dina?"

"They didn't say."

"I'm not expected at any other meetings right now, am I?" said Quill with hope.

Dina shook her head. "Nope."

"You think I should go out there."

"Yep."

"And John's where?"

Dina picked up the pink message slip Quill's nervous fingers had let drop on the desktop. " 'At the site. Kitchen came. Here all day. Took PC.' "

"The rat," muttered Quill. "The big rat. I would have been happy to go out to the site and supervise the kitchen install. I'm good at that."

"He didn't know about. . . . that before he left." Dina waved vaguely in the direction of the gazebo. A distant sound of applause—and a few belligerent "Right ons!"—drifted through the open door.

"Well, okay," said Quill.

She walked through the lounge and stopped at the doors leading to the patio. She had a very good view of the gazebo from here. To the left lay the rose garden, the fountain in the middle of the koi pond sending glittering drops into the sunny air. To the right was the curve of the Inn itself, and beyond that, the path over the bridge to the village. In the center, of course, were what looked like the Inn's entire staff (dressed, Quill noted with burgeoning hope, in dining room and kitchen kit). Doreen stood conspicuously apart. She was carrying a sign that read THROW THE BUM OUT! which Quill surmised referred to Mr. Stoker, although given Doreen's attitude toward Quill the past few weeks, she wasn't entirely sure.

Axminster Stoker stood in the middle of the gazebo, which gave him a two-foot advantage over the heads of the crowd. Quill stretched on tiptoe. Seated behind Axminster in the latticed recesses were Mr. Sakura and his faithful shadow, Motoyama.

Quill cracked the glass doors open and peeked around the corner.

"Empowerment saves jobs!" Axminster's voice had astonishing carrying power. "It is your right to be in on decisions which affect your future!"

Doreen raised her sign, blew a gigantic raspberry, and shouted, *"Three cheers for the boss!"*

Quill breathed a small sigh of relief.

"What's going on?" Georgia's voice was amused.

"Are you all right?" asked Meg. "We heard all this hoo-ha through the open window. What is it?"

"An employee meeting."

"I can see that, stupid. They look mad."

"They do."

"About what?"

"The discount mall, I should imagine. Their investment."

"They care about money? Now!? With the kitchen just reopened? How long is this meeting going to take?"

"Well, you know what Axminster told us about empowering the employees, Meg, these things take time. Problem resolution can take weeks. Months."

"Bullshit. They want a solution? I'll give them a solution."

"Remember our values statement, Meg. Concern. Caring. Commitment."

"Try Cooking, Cleaning, and Doing Your Damn Job!"

"Well, heck," Quill said to Georgia and crossed the flagstone patio behind Meg, with (she hoped) firm and unfaltering steps.

"It's just Stoke," Georgia said comfortingly. "Doing his thing."

"Hey!" Meg marched up to the edge of the crowd and elbowed her way purposefully through. "Bjorn. Frank. What the heck are you guys doing here? You called in sick!"

"We're not sick, exactly," Frank said. "We just got notice of this meeting, and thought maybe we should be here."

"It is the employee's right to strike!" said Axminster excitedly. "When deceived and burdened by the unfair practices of management, it is the employee's right—no, I should say the employee's *duty* to establish direct and unambiguous lines of communication."

"*Boo sucks to you?!*" yelled Doreen.

"Boo what to whom?" Meg said. "Is everybody crazy? *Hey!*" she shouted suddenly. "Stoker!"

"And here is management now!" Axminster beamed. "Come, I would wager, ready to sit down and discuss this issue with the goodwill and trust that characterize the finest Quality leadership in the finest companies. Remember, team. Concern! Caring! Commitment!"

Meg, taking care to avoid the sweet peas, marched into the gazebo, elbowed Axminster out of the way, and leaned out to address the troops.

"You! Bjorn. Frank. We've got dinners to cook tonight. Get back in the kitchen."

"But, Meg," said Kathleen, her hands twisting nervously in her apron. "About the mini-mall investment—"

"Who wants out?"

Several of the employees raised their hands.

"See Quill. She'll give you your money back. Anything else?"

"Margaret! We are trying to establish a dialogue here. This is simply not demonstrating proper concern for the integrity of the employees."

"Anybody else want out?"

Doreen, scowling ferociously, waved her sign (to the imminent danger of two waiters nearby) and hollered, "I'm keepin' mine in it. I tolt you bozos not to listen to this sorry sack of horse poop!"

"Well?" Meg demanded of the crowd.

Most of the employees shook their heads.

"Anytime anybody wants out, see Quill. Or John. Anybody else want to say anything?"

There was a general murmur which indicted a negative.

"Good." Meg turned to Axminster. "Solution presented. Meeting's over. That's it, guys, back to work." She gave Axminster a shove which was not quite a blow. "You can go give Doreen a hand with the rooms, since you've thrown the cleaning schedule totally out of whack with this stuff. Doreen? You have an extra vacuum cleaner?"

"I got scrub brushes and filthy terlits."

"My goodness," said Axminster in great distress. "Of course, I am ready to put my hand to any task in the pursuit of productivity, but. . . . Sakura-san, I appeal to you. Please. Tell her what she has done."

Mr. Sakura rose solemnly from his bench, put his hands together, and bowed to Meg. "Vely good work. Vely. Quick!" He snapped his fingers. He turned to Axminster. "You watch. She is good. Vely good. *Arigatoo gozai-mashita,* Stoker-san. It has been vely interesting. Vely. Mis

Quiriam is vely good to suggest crean *obenjo, nei*? You help that one." He chuckled genially, but the way he jerked his head toward Doreen was not genial at all. "Team-werrrk! *Hai!*"

Axminster clicked his heels together and stood at parade rest. Quill resisted the impulse to pat him sympathetically.

Mr. Sakura clapped Meg on the back. "Many. Times. I. Have. Fert the same." He bowed. Meg bowed back. "As you Amerr-icans say, *Sayonara* for now. Motoyama!" He snapped his fingers, and the two followed the dispersing crowd of employees into the Inn.

Doreen poked Axminster in the back with the sign. "Take this, you, and follow me."

Axminster turned just before he and Doreen disappeared around the corner on their way to the utility shed. "May we discuss this further on?"

"Of course," Quill called. "Any time."

"More meetings?" said Meg.

Georgia's laugh rolled across the lawn.

"Actually, it should work out well. I have a little job from Myles, which I swore I wouldn't tell either of you about, or I would, and more meetings will give me a great excuse to talk to each of the employees individually."

"To find out if anyone saw who gave Carlyle the poi-soned finger?"

"Well, yes. But please don't tell anyone else, Meg, or you either, Gee. I'm sort of on assignment."

"I've got an assignment. I'd take it on myself if I weren't going to be so busy with the new restaurant." Meg looked at Quill, her brow furrowed. "Why was Axminster so quick to do what Mr. Sakura told him to do?"

"I don't know. Does it matter? He worships the ground the man walks on obviously, because of his Key Operating thingy, I suppose."

"That doesn't make sense. Would you go clean toilets if Picasso told you to?"

"Never mind that he's dead, why in the world would Picasso ask me to clean toilets?"

"That's it exactly, isn't it? Come on, Georgia, I'll get you some breakfast."

CHAPTER 13

Quill had several hours before she was due to visit the construction site with Georgia and sit in on the Society for the Advancement of Jell-O Architecture committee meeting. She used them to interview employees one at a time in her office. She kept scrupulous notes (guiltily aware that she really ought to pay as much attention to her note-taking responsibilities for the Chamber) and, a short time before Georgia was to pick her up, leaned back and looked at the result of her efforts in bewilderment.

Every suspect had passed that corner of the Inn at or around seven o'clock.

The *sous* chefs had been in the kitchen and hadn't noticed a thing, although several of them volunteered—strictly in the spirit of empowerment and team efforts to improve productivity—that if Meg could be persuaded to let them take coffee breaks outside at suitable intervals, they would be able to watch the corner of the Inn with a great deal of attention. Quill, doubtful that Meg's Simon Legree style in the kitchen could be modified enough to accommodate these modest demands, said that she'd see what she could do. Meg was prone to utter a maxim about art and sweat which—although she stoutly maintained it was a favorite saying of the French composer Claude Marie de Courcy's—Quill knew very well she'd made up.

The waiters and waitresses, whose schedules fell under John's purview, were much more helpful. Peter Hairston, strolling in the front garden for a ten-minute break just after

six-thirty, had seen Mr. Sakura and the faithful Motoyama
come from around the back of the Inn to the front, presumably to reenter the Inn through the front door, although he
wasn't sure. Marco DeMarco, in desultory conversation
with Axminster Stoker, had been smoking a cigarette in the
drive. Kathleen, whose break followed on the heels of Peter's, had seen the Kiplings in full Victorian dress, sweeping through the rose garden in the direction of the corner
of the Inn where Carlyle and Hedrick were to follow some
moments later. It was, Kathleen thought, about five minutes
to seven, and all of the Kiplings were together: Mr. and
Mrs. Fairbanks, Jerzey Paulovich, Miss Kent, and Mrs.
Hardwicke.

The times were wrong. Quill stuck her pencil in her hair.
The Kiplings were at the party by seven; she'd confirmed
that by her own watch. But Hedrick and Carlyle had arrived
some five minutes later, again confirmed by her own watch.
She looked at her watch and checked the accuracy against
the clock on her office wall. They were within a minute of
each other. Mr. Sakura and Motoyama had come through
the lounge and out into the patio at about the same time
Carlyle and Hedrick arrived on the the lawn side. And Axminster and DeMarco had come in separately, DeMarco
from the lounge, Axminster from the other side of the gazebo, which meant he must have walked through the perennial gardens and past the kitchen, the long way round.

Why would he take the long way round?

Where had Hedrick and Carlyle been for that extra five
minutes? None of the staff could account for the missing
time. No one had actually seen Carlyle encounter any one
of the other guests, except in the patio itself.

"You ready?"

Quill jerked upright with a start. "Georgia! Is it time
already?"

"Just about. It's about ten minutes to the site, isn't it? It
was roughly that in the van, at least, when we went down
on the day Mrs. Conway was thrown in the river, poor
soul."

Quill gathered her car keys, purse, hairbrush, and notepad. She ducked and peered into the small mirror hanging

on the wall near her office door. "Do I look okay? My hair frizzes up like thistles in this heat."

"That's not a perm? Gawd! What I wouldn't do to have naturally curly hair. So, other than employee revolutions, how's the morning going? I saw Myles leave rather early this morning."

Quill smiled.

"Oh, Quill," said Georgia.

"What?"

"Just. That look. I'm glad for you, sweetie."

"Well, hang on to the feeling. You're about to meet Adela Henry, first lady of Hemlock Falls." On their way out to the parking lot, Quill gave an animated description of Mrs. Henry's social career, which bore a close resemblance to Sherman's.

"As in General Sherman, the fella that marched from Atlanta to the sea?" Georgia's round face was red with laughter. "I can't wait."

"At least the Jell-O mania isn't as tacky as the Little Miss Hemlock Falls Beauty Contest, Gee. Remind me to tell you about that some time."

They walked to Quill's Olds in a companionable silence, Quill accommodating her steps to Georgia's slower ones. She waited until Georgia had eased herself into the passenger side of the car, then, as she pulled out onto the road that led to Route 15, asked her if she'd run into Carlyle and Hedrick the night of the murder.

"We all did. Not literally, of course, but we saw them come in. Lila Fairbanks likes us all to arrive at the same time whenever we give a performance. Makes a more impressive effect, although she'd never in this world admit it. So, wherever we go, we're accustomed to being ready a little before we actually need too. We wait until the crowd's panting with anticipation and come in together."

"You did have a splendid entrance at the party," said Quill. "I'm so sorry we didn't get to hear the performance."

"You just might yet, if you don't manage to avoid Lyle for the next couple of days. He didn't think it was suitable to request a second chance until a day or two had passed, but I met them this morning at breakfast, and some wistful little hints were dropped.''

"Gosh," said Quill vaguely. "Anytime. Although we're going to be pretty busy with the opening-day ceremonies tomorrow, and the Society's just due to stay until the end of the week. Maybe next time?"

Georgia, who was wearing flamboyant rhinestone sunglasses, dropped them lower on her nose and rolled her eyes sternly over the tops. "Confess. You don't want to hear the Master's poetry condensed into an hour-long performance?"

"Georgia, I . . . well. No. No, I don't. Anyone who can write something as smarmy and sententious as *If.*"

" 'If you can keep your head when all about you are losing theirs,' " Georgia intoned.

"Then you haven't seen the fire, and everybody else has already found the exit," Quill said somewhat tartly. "Has everyone been together a long time? The Kipling Society, I mean?"

Georgia shot her a shrewd glance. "Still detecting? You can apply the rubber hose yourself, if you want to. They're visiting the site today, with Mr. Sakura, who, it appears, is eager to join our little band. If I do decide to move to Hemlock Falls, he'll take my place in the group. Anyway, they talked Meg into making them a picnic lunch to take to the site today. They love that little woods next to the mall. It's a rehearsal, technically, and I should be there, but," she added complacently, "I have this Ladies meeting instead. Which suits me just fine. At least it'll be out of the sun.''

"Is there a limit to the number of members?"

"Oh, no. But a certain degree of consanguinity is required to make a happy little team. The common denominator is probably money. To get to your question—you are a tenacious woman, in your own way, Quill—I've known Lyle and Lila for years. Lyle was a great friend of Doug's and mine. And Kipling's been a favorite of Lyle's forever. So, after Doug died. . . . '' She fell silent. The round, cheerful face flushed. Her voice was sad. "It was so hard. I still miss him. Every day. Every day. Anyway, Lyle'd retired and pulled this crazy bunch of people together and I just decided to join them, for the travel and the companionship, mostly. It's been fun.''

"So Lyle's the founding member. What about Miss Kent?''

"Aurora? Golly, let's see. She's Worthington Mill money, you know, out of Vermont. I think she met Lyle and Lila on a cruise to St. Thomas three or four years ago. That must have been around the time that Jerzey joined, or maybe it was a little later. He's a heck of a bridge player, by the way.''

"Jerzey has money, too?''

"I expect so. I told you we were all loaded.''

"Where'd the Fairbanks money come from?''

Georgia burst out laughing. "With that accent? You have to ask? Oil, honey, oil.''

"Was Doug in oil, too? Is that how the four of you were friends?''

Quill got the look over the sunglasses again. "I've been meaning to ask you. That dishy sheriff?''

"Myles?''

"You come to an understanding, as they say?''

"Sort of.''

"Well, I'm glad. But you tell him from me that Doug and Lyle met over a yearling filly at Saratoga Race Week some years back, bid against each other on the horse. I don't remember who actually ended up buying her—it might have been us—but one of 'em lost I don't know how many thousands on the damn thing, and they went out together on a three-day toot and were fast friends ever since. Men.'' Georgia shook her head. "Can't live with 'em, can't live without them.''

"When did the trip to Tokyo happen?'' Quill, chafing under Myles's stricture not to tell anyone that she was investigating, was finding it difficult to keep up the appearance of aimless chatter. Georgia's eyes were too shrewd.

"Japan was actually a business trip for Lyle. I hadn't joined them yet. Isn't that your turn here? Quill, that's a darn pretty mall, if I do say so myself.''

"Well, why wouldn't you?'' asked Quill affectionately.

"It is nice, isn't it? Although, if we accept Mr. Sakura's offer to buy it, I won't feel quite the same about it as I do now."

"If the parking lot's empty for months on end because of that new mall down the road, you're not going to feel the same about it, either."

"The parking lot's not empty enough, now. Look. There's the Horrible Hedrick's Cadillac. And the Inn van, too. The Kiplings must be here already. It looks like the work crew's gone, though."

"Oh, my, look at the tent! I love this!"

They got out of the car. A huge gaily striped awning tent had been set up in the meadow south of the mall itself. The sod had been delivered that morning, and the scent of freshly turned dirt filled the air. The backhoe was parked near the septic tank, and the bulldozers were gone.

The tent was red and white. A large banner draped across the front entrance shouted HEMLOCK FALLS VERY OWN! The Mall at the Falls!

"Why didn't the Ladies Society just use the atrium in the building for the exhibits?" asked Georgia.

"That was a battle," said Quill. "This is a small town, remember, and all our investors are from around here. The wives didn't want anyone messing up the stores with the food exhibits."

"Did you say food?"

"Oh, yes. We don't have a county fair in the Falls, although Esther West has been talking about starting one up, so the opening is being treated as sort of a dry run. We've got a baking competition, and jams and jellies, and, of course, the Jell-O Architecture Contest."

"Is there any food to eat?" asked Georgia. "I'm feeling a bit peckish, as a true Kiplingite might say."

"The restaurants will be serving tomorrow. Ours and of course the McDonald's. And I think the Agway will have a beer booth and hot dogs."

"But I'm hungry now!"

Quill chuckled. "I think there's a diner wagon for the work crew. Maybe it's still here. Shall we walk over and see if they're still open?"

"Are you hungry?"

"Well, no," Quill admitted.

"Then I'll go. You go in and tell the ladies I'll be with them shortly. You want anything?"

"Some iced tea, if they have it. I'll see you in a few minutes."

Quill walked to the tent, and into the meeting. The Falls's *cognoscenti* (Marge Schmidt and Betty Hall, mainly) were of the opinion that the Ladies Society for the Advancement of Jell-O Architecture was the saving of Mayor Henry's marriage, not to mention the Hemlock Falls political structure. Up until the creation of that body, Adela Henry, the mayor's wife of some thirty years and a masterful woman, had been known to meddle with varying degrees of success in village affairs. While no one would deny that Adela's Vigilante Group (an organization dedicated to sweeping the lockers of the local high school for illicit substances, which had resulted in the confiscation of several dozen packets of No-Doz at exam time) or the Hemlock Anti-Alcohol League (which had circulated an unsuccessful temperance petition for the whole of Tompkins County) had roots in worthy enough values, everyone took mild exception to the high-handedness with which Adela enforced her views. She was a tall woman, with prematurely white hair tinted blue at the Hemlock Hall of Beauty once a month, and a piercing voice. Meg thought she would have made a great prime minister of some unsuspecting republic.

Quill waved to Adela as she entered the tent. Adela, dressed in a cotton print dress and a large straw hat, motioned her to the long table set in the center.

"What do you think?" she demanded without preamble. "You have an Eye, Quill. No one"—she swept the assembled members of the Society with a commanding glance— "no one would deny your Eye."

A long table was set squarely in the middle of the tent. Each of the displays was tastefully arranged on felt-covered pieces of cardboard.

"They're just the most *interesting* buildings I've ever seen." Quill walked around the table with her hands clasped behind her back. The buildings quivered as she walked. She stopped in front of a particularly teetery one. "Is this Eiffel Tower yours, Esther?"

"*Mais oui*," said Esther anxiously. "I had a bit of trouble with the top, as you see."

The edifice, made of either strawberry or cherry Jell-O, Quill wasn't sure which, had a peculiarly thick look to it.

"How did you get it to ... to ... tower?"

Esther darted a hesitant look at Adela. "Concrete," she said defiantly.

"You are supposed to be able to eat it," said Adela coldly. "We agreed."

"I'm going to," said Esther. "Concrete won't hurt you. I asked Dr. Bishop. Not quite what it should be for the digestion, but no harm will come to me, he said."

The sun, coming into the tent through plastic skylights in the tent top, struck blueberry, grape, orange, and lemon highlights from the tiny buildings.

"Now this is ... is ... most interesting," said Quill "It's obviously, um ..."

"Mount Fujiyama," said Adela. "The coconut is the snow, of course."

"And the, um, fixative?"

"If you mean by that, what did I use to achieve the height, in a food that is essentially, well, essentially Jell-O, the answer is Rice Krispies. Which are highly edible."

Esther, with a great show of unconcern, took a teaspoon from the coffee tray and nibbled at the Eiffel Tower.

"We thought that perhaps you might consider the position of judge," said Adela, a hint of warmth creeping into the frostiness of her demeanor. "You are, I understand from that extremely attractive young Japanese man at the Inn, an Artist of the First Rank."

Quill who'd always been fascinated by Adela's ability to speak in capitals, murmured something deprecating. The thought of judging the contest struck her bones to, well, she thought, Jell-O.

"We have Artistic Standards," said Adela, correctly interpreting Quill's muttered demurral. "I had them printed up. By that excessively rude young man who took over Our Newspaper from Pete Rosen."

"He took some pictures," volunteered a young, timid matron whom Quill didn't know, but thought perhaps was a Peterson. "We'll be in the paper."

"We shall see," said Adela. "Monica. Perhaps you would provide Ms. Quilliam with the Rules and Regulations."

Quill accepted the sheet with the meekness that Adela seemed to engender in anyone who swept into her orbit.

"I see you've established one-hundred-point ratings, Adela. Twenty points for creativity in color. Twenty points for edibility. Twenty points for suitability. And the remainder for Aesthetic Appropriateness." Quill coughed. It didn't help. She coughed again.

"The judging will take place tomorrow, at the conclusion of the opening day ceremonies. The mayor"—Adela hadn't used Elmer's given name since the day he was elected— "will announce the winner after the speeches and the talent show. The other foods"—she indicated the jars of jellies, the baked goods exhibits, and the flower arrangements lined up on various tables around the tent—"will be announced first. Are you all right, my dear?"

"Just. Something. Caught. In my throat. 'Scuse me. Friend's bringing me some tea." Quill ducked out of the tent and into Georgia, who spilled the tea she was carrying onto her bare ankles.

"What!?" Georgia demanded.

Quill, who was laughing so hard she couldn't stand up straight, grabbed her arm. "Georgia. Georgia, as you love me. Judge that contest!"

"Who, me? I don't know a thing about Jell-O!"

"Who does? Take a look in there! Don't let them see you!"

Georgia peered cautiously around the opening.

"What do you see?"

"A bunch of nice middle-class ladies around a table full of Jell-O. What do you expect me to see?"

"My Fate!" said Quill dramatically. "Every woman in town who has anything to say about anything has entered that darn contest."

"So? Shut your eyes and give one of 'em a blue ribbon, one a red—"

"You don't understand! Do I give the blue ribbon to Esther? Who should at least get it for having the balls to eat concrete so that she can win . . ."

"Concrete!"

". . . and have Mrs. Mayor mad at me for the rest of my life? Do I give it to Miriam Doncaster, who's a dear dear friend and appears to have attempted a train wreck—unless it's L.A. after the quake. I'll be damned if I know which— and have Esther cut me dead in the street for the next three years? Help!"

"Oh, Gawd. I see what you mean. Here, drink what's left of your tea. You know what we should do?"

"No. What?" Quill drained the tea, which was warm.

"Run like hell."

"We can't run like hell."

"Sure we can."

"I have to check with John, to see how the boutique's coming."

"Then we'll run like hell in there."

"You know what?" said Quill. "I think that's the best idea I've heard all day."

John, with his usual air of unruffled calm, was installing the faucet in the kitchen sink when Quill and Georgia arrived breathless at the restaurant.

"Wow!" said Quill. "When I was in here yesterday the kitchen was bare walls and pipes."

"Took a couple of hours," said John. "No more than that. Everything dropped into place. DeMarco had the plumber here and ready to go, and the whole thing—wait a second . . ." He pulled the faucet handle up. There was a burp, a stutter in the pipes, and a gush of water. "Everything works."

"How come you had to install the faucet?"

"The crew was scheduled to quit at twelve noon, and twelve noon it was. The only worker left here is DeMarco himself, and he's setting the top of the septic system on right now. It was the penalties for overtime that did it. But they finished on time."

"Good old sympathetic you." Quill sighed happily. The kitchen was a stainless-steel, self-contained model that fitted tightly together like an elegant little puzzle. Meg would love it. "It's just beautiful. Is her cookware coming in soon?"

"Mike's going to bring it back in the van when he takes the Kiplings and Mr. Sakura home."

"Have you seen him? Have you thought more about the offer? Shall we take it?"

John's glance at Georgia was casual. He paused but said readily enough, "Yes. I do think so. It's a fair offer. It means that everyone will get his or her money back, with a very slight premium attached."

"How much?" asked Georgia. "Sorry, I don't mean to butt in, but I might be interested in doing something about all this myself, you know."

"In that case, let me show the numbers to you." John drew them to the table where his PC sat glowing. "Mr. Sakura has a lot of information about the costs involved. It makes me a little curious as to where he got the information, but that's neither here nor there for the moment. Besides, I can make a good guess."

"I've been wondering who gave Hedrick all that dirt for the goods book," said Quill. "Do you think it's the same person?"

John shook his head. "I don't know. Myles's guess is that the source for the gossip and the source for the information about the investment package are two different people, but he wouldn't tell me why. Now that I think I know who, I'm not certain Myles is right. Anyway, here's a list of the amounts listed by the name of each of the principals in Mall, Inc." He tapped the keyboard and a list of names and figures appeared on the screen. "Quill, Meg, and I put in three hundred thousand from savings, Georgia; we added fifty thousand as a pledge from employees, for which the Inn took out a banknote. Bottom line to get in was a quarter million.

"I input Mr. Sakura's offer this morning while the kitchen was getting set. It breaks down like this." He tapped. A second column of figures appeared to the right of the names. "And when you match the investor's original contribution against the Sakura offer, the payout's like this." His finger moved rapidly, the screen split, and the list of investors and their cash pledges was matched by a payout figure. "You notice anything?"

Georgia cast a practiced eye at the screen. "Howie Murchison's payout is twenty percent over his investment. Everybody else averages about the same. One percent."

"Right."

"Howie! Howie's been going behind everyone's back to talk to Mr. Sakura! I don't believe it!" Quill remembered, suddenly, Miriam's nervous shredding of the tissue at the chamber meeting three days ago. "Howie!" she said again, the disbelief replaced by anger.

"Don't jump the gun here, Quill. That could be in lieu of a broker's fee—it's a tax issue I won't bore you with. And if, as I suspect, Howie knew about the competing mall a few months after we'd all committed to this, you have to hand it to him. I'll bet he looked for an investor to save not only himself, but the rest of the town."

"That answers another question," said Quill. "I wondered why Mr. Sakura knew about this before he showed up here." She sighed. "So you think we'd better take the offer."

"I do. If Mr. Sakura understands the situation here, he could've taken advantage by waiting a year until the other mall was completed, and then offering us all twenty cents on the dollar. He didn't. Bad business practice, I have to say."

"Bad business to give us our money back!"

"Oh, he's a good man. That's different." John grinned slightly. "The short form of the offer which Howie passed out yesterday provides for a sell-out of the equipment each of us put into the stores, and a one-year lease, which can be terminated after twelve months, with fifteen days' notice. That's a little rough."

"Maybe he won't want us to move," said Quill. "Maybe the mall will work despite the discount place down the road."

"Maybe. And maybe Mr. Sakura is thinking of building a golf course."

"A golf course? A *golf* course?!"

"Or a resort. Japanese investment in American real estate isn't just for big cities, Quill. This is an ideal spot for a resort. And to the Japanese, who are used to land prices ten to twenty times what we pay here, this looks like a pretty good deal. Mr. Sakura's grandchildren are here. His son's here. What better place for a former director of Sakura Industries to retire part-time?"

"Well. None, I suppose. But a golf course?"

"Could be a very good thing for the town. And for the Inn."

"Did I hear a new project?" Marco DeMarco appeared at the open door and walked in. He nodded to Georgia. "How do you do?"

Quill smiled at him. "This is Georgia Hardwicke, Mr. DeMarco."

"We met at the party the other night. You were wearing quite a dress."

Georgia laughed. Quill, remembering Georgia's geezer speech, had a sudden, happy inspiration. They were roughly the same age, and they even looked a little bit alike. Although Georgia's hair color owed more to a bottle than to nature, their coloring was close.

She darted a swift glance at DeMarco's ring finger. Bare. "Mr. DeMarco, everything looks just wonderful. And you finished on time!"

"In the nick of," he agreed. "Just stopped in to tell you I'll be locking up, and to take a last look around. I just buried the septic tank, and I want to flush a few toilets, see if they work. Otherwise, I'm finished for the day. I'll be back for the ceremonies, of course."

"When you've finished here"—Quill glanced at Georgia with a mischievous look—"why don't you stop by the Inn for dinner? We can celebrate the opening of the mall. And the fact that we seem to be going to sell it."

"Heard about that. Kind of sorry. It's a great little project. If I could take a raincheck on the dinner, I'd appreciate it. I'd like to get back to Syracuse tonight. I've got a bid to get in.''

"Anything we should know about?'' asked John.

DeMarco winked. "Big mall going up down the road, I hear. Ms. Quilliam? Mrs. Hardwicke? Be seeing you.''

The sun was setting over the treetops when Quill and Georgia walked to the Olds to go home. The site was quiet, the awning tent empty. The grounds held an air of expectancy. The parking lot was empty except for Quill's Olds and Hedrick's Cadillac. Quill frowned at it. "Maybe we should tell Mr. DeMarco that Hedrick is still around. Skulking in the bushes with his little goods book, I should think.''

"I'm sure DeMarco will flush him out. You look happy,'' Georgia commented abruptly.

"Tomorrow should be fun,'' Quill said. "And yes, I'm happy. Now, tell me the truth, Georgia, about DeMarco. Kinda cute, huh?''

"Not bad for a geezer.''

"And he'll be around for a while if he gets the bid on the discount mall project. Are you still thinking of sticking around Hemlock Falls after the Kiplings wend on their way?''

"I wouldn't,'' said Georgia, "think of settling anywhere else.''

CHAPTER 14

The morning of Hemlock Falls Mall at the Falls Opening Day Ceremonies dawned to all the auguries necessary for success. The sun shone. The sky was blue. The Inn was host to Harvey Bozzel's dignitaries: two State Assembly persons, and the second secretarial assistant to the Congressman from New York. (Helena Houndswood, star of stage, screen, and television, had sent an uncharitably worded note of regret.) Meg threw two major snits before breakfast and a spectacular temper tantrum at nine o'clock, which meant she would cook superbly.

Quill came from the kitchen to join Myles, Andy, and John in the dining room with a huge smile and an exquisite sense of well-being.

"The menu for the opening of the boutique," she said as she settled into the chair next to Myles, "is going to be terrific."

"Gazpacho?' asked John, with hope.

"And vichyssoise. A hot ratatouille, and stuffed mushrooms. Dilled cucumber dressing for the salads. Creme brûlée, mousse, and caramel flan." Quill reached for a small brioche and buttered it. "It's all transportable, so actual cooking should be at a minimum." A shriek and a crash from behind the swinging doors to the kitchen broadened her smile. "It's the crab clouds, I think. They delivered the crab here, instead of the mall, and there's not enough ice. And she doesn't think she has enough cornmeal."

"Crab clouds?" Myles asked.

"You missed out on those, didn't you?" said Andy. "Meg created them last month while you two were still on the outs. My guess is they'll help get her that fourth star. They're fantastic. And she's got some ideas for the Christmas season that really sound incredible. You're not going to have to wait long for that final rating, Quill. Next year at the latest."

"So she's not . . ." Quill stopped.

"Thinking of leaving the Inn when we get married? Not on your life. The woman's a genius in the kitchen."

"Married? You're talking marriage?" Quill's feelings were mixed. Glad for Meg. Unhappy that she hadn't told her.

"Not directly, no. But now that you and Myles . . ." Myles's foot moved sharply under the table. Andy winced and changed the subject with no subtlety at all. "Is there anything I can do for you today, Quill? I'm covered at the hospital, so I'm completely at your disposal."

"Do you mean, Andy, that Meg put off discussions of your future because of me?"

Andy looked at John, then Myles, with a hint of what Quill had always characterized as male panic in the face of the Female Unknown. "Not exactly. But you two have been a team for so long . . . like this detective business, for example. How's the investigation coming?"

Quill, struggling with a sudden understanding that should have come to her long before, rather absently took a crêpe from Myles's plate and began to eat it.

"Hey," said Myles. "That's mine."

"I'll accept your diversionary tactic, Andy," Quill said sternly, "for the moment. But at some point in the very near future, my sister and I are going to have a talk. And to answer your question, our investigation, *my* investigation at least, is going nowhere."

"I wouldn't say that." Myles, in lieu of his second crêpe, picked up a muffin. "You and John cleared up a lot of ancillary issues yesterday."

"You mean you know who did it?"

"I've got a better sense of how the murders were committed. And a strong hunch as to who carried them out. I have no motive. And I have no proof.'' He rubbed the back of his neck with a weary gesture. ''And time's running out.''

''It's Hedrick,'' said Quill. ''It has to be. Did you get any information about his stepfather's death? Does he have a record?''

''Hedrick was never indicted. I talked to Jerry Matthews last night, who's with the force in Palm Beach; there was a lot of suspicion when Hedrick's stepfather died, and a lot of gossip. The autopsy reports indicate botulism as the cause of death, from a gift set of jellies given to him by a friend at Christmas. The woman—unrelated to Louisa or Carlyle—was cleared of any culpability. It went down as an accidental death through the carelessness of an amateur cook. Jerry's take on it was that Conway was a rich man, and every time a rich man dies without an easily discernible cause, suspicions flourish, as he put it, like kudzu in a vacant lot.''

''Hedrick told me he never eats anything canned,'' Quill recalled suddenly. ''I thought it was just another part of his charm.''

''Jerry did tell me something interesting, though. I asked for a list of people who were at the party where Conway finally keeled over. Botulism takes what, Andy, twenty-four to thirty-six hours to kill?''

Andy nodded. ''Lot depends on the usual: age, weight, gender, prior physical condition.''

''Conway died late Sunday evening. There'd been a house party at his mansion on the beach which began Thursday night. Conway ate the jellies sometime that evening and developed flulike symptoms the next morning. He drank quite a bit—Jerry said that the entire crowd was notable for the amount of alcohol consumed at these parties—and drank heavily the next day. By Sunday he was semiconscious. Louisa, for whom Jerry has little or no affection, kept insisting he was drunk and to leave him alone. By Sunday evening Conway'd passed into a coma. He died early Monday morning.''

''Which of the Conways were at the party?'' asked Quill.

''Hedrick, Louisa, and Carlyle, who was there with the

heir to a Mexican cattle fortune, and who was suspected of dealing drugs.'' Myles took a swallow of coffee, then set the cup down deliberately. ''And Lyle and Lila Fairbanks.''

''The Fairbanks!'' Quill took a deep breath. ''They never mentioned it! Hedrick never mentioned it!''

''No. They didn't, did they? Hedrick never went near them at the party where Carlyle was killed. And when I interrogated him afterward, he didn't say a word about having known them before.''

''Who,'' asked John, ''made the jelly?''

''Lila.''

The mall parking lot was jammed with vehicles. The Monster Truck Rally (SEE! THE MIGHTIEST MACHINES! IN COMBAT!) had attracted six entrants, and the huge vehicles occupied, Quill thought with irritation, far more parking space than they should have. Mr. Motoyama stood lost in admiration before them, his hands clasped behind his back, looking smaller than ever against the eight-foot tires.

Hedrick had had the foresight to reserve the same spot he'd had yesterday. Quill toyed with the idea of parking her Olds behind him, so that when he came looking for her, she'd have an opportunity to engage in a little artless questioning. ''Did you switch Lila Fairbanks's jelly jar for one of your own in Palm Beach six years ago?'' might be a good conversation opener.

Quill watched Lila Fairbanks wind her way through the clustered vehicles across the parking lot to the awning tent. She was wearing one of an apparently endless supply of white gauze dresses, this one trimmed with rose-colored ribbons. Lyle, as usual, hovered beside her, carrying a matching parasol to shield her from the bright August sun. She couldn't believe that this small, feminine woman with the sweet face could have made killer jelly on purpose. She said as much to Georgia.

''Myles wouldn't like it, if he knew you told me.'' Today's caftan was bright pink, with blue and green embroidered trim at the neckline. Georgia looked tired and strained despite the cheerful colors. ''It must have been an accident,'' she said stubbornly. ''I remember that Lila went through a real Martha Stewart period, canning, drying flowers, baking bread from scratch. It drove her housekeeper wild. She's vague and a little silly, Quill, but she's no more a murderer than I am.''

"And she never said a word about knowing the Conways from before?''

"The rich travel in small, tight circles, Quill. I went into a real moult after Doug died—I wasn't much of a partygoer in the first place. You know me, give me a good book, a plate of Meg's food, and a nice lounge chair, and I'm set for life. But it doesn't surprise me that the Fairbanks drifted in and out of café society. There's a handful of the really rich who all know each other—and Lyle's one of them.''

"I guess I won't.'' Quill maneuvered the Olds onto the grass verge and turned the ignition off.

"Won't what?''

"Park behind Hedrick. I'm going to find him and ask a lot of seemingly artless questions about his stepfather's death.''

"Do you think that's a good idea?'' Georgia's forehead creased with worry. "It might be dangerous.''

"Pooh! as Meg would say. How dangerous can he get in this crowd?''

"Well, I'm going to stick with you like glue. I don't want your body found in the river with a neat little bash in the temple.''

"In that outfit I think you should stick to Marco De-Marco,'' said Quill with a grin. "You're sure that on the day Louisa was murdered, neither Lyle nor Lila wandered off in the direction of the septic system?''

"Positive. Jerzey can confirm it. As a matter of fact, so can Axminster Stoker and Mr. Sakura. We wandered around in a group the whole time, gawking at the construction and getting in the way of the work crew.''

"And DeMarco wasn't even there. He was in San Francisco. You know what I think?''

"What?'' They began to stroll toward the awning tent. Outside, the Hemlock Falls High School Marching Band swung into a spirited, if flawed, version of "The Stars and Stripes Forever.''

"We should just enjoy the afternoon. Forget all this."

"Georgia, we're close to a solution here. Suppose the Fairbanks are killing off Conways as revenge for Mr. Conway's murder? If I can find Hedrick and get him to explain a few things, we might nail them."

"Like what?"

"Well, for one thing, who knew of Carlyle's little party trick?"

"The Fairbanks, probably."

"And why did he refuse to let anyone here know he'd known the Fairbanks before? It's very suspicious, don't you think? If I'd been a fragile little person like Lila Fairbanks, you can bet your bottom dollar I wouldn't acknowledge the man who had substituted poisoned jelly for the good stuff and tried to get me implicated in a murder, either. And if Hedrick is guilty of that first murder, it makes sense that he wouldn't want to acknowledge them, either. So, when I find 'this reporter,' I'm going to ask him the sixty-four-thousand dollar question: Since he murdered Mr. Conway, why the heck doesn't he admit it?"

Georgia threw back her head and laughed, then looked at Quill with great affection. "Just don't," she warned, "see the little blighter alone. What does Myles think of all this?"

"He said to stay out of it. To stay away from the Fairbanks and from Hedrick and let him wrap up the case. There's something," Quill said in frustration, "that I've missed. He told me Hedrick was dangerous. But if Hedrick did it—where's the motive? He doesn't have any money. There's something I've missed. Some vital clue."

"Whatever it is, it'll have to wait until the Jell-O contest is over." The Sousa march came to a crashing conclusion. "And what the devil is that noise?"

" 'The Stars and Stripes.' Sousa. The piccolo's got the flu." Quill heard Elmer's amplified voice testing the sound system from inside the tent. "It's just on two o'clock. Hedrick's probably in there getting pictures for the loathsome rag. Will you help me find him?"

Georgia gave a gusty sigh. "Okay. But 'don't go into the basement.' Promise?"

"Promise."

Despite the fact that the tent was open on four sides to the afternoon breeze, the crush of people made the interior stifling. Georgia took the lead, and the crowds parted before her pink caftan like tuna before a trawler. Quill scanned the crowd, waved to Marge Schmidt and Betty Hall, smiled at Chris Croh, and smiled again at Monica Peterson, architect of a Jell-O building Quill had been unable to identify the day before. Monica semaphored urgently. Quill smiled vaguely and tried the Dodge, a trick she'd observed Helena Houndswood use when greeting the legions of fans (six, including Esther West's poodle) that had greeted her on Main Street the week of her ill-fated visit to Hemlock Falls the year before. Basically, the Dodge consisted of a broad grin, eye-contact just above the petitioner's forehead, and a graceful turn-and-wave maneuver Quill had much admired.

"Didn't you see me?" Monica demanded, planting herself directly under Quill's chin.

"Monica! Isn't this wonderful!"

"Mrs. Henry wants you," said Monica despairingly. "She's been wondering where you are. She's a little upset that you haven't judged anything yet."

"Um," said Quill. Georgia, who'd successfully made her way to the small stage set up at the front of the tent, was looking over the heads of the crowd for Quill. Quill raised herself on tiptoe and waved energetically. Georgia caught her eye and mouthed "no Hedrick."

"Quill?"

"I didn't exactly agree to judge the Jell-O Architecture Contest, Monica. I mean, I'm sure there are a lot of people more qualified than I to decide who built the best building." She had an inspiration. "What about Mr. DeMarco? He's in construction."

"Mrs. Henry says the buildings are art. And you're an artist. Could you come over pretty quick, please?" She craned her neck up and whispered in Quill's ear. "Esther's not speaking to her. Miriam's so mad she's sitting on a chair reading a book, because Adela disqualified her entry—it was an homage to Agatha Christie, with the cutest little train out of Knox Blox—because her fixative is Super Glue and you can't eat Super Glue. And even Mrs. Shuttleworth is getting a little cranky. She said, 'Oh, God! Adela,' in this cross way, twice. It's terrible!!''

Quill resisted the temptation to pat Monica on the head and say "there-there." Instead she said confidingly "I'll tell you what the trouble is, Monica. It's that I can't be objective about this contest, knowing everybody that I do. And a judge has to be objective. What about Howie Murchison? He's town justice. And Doreen told me this morning that everyone's mad at him anyway because of . . . never mind. Forget I said that.''

"Mr. Murchison said he'd rather shave a bear's behind with a buzzsaw than judge." Monica's eyes sparkled with tears. "Mrs. Henry is just going to be so mad! It'll wreck everything.''

"What we need," muttered Quill, "is an objective *panel* of judges. Wait here.''

She found Elmer frowning over a sheaf of much-folded paper. "Quill, d'ya'll think I should greet the second secretary to our Congressman before I present the Assemblymen? Or should I present the Assemblywoman before the second secretary? This-here protocol's tough.''

"The Assemblyman and -woman first," said Quill. "They're the elected officials. Elmer, may I make an announcement?''

"What kind of an announcement?" A look of what Quill could only call terror crossed his face. "Not the results of the Jell-O Architecture Contest? You didn't give the blue ribbon to Esther or anything, did you? I'm telling you, Quill, it's a terrible bidness to have the wife involved in something as important as this.''

"No," soothed Quill, "and I'm not going to. Judge, I mean. I want to ask the Kipling Condensation Society and Mr. Sakura to judge the contest.''

"Hah? You mean outsiders?''

"Elmer! What better way to handle it? They'll all be gone in a week!''

"I get your drift, Quill, I get your drift. It's an excellent plan!" He looked a little wistful. "You think maybe I could

announce it? Lot of the folks around here are kinda mad
on account of what happened with the mini-mall. But
Howie said—''

"Later, Elmer. I think it'd be terrific if you got up, welcomed everybody, in a general sort of way you understand,
not''—she eyed the dozen or so handwritten sheets in his
hands—''the whole speech, but just that you'd like to ask
our out-of-towners, the Kipling Condensation Society, and
Mr. Sakura Toshiro, the famous former managing director
of Sakura Industries, to contribute to the day's festivities
by judging the contest. Oh! And be sure to read a copy of
Adela's Rules and Regulations, so they know what they're
judging for."

"Got it." He squeezed her arm in fervent gratitude. "I
owe you one, Quill. You're a true pal."

In subsequent years, when the Jell-O Battles had passed
into town history, and the pros and cons were discussed
with the cooler attitudes that the mere passage of time
brings, the citizens of Hemlock Falls were unanimous in
one thing: Elmer Henry started it. This was unfortunate,
and may have had something to do with the closeness of
the race for mayor fought the following year (Henry versus
Henry) because, as no one but Quill and the mayor knew,
it was really all her fault.

"Terlits," said Doreen in Quill's ear, while she watched
Elmer ascend to the podium.

"Doreen! I'm glad you finally got here. Did you come
by yourself?"

"I tolt you that there Stoker was follering me," said
Doreen obscurely. "But the terlits is backed up."

"At the Inn? Again? Darn it! Is Petey Peterson here? I
know he was scheduled to drive in the Monster Truck Ral-
ley. Maybe you can persuade him to go back and pump the
septic out."

"Ladies and gentlemen!" Elmer's voice boomed, faded,
and then came back at a tolerable volume. "I have an announcement to make. Please do not use, I repeat, do not
use, the toilets. We have a tempr'y back up in the system . . . what?" He turned and bent down to Marco De-
Marco, who was, Quill was pleased to see, standing next

to Georgia. They already looked like a long-married couple. "Mr. DeMarco here, is having PortaPotties come in, but it'll take about a half hour. In the meantime please, ah, use the woods. Thank you. Thank you."

"Terlits," said Doreen again. "What I want to know is, how come? All of a sudden we're having all this trouble with terlits, when we never did before."

"Probably something stuck in the system," said Quill, knowledgeable after her septic system lecture from Eugene. She rubbed her forehead. There was something Eugene had told her about the system . . .

"Quiet, please!" said the mayor. "I would like to welcome you all to the Opening Day Ceremonies of this fine mini-mall . . . what? Oh, Howie says it's more like a *de minimus* mall, 'cause it looks like we've agreed to accept Mr. Sakra's offer. Anyhow, I'd like to ask some of our out-of-town guests to he'p us here, with an effort the ladies of this town have made to memorialize some of our greatest memorials."

The Kiplings, Quill discovered, were more bewildered than flattered, but in the true Victorian spirit, up to the challenge. Mr. Sakura (followed by the inevitable Motoyama) with many bows and nods, joined them as they solemnly marched up and down the display table to judge the Jell-O contest. Each of the ladies stood more or less proudly beside her creation, except for Miriam Doncaster, who rather elaborately ignored the whole thing and continued the charade of reading her book. Somebody had upended a bucket over her train.

Mr. Motoyama, trailing his boss, growled, "Jer-ro."

"I beg your pardon?" said Mrs. Henry.

"*Jer*-o. Jer-*o*! Jer-*rooooohh!*" howled Mr. Motoyama, with sudden ferocious intent. He snarled. Shook his fist. Dashed out of the tent. In the stunned silence Quill heard a shriek, and clatter, and the ominous sound of a Monster truck being gunned to ear-splitting pitch.

Fortunately, most of the crowd dashed outside, the men, bored, in the hopes that the Monster Truck Rally had started without them, the women, Quill later believed, out of an atavistic survival impulse present in the most obdurate feminist whenever an enraged male is around a large truck.

Motoyama barreled the shiny red truck through the south opening and headed straight for the display table, knocking over the jellies, the baked goods, the soft drink stand, and the flower display on its way. Women screamed. Elmer bellowed. Outside, the several deputies who'd been directing traffic jumped in the black-and-white and turned on the siren. Motoyama, with sporadic cries of *"Jer-roooh!"* threw the truck in reverse (flattening a tuba that had been left carelessly near the Coke machine) and rammed the display table again. The gears clashed. The motor revved. The truck jumped forward like a bull out of the chute and slammed into the tent pole.

The awning collapsed in billows around the truck. The engine died. Shouts, curses, and imprecations issued from various spots under the fallen tent.

"Jerroooh!" snarled Mr. Motoyama, muffled, but undefeated.

"It was Mrs. Henry's replica of Mount Fuji," said Andy, applying a small Band-Aid to a cut above Quill's brow. "Nearly as we can figure out, he thought it was a sacrilege."

"Well, it *was* sacrilegious," said Meg tartly. "What do you think poor Dookie would have thought of a Jell-O crucifix? It was in lousy taste. I'm just glad nobody was seriously hurt."

"Has everybody gone home?" Quill got up and wandered around their restaurant. The staff had decorated it with balloons and crepe paper. The glassware on the café tables shone sparkling clear. The menu on the blackboard displayed the opening day specials. A scent of tarragon and crab made the area pleasantly reminiscent of the kitchen at the Inn.

"Almost." Andy tried, but couldn't suppress a grin. "Between the toilets malfunctioning and the tent collapse, Myles decided it was better to reschedule the event for next week. I co-opted the Inn van, Quill, to run some of the elderly back to the village. So the Kiplings and Mr. Sakura are outside, waiting to get picked up. Myles sent Mr. Motoyama to the lockup with Deputy Dave.''

The drone-shove of the backhoe in operation in the distance attracted Quill's attention. "Is the plumbing really messed up? Are we going to be able to open next week?''

"John and Myles are down at the septic tank now." Andy packed up his black bag and snapped it shut. "Whatever the obstruction was, it didn't seem to be in the pipes leading to the system. Myles asked DeMarco to take off the top of the tank.''

"Wow!" Meg shook her head. "When I think of what the Horrible Hedrick is going to do with the headlines! You know, if we'd been thinking, we'd have created a plan to get him out of the way today.''

"Somebody already did," said Myles. He walked through the open door. His uniform was streaked with dirt. "Andy? I'm going to need you down at the septic tank. Looks like he's been in there at least overnight.''

"Christ." Andy picked up his back. "What's your best guess?''

"Hammer blow to the head. Same MO as the first one. Rigor's set in and gone, but there's no bloating. I'd say twenty-four hours or less, but you're the expert. Whoever put him in there must have been in a hurry. The body's shoved up against the outlet valve and blocked the waste line from the building. Quill? Unless you want to come down to the pit with us, I'd appreciate it if you'd go back to the Inn.''

Quill watched his eyes. "Myles. It's not your fault.''

"Dammit, Quill." He looked at the ground at his feet, then back up at her. She started toward him, then stopped. "I don't have an excuse. Don't you understand? After I talked with Matthews in Palm Beach last night, I knew. Instead, I . . .''

He'd come to her.

"Lila Fairbanks," said Meg softly. "Golly. And her husband, too, I bet.''

"It fits," said Quill in an undertone. "They were here yesterday, with the others.''

"Do you have proof, Myles?" asked Andy.

"No. No proof. It's been a series of clever crimes. But,

goddammit, I could have stopped this."

"How?" asked Quill gently. "You said he'd been in there more than twenty-four hours. When did you talk to Matthews?"

"After dinner. Around eight."

"Then he was already dead," said Meg bluntly. "Quill, are you coming?"

"I'll stay here. I'll make coffee."

Myles looked at her. "Has everyone gone? Quill? I don't want you here alone."

"I'll be fine, Myles."

He made a movement, impatient to be gone.

"Go on, all of you. I'll be here when you get back. Meg? Can you wait just a second?"

"Sure. I'll be with you in a minute, Andy."

"The Kiplings are in the parking lot. I'd better get them and bring them in here until Mike gets back with the van."

"But the Fairbanks! Quill! You're not going to feed a murderer!"

"Did you see Myles's face? He thinks Hedrick died because I distracted him. It's my fault, Meg. He blames me. If he'd been concentrating on his job instead of what was happening to me, I know he thinks this never would have happened. The Fairbanks don't know that he's on to them, but there's a chance, just a chance, that they'll try and slip away now that Hedrick's been found. I'll just keep them altogether and give them a meal and make sure that Lyle and his wife get back to the Inn with the others."

"I'd better tell Myles they're here," said Meg.

"Okay. Just wait for the right moment. Not in front of anyone else. I can't stand to see him like that."

Meg reached out and hugged her. "Okay. Serve 'em a meal and keep 'em happy and oblivious."

"Just tell me what to serve."

"Cold soups and salads are in the frige. Don't try the crab clouds. You can heat the ratatouille in the microwave. Three minutes and stir, three minutes and stir again."

"Got it. Georgia can help me."

"Okay, I'll send them all in."

Quill went to the refrigerator and began to set out the

gazpacho and the vichyssoise, then put two portions of the ratatouille in the microwave. Meg had a large supply of sourdough bread stocked in a cupboard, and she removed a loaf and began to slice it into chunks.

There was a whisper of movement across the flagstone patio outside.

"Gawd," said Georgia.

The Fairbanks, Miss Kent, and Mr. Sakura filed in behind her. Marco DeMarco arrived with Georgia, the two of them looking reassuringly solid. "Not much more I can do down there," DeMarco said in response to her inquiring glance. He shrugged. "And Meg said you were serving food. Sorry to bust in like this, but I was hungry. The poor guy."

Quill looked at Lila. The delicate face was flushed, the eyes a little wild. She drew the ribbons at her waist through her fingers, back and forth, back and forth. She never left her husband's side. Lyle cupped her elbow protectively with one hand.

"You all are getting quite an impression of Hemlock Falls," said Georgia lightly, to break the uncomfortable silence.

"We will not talk about it," said Miss Kent firmly.

"Sit anywhere, please," said Quill. "I thought I'd get you a little early supper while we're waiting for Mike and the van."

They settled into the chairs like large birds.

"Did anyone figure out why poor Motoyama went berserk?" asked Georgia with determined cheerfulness.

Quill shot her a grateful look. "Well!" she said, lightly. "It was typically Hemlock Falls, Gee. I hope it adds to your already fervent desire to come and live among us. It was the Jell-O exhibits." Quill arranged the arugula on plates and removed the vinaigrette cruet from the shelf. "You'll have noticed, I'm sure, the *verve* and personal attention which each of the ladies gave to their exhibits. Miriam, for example, is town librarian and a mystery fan, so she did a replica of the train in *Murder on the Orient Express*..." The quality of the silence shifted, like a great weight.

She stopped in midsentence.

The bread knife fell from her fingers.

Quill turned. Stared at them. They stared back. All of them, with the unwinking eyes of predators.

Georgia's hand jerked up. Lyle Fairbank's eyes were steady. Miss Kent coughed a little and shifted in her seat.

Georgia rose from her chair.

Quill backed up and hit the counter. She could go no farther. The end of a terrible story she had read once, long ago, came to her, like jaws snapping shut in a trap. She thought.

> *"No!" Tess cried. "It isn't fair!"*
> *And then they came for her.*

"Georgia! You!" Quill pushed back a sudden spurt of tears. "He's your brother," she said, pointing suddenly at DeMarco. "The resemblance. It's not the coloring. It's the shape of the skull. The ears . . ."

"The painter's eye," said Georgia.

"It's you," said Quill huskily. She cleared her throat. "It's all of you."

The Kiplings watched her, with that alien stillness.

"It couldn't have happened any other way. You were all together when Louisa died. You were all at the party when Carlyle died. And yesterday . . ." She took a deep breath. "Yesterday you went into the woods. Together. And Hedrick followed you there."

"Yes," said Georgia. Her face was patched with high, bright color.

"Gee," DeMarco ordered. "Shut up."

"No. I want to explain." She stood, hands crossed over her chest, fists clenched, the pink caftan an incongruous flare of color. "And it's my call. You know it's my call. Can you stop me? Can you?"

No one spoke.

"Explain?" Quill, her heart beating so hard she could feel it in her throat. "Explain three murders?"

"There were more deaths than that," said Georgia. "Far

many more than that. We just stopped them, the Conways, from killing again.''

''But *why?!*''

Georgia's face closed shut, like a fist. ''I was Douglas Conway's first wife. The one he divorced. To marry that rapacious little bitch Louisa North, with her slut of a daughter, and her murdering bastard of a son.'' Her voice, shaking so badly that Quill could barely understand her, faltered and died away.

''You lied to me!'' cried Quill. ''You said he died!''

''And so he did, for me, seven years ago.''

''I,'' said Lyle Fairbanks, ''was Doug Conway's best friend. And my wife, Lila, was the woman the Conways tried to pin Doug's murder on.''

''I was Doug's sister,'' said Miss Kent. ''And Louisa Conway stole the only man I ever loved.''

''And you. Mr. Sakura.'' Quills voice was just above a whisper.

''Hedrick Conway and his women.'' His black eyes glittered at her with a wise and angry intelligence. ''A scandal, brought on by my . . . association . . . with the rapacious Miss Carlyle.''

''All of them deserved to die,'' said Georgia, a terrible satisfaction in her voice. ''When they'd drained Doug, and finally killed him—because, Quill, it was murder, no matter what your lover tells you, what those investigators in Palm Beach tell you—they poisoned him. I contacted each one of my friends that that miserable little crew had injured, one by one. And we decided that at the right place, at the right time, they would help me. They would help me get justice.

''I was fifty-two when Louisa North and her poisonous little slut of a daughter crossed Douglas's path. We'd been married almost thirty years. I was Douglas's first and only love. He was a genius, and his partner—my father, Stephen Hardwicke—knew how to parlay Douglas's genius into the empire that they both built. We were rich. We were happy. Douglas had never even been with another woman. Not until that bitch and her brood showed up.''

There were no tears, Quill noted. Just a bright, hard blaze behind Georgia's eyes.

"We came across them at one of those parties I'd told you about. We were traveling quite a lot, that year, trying things we hadn't needed to try before. Douglas was dried up. Out of ideas. Spent. He loved his work and there was no more that he could do, so we traveled. We had everything material we could ever want. Except youth. Except change.

"I told you about the circuit for the very rich. And that's what we were, what I still am, the very rich. We accepted an invitation to a party on a yacht in Greece. For a week. I knew, once we got there, that I had to get him home. I knew, once I walked that deck and saw the human garbage tanning in the sun, that this was no place for us, no place at all. But I didn't act on what I knew. And when I found them together—Louisa, Carlyle, and my Douglas, naked in a stateroom—my Douglas, with that thinning hair, those ridiculous glasses . . ." Georgia closed her eyes.

Miss Kent smoothed her linen skirt over her knees and took a sip of water.

"I never should have divorced him. I know that now. Carlyle was into all kinds of drugs. She and her harpy mother battened on him, and then they sucked him dry.

"He was generous in the divorce settlement. He could afford to be. What I told you was true. He died for me that day, seven years ago, he died for himself that day, seven years ago, although his physical death didn't happen until a year later. At that party. In Palm Beach."

"Doug and Gee were talking about getting back together. It's what precipitated his murder, you see," said Lyle. "He was talking on the phone every day to Gee, here, trying to shake the drugs those three had gotten him on to, and there would have been hell to pay for that little tribe, you can bet, if Gee'd come back into the picture. Those of us that loved Doug—and I'm not ashamed to say that I loved him, as nuts as he went for that year—well, were doing our best to get him and Gee back together."

Lila Fairbanks touched her husband's hand. "We think what happened then is that Louisa, Hedrick, and Carlyle decided to kill him that weekend and arrived prepared. Botulism is easy enough to manufacture. You can do it in your own kitchen. When our own children were grown, and out of the house, I took up, oh, all kinds of things to feel as though I were still ... womanly ... I guess is the word, and it may sound silly to someone like you, Quill, coming from me, who has so much in the way of material things, but I just wanted ... to be ordinary. So I brought Doug some of my canned jellies ...''

"She'd made a habit of it, the past year." Lyle rubbed his wife's shoulder. "It was kind of a joke around that group—well, not a joke exactly."

"Bored, brittle, sophisticated, and, as Georgia said, human garbage." Miss Kent's voice was crisp. "It was a joke, dear Lila, only to people who hadn't had normal feelings for years, if ever. I, myself, always loved your jellies."

Quill didn't know whether to laugh or cry.

"So they tried to make you responsible for the murder, Mrs. Fairbanks?"

Lila nodded.

"Set her back quite a bit," said Lyle gruffly. "Ended up in the hospital for a while."

"It was a mental institution," said Lila, trembling. "A house for crazy people."

"And as for the rest of us," said DeMarco, "you don't need a detailed drawing, do you? Louisa and Carlyle had a spat soon after they'd snared Doug, and Louisa turned her out without a penny. Mr. Sakura, here"—he coughed—"well, Carlyle tried a bit of blackmail on him."

"And it worked," said Mr. Sakura. "My position, gone. The honor of my house was shamed."

"At least the bastards didn't end up with much," said Miss Kent cheerfully. "Sakura-san didn't pay her a plugged nickel, and Gee's managed to tie up the fortune in litigation for a long while."

"But Louisa and Cay?" said Quill.

"Oh, yes," said Miss Kent serenely. "Cay wormed her way back into the fold. My guess is that Cay tried a bit of blackmail on her own mother. Louisa's appetites were notorious, and after she threw Cay out, let's just say that

Douglas, as besotted as he was, would have divorced her if he'd known what Cay did about her mother."

"And you, Miss Kent?" asked Quill. "Why did you hate him so?"

"I would prefer, my dear, not to go into that. But I can tell you . . ." She raised her finely boned face to Quill's. Her lips drew back from her teeth. "I can tell you. *I had a hell of a reason!*"

"Mr. Paulovich?" asked Quill.

"Cover," Georgia said, her grin white.

"But the law. Couldn't you have gone to the police?"

"Don't be naive!" Miss Kent snapped. "What possible recourse could we have had? Douglas was of age. He was mentally competent. In my own case—" She bit her lip. "There was no proof, you see. Absolutely no proof. There is no law to deal with the ruination of a man. Only laws for his physical demise. So we took, in the classic manner, matters into our own hands."

"You can't," said Quill. "You can't."

"We can," said Lyle, "and we did."

"But you've told me," said Quill recklessly.

"We have, Quill," said Georgia a little sadly. "But no one will believe you, without proof, without another witness. These's no jury in the country that would convict us on your word alone. And your sheriff's a good man, Quill, but we were very, very careful And we will back each other up. There's too much at stake for us, you see."

She took a deep breath. "When you remember me, when you remember our friendship, you'll see that I never lied to you. Never. Not once. I didn't betray that trust, Quill, and as strange as this may seem to you now, it's important that you know it." She looked at the others, and without a word exchanged, they got to their feet. "Do you think Mike's here with the van?"

Quill spread her hands.

"Then we'll see ourselves out, my dear. Thank you." Miss Kent patted her cheek. Her fingers were scented like violets.

Quill watched them leave, heard their footsteps whisper-slide over the cobblestone court.

She waited, as the darkness gathered in the little restaurant, and the sounds of a summer evening filled the quiet. She waited, and Myles came in exhausted, with lines around his mouth where there had been none before, and she said, as he walked in, a question in his eyes at finding her alone in the darkness:

"The thing is, they forgot Mr. Stoker."

CHAPTER 15

There were days in August which carried a melancholy hint of fall. Quill sat in the waiting room of the tiny hospital that served the Falls and the surrounding small communities and thought about the quality of the light: it was gold, round, autumnal. The warm air had lost the round fullness of humidity. An occasional current carried the coolness of September.

Next to her, Meg was restless, fidgeting in the uncomfortable chair, picking at her shoelace. She relaxed. "There they are."

Quill turned and looked over her shoulder. Andy, remote in his hospital whites, came down the hall. His face was somber. Myles walked beside him.

"Let's go into my office." Andy preceded them. It was small, the bookshelves crowded with medical texts, the desk overflowing with journals, magazines, and patient folders. There was a faint smell of antiseptic. Quill settled next to Myles. Meg stood at the window, looking out at the football field. The high school team had started practice. The shouted exuberance of the young was monitored by the coach's whistle, a shrill imperative.

"How long has she got?" asked Myles.

Andy flipped through Georgia Hardwicke's chart. "It's hard to say. Six weeks. Maybe two months."

"So that's why she signed a confession." Quill rubbed her forehead. "She must have known about this. Last year. When she began to hunt the Conways."

Andy raised one eyebrow. "She says not."

Quill was brusque, fighting tears. "Of course she knew. Why else did she wait six years to take revenge? It's pituitary cancer, you said? Metastasized to the liver? Of course she knew. I don't think the rest of them did. If they had, if they knew that she planned to confess all along, do you think they would have helped her? She convinced them, I know she convinced them, that they'd be safe. That they'd be able to plan to kill and get away with it." She looked at Myles. "Will the others go to trial?"

"I doubt it. Lila Fairbanks might be ready to talk, but her lawyers have her sequestered. The others. . . ." He shrugged. "Silence. The evidence rests on Georgia's confession—which denies the complicity of the others—and on Stoker's affidavit that they'd paid him to follow Hedrick Conway and his family and report back on their activities. We've got Stoker's expense acounts, which show that he followed them everywhere for the past year, and copies of his reports on the Conways' activities, but nothing to support a charge of murder, or even conspiracy to murder. Everything can be explained by the civil action the Kiplings have brought against Douglas Conway's estate. Sakura's attempting to recover the income he lost from Carlyle Conway's blackmail scheme. Georgia's suing to have the will contested because of Louisa's and Carlyle's undue influence. Her brother, who's heir to Georgia's fortune, has a legitimate interest in her fiscal status. The Fairbanks claim they were conducting a private investigation to pin Douglas Conway's murder on the Conways so that Lila's name could be cleared. Everyone except Miss Kent had logical—not fair—but logical reasons for having Conway followed by Axminster Stoker. Nothing actionable there. And, as I said, impossible to prove conspiracy."

"Do you suppose we'll ever know about Miss Kent?" asked Meg.

Myles shrugged.

"It's the ruthlessness of it," said Meg. "Poor Stoke. The poor man had no idea he was being used as a stalking horse for murder."

"I was blind to it," said Quill, rousing herself from a

fixed concentration on a replica of a human skull on Andy's desk. "They all referred to him as 'Stoke.' The family resemblance between Georgia and DeMarco. The connections between HC Pharmaceuticals and the Conways. The fact that all of them were nearby when each of the murders occurred. The lies they told! The lies!"

"The rich," said Andy," are different from you and me. Quill? Georgia would like to see you."

"Now, Andy?" asked Quill.

"I'm going to transfer her to the prison hospital at Attica this afternoon. She's in three-eleven."

The halls had the hushed silence peculiar to hospitals, blanketing the constancy of its purpose, distancing visitors from the world of life from the reality of death.

Georgia was pale, her face drawn, but the smile was there, and the booming, generous laugh. One of the nurses turned away from her bedside with a grin and a shake of her head as Quill pushed open the door and entered the room.

"Could you excuse us for a second?" asked Quill.

The nurse left on noiseless feet.

Georgia's smile died. "Well, Miss Sarah. This has shaken you up, hasn't it?"

"That's an understatement."

"An inadequate understatement. Not my style at all." She nodded to the visitor's chair. "Sit down."

Quill sat carefully and clasped her hands in her lap.

"You feel betrayed."

"I do."

"And what else? Disgusted? Revolted? Furious?"

"All those."

"I don't expect you to understand. I don't expect you to forgive me. But I want to tell you something. Gawd. I hope I get this right." She reached to the table beside the bed and drank from the tumbler of water. "Yes, I used some people who trusted me. I traded on love, affection, loyalty, friendship. With you. And Stoke. I used poor old Stoke, who thought that he was cooperating in an effort to embarrass Hedrick and those harpy women. Stoke wanted to right a wrong that'd been done to a man he'd revered for twenty years. But that doesn't mean I'm a liar. It means that I made a choice. I know exactly what I've sacrificed, Quill. I know what's been taken from me, as a person, because I did what I did. But I knew what I was doing. The Conways would, *did* get away with it. This''—she swept her hand down, across her chest and belly—''this cancer condemned me, and freed me all at once. I was sentenced before my crimes were committed. And once I decided to kill them—and I killed all three of them, Quill— I had no choice but to use the people I loved. Didn't someone once call them little murders, the crimes we commit against the healthy living?''

''A comedian,'' said Quill dryly.

''So you see.''

Quill shook her head. ''Why involve the Kiplings? Why not''—she stopped—''just do it yourself?''

''Because that bitch had to know it wasn't just me.'' Georgia's eyes narrowed, and that flat glittering stare would remain with Quill a long, long time. ''Louisa. In the woods. We followed her. I can move quietly, you know, for all my size. She turned. We stood there. Silent. All of us. And I swung the hammer. And Carlyle, on the floor, with all of us around her. We were the last thing she saw, and she *knew*. For a long time. She *knew*. And the brother. He screamed. Like a rabbit. Like a rabbit.''

''It isn't fair!'' cried Tess.
And then they were on her.

''You've lost something,'' said Meg when Quill told her what had happened. ''I hope to God you get it back.''

''What?'' said Quill. ''What have I lost?''

They were in the kitchen. The copper pots hung from the wrought-iron hooks like billy clubs. The herbs had a stale graveyard smell. The afternoon light had died, and night crouched behind the falls.

Meg pulled a comic face. ''Your sunny faith in the essential goodness of human beings?''

''I'm tired,'' said Quill. ''I'm not up to light chat.''

''Sorry. Sorry. I guess neither of us is especially good at

looking into the pit. Now, dancing around the edge of the pit, jester bells in hand, *that* we're good at.''

"It was all of them. All of them. Smiling, genial, good humored . . .''

". . . and lethal.''

"I always thought there were things normal people wouldn't do.''

"Myles knows better. One can smile and smile and be a villain.''

"But Georgia was good. I loved her.''

"Things fall apart,'' said Meg, "the center fails to hold.''

"Shut up,'' said Quill fiercely.

"All right. I'll quit the oblique and we'll tackle this head on. If there's a fixed and eternal good, Quill, you won't find it in people. You'll find it in yourself. And your self needs your painting. Take a month. Go back to New York. Paint. And come home.''

"And Myles?''

"And me? And John and the Inn and Doreen and all those things you think you're serving because we're good? Pooh. You'll know what to do when you come home. Do it. Leave us. And come back.''

CHAPTER 16

Quill signaled a right turn and pulled into the long driveway that led to the Inn. Bronze and pink chrysanthemums bloomed on either side of the door, and trees were a fireworks of scarlet, bronze, and yellow. There'd been a heavy frost the night before, and the last of the autumn lilies shivered in the October air.

Doreen, her apron filled with late potatoes, stumped around the corner of the old building. She grinned and dumped the potatoes in a tidy pile by the ivy trellis. "You're earlier than you said."

"The thruway was clear. And everybody's driving seventy anyway these days, Doreen."

"Ayuh? You get another ticket?"

"No, I did not get another ticket."

"You got that suitcase?"

"It's in the back. Along with"—Quill paused, a little shy—"a few sketches."

"Huh." Doreen opened the back door and slid the portfolio out. She flipped it open and stood considering. "Like the way you handled the water. Foreground perspective's off some."

Quill gaped at her.

"Sher'f talks about his art classes some at dinner. That Stoke's thinking about takin' a few." She sniffed.

"How's he doing?"

"Ast *him*. Once he stopped fooling around with that Quality stuff, he started talking like a sensible person, I

242

guess.'' She hoisted Quill's suitcase.

"Meg wrote that he's found a little house to buy in town.''

"Pension'll go to that, I guess, now that he's not pretending to be a rich guy.''

"I'm glad he decided to take over the newspaper.''

Doreen sucked her teeth, whether in disapprobation or indifference, Quill couldn't tell. "Wait'll you see it. It's somethin'. Go on, they're waiting on you in there. Sheriff'll be along soon.''

Quill walked into the foyer. The vases were filled with autumn leaves. A fire burned steadily in the cobblestone fireplace. The small sign they used to welcome guests read WELCOME! ARTIST SARAH QUILLIAM! with two lines underneath: CHAMBER OF COMMERCE WELCOME HOME DINNER 7:00 P.M., and then, QUILLIAM EXHIBIT, THE SAKURA MALL AT THE FALLS EXHIBITED DAILY underneath.

"We wasn't sure you wanted your pitchers hung here, so Meg and the Sher'f hung up 'em down to the mall.''

Quill cleared her throat and smiled.

"And the terlits are workin', which is a mercy.''

"I take it that's not a comment on the quality of Sarah's work,'' said Axminster crisply as he came down the stairs from the upper floor. He'd shaved his mustache. He was wearing an Aloha shirt.

Doreen muttered what Quill took to be an imprecation and abjured Axminster to shake a leg and get the luggage.

"Please don't bother,'' said Quill. "I'll take care of it.''

"We're glad to see you back, Sarah.'' He kissed her cheek. "I'd be delighted to assist you with the luggage. Andy, Meg, and John are in the kitchen. I'll be along in a moment.''

"You hustle,'' said Doreen. "We got to get ready for that Chamber dinner.''

Axminster snapped a salute and carried Quill's case back upstairs.

"Doreen, just because poor Mr. Stoker isn't as rich as we thought, there's no need to make a . . . a . . . *slave* out of him.''

"Gotta learn, don't he? One gol-durned thing I won't

put up with is a lazy husband.''

Quill stared at her. "A what!?''

"Well, I married him, din't I? Somebody had to give the bozo a hand with that-there newspaper business. Durn fool can't keep accounts to save his life.''

Quill burst into the kitchen. The thymey smell of *boeuf bourguignon* curled through the mixed scents of the wood fire, fresh bread, and spicy chrysanthemums. Meg shrieked and kissed her. Andy grabbed her in a bear hug. John nodded, smiled, and smiled again.

The back door banged open.

"Well, Myles, my dear," she said. "I'm home."

CRAB CLOUDS

from the Inn at Hemlock Falls

one cup fresh Dungeness crab, shredded
2 tsps. cilantro, chopped
1 tsp. fresh parsley, chopped
2 tsps. sweet red pepper, chopped fine
1 tsp. green pepper, chopped fine
2 tsps. Vidalia onion, chopped fine
2 cups cornmeal and flour, mixed in equal parts
½ cup whole milk
one medium-sized egg
one-half cup unsalted butter
several teaspoons each of unsalted butter and olive oil,
    for sautéing

Steam Dungeness crab for six minutes. Crack claws and body. Set crab meat aside.

Chop spices and peppers and mix together. Add to crab. Sauté onion for five minutes in butter, until onion is clear and transparent. Add to crab. Mix crab mixture well.

Measure cornmeal-flour mixture into glass bowl. Place milk in separate bowl. Separate egg. Beat yolk to thick froth. Beat egg white to soft peaks. Carefully fold egg into milk until smooth and very thick. Melt butter in pan, slowly, until it has separated into milky/clear liquid. Let butter cool slightly and whisk it into the cornmeal mixture, being careful not to curdle the egg, and to keep mixture thick.

Put a few teaspoons combined sweet butter and very pure olive oil into crepe pan and heat until it sizzles around the edges. Add three or four tablespoons of cornmeal to the pan and flatten with back of spoon. Cook as you would a pancake, until the edges of the crab cloud dry and curl sightly. Place a few tablespoons of crab mixture in the center of the crab cloud, leaving an eighth-of-an-inch edge all around. Flip the crab cloud over and sauté until corn-flour mixture is cooked through.

Serve with condiments such as tomato or mustard chutney.

Welcome to Hemlock Falls...a quiet town in upstate New
York where you can find a cozy bed at the Inn, a tasty home-
cooked meal—and murder where you least expect it...

THE HEMLOCK FALLS MYSTERY SERIES

CLAUDIA BISHOP

with an original recipe in each mystery

__A PINCH OF POISON   0-425-15104-2/$5.99
When a nosy newspaperman goes sniffing around town, Sarah
and Meg smell something rotten. It's worse than corruption—
it's murder. And the newsman is facing his final deadline...

__A DASH OF DEATH   0-425-14638-3/$4.99
After a group of women from Hemlock Falls win a design
contest, one disappears and another dies. Just how far would
television host and town snob Helena Houndswood go to avoid
mixing with the déclassé of the neighborhood?

__A TASTE FOR MURDER   0-425-14350-3/$5.99
The History Days festival is the highlight of the year in Hemlock
Falls, with the reenactment of the 17th-century witch trials. But
a mock execution becomes all too real when a woman is crushed
under a pile of stones and the killer is still on the loose...

__MURDER WELL-DONE   0-425-15336-3/$5.99
Big trouble comes to Hemlock Falls when a sleazy ex-senator
holds his wedding reception at the Inn. It's a success—until his
body is found tied to a barbecue spit.